"I'm thrilled to present Piper Starling and Sawyer Stratton!" country icon Sara Gilmore exclaimed.

As the lights came up and the music started to play, Piper reminded herself that the stage was home. Nothing could hurt her here.

Piper sang the song, holding nothing back. The song was about fear—the fear of letting go. Piper was very much afraid, but this time of having to hold on.

As the song neared the end, her gaze locked with Sawyer's. He stepped closer. Piper froze. At rehearsal, they had decided he would back away as the music faded. He was clearly changing the plan here.

Piper's heart pounded. Sawyer pushed the guitar behind his back then reached up and cradled her cheek in his hand. The blood thumped in her ears. She had no idea what he was doing. As the lights began to dim, he leaned forward, his lips inches from hers.

The crowd gasped and then exploded into thunderous applause.

Piper blinked and everything went black.

Dear Reader,

I am so excited to finally get to share Sawyer and Piper's story with you. The Grace Note Records series has been a joy to write because even though the books are tied to the same record company, every character faces different challenges.

When I started writing this series, I knew the combination of the Nashville music scene and the small-town setting would create a dramatic backdrop for romance. Thankfully, it delivered! This story takes us out of Grass Lake and into the world of country music. It was fun to explore the behind-the-scenes life of a country performer... and to throw some pretty huge obstacles at our hero and heroine. I hope you enjoy my latest love story and survive the roller coaster of emotion Sawyer and Piper experience along the way!

I love to hear from my readers. You can find me on Facebook at Facebook.com/amyvastineauthor, or you can visit my website, amyvastine.com, where you can sign up for my newsletter, receive release information, enter contests and giveaways, and learn about promotions. There's also a list and link to all my backlist titles.

Welcome back to Grace Note Records. I hope to see you again!

Amy Vastine

HEARTWARMING

Love Songs and Lullabies

———

Amy Vastine

Recycling programs
for this product may
not exist in your area.

ISBN-13: 978-1-335-63357-6

Love Songs and Lullabies

Printed in U.S.A.

Amy Vastine has been plotting stories in her head for as long as she can remember. An eternal optimist, she studied social work, hoping to teach others how to find their silver lining. Now she enjoys creating happily-ever-afters for all to read. Amy lives outside Chicago with her high school sweetheart turned husband, three fun-loving children and their sweet but mischievous puppy dog. Visit her at amyvastine.com.

Books by Amy Vastine

Harlequin Heartwarming

Grace Note Records

The Girl He Used to Love
Catch a Fallen Star

Chicago Sisters

The Better Man
The Best Laid Plans
The Hardest Fight

The Weather Girl

For my dad.

Thanks for always being there for me and teaching me the importance of always putting family first.

CHAPTER ONE

"WHAT DO YOU MEAN, I'm pregnant?"

Piper Starling felt like she'd stepped outside her body. Her stomach rolled. The walls of the exam room inside Nashville General Hospital's ER began to close in. This could not be happening.

"Miss Starling—" The doctor took a seat on the stool beside the exam table.

"You must be mistaken." Piper tried to control the shakiness of her voice and hang on to the single shred of hope from which she dangled. "I'm here because I twisted my ankle. I'm waiting for an X-ray, not a pregnancy test."

She had bumped into Sawyer Stratton onstage while setting up for rehearsal and twisted it. High heels and poor balance did not mix well.

The doctor scratched at his closely cropped gray beard and gave her a sympathetic smile. "I know why you came in, Piper. I think perhaps my nurse failed to mention a pregnancy test is part of the routine bloodwork we perform here in the ER."

Piper crinkled the paper covering the exam table in her fists. *Pregnant.* This made the possibility of a broken ankle seem like nothing. She could barely absorb what the doctor was saying as he went on about soft-tissue damage and the necessity of prenatal vitamins and a more balanced lifestyle going forward.

A sharp knock on the door made Piper jump. Before the doctor could get to his feet, her father pushed it open. Piper's heart flew into overdrive. She might be a grown woman, but her father's opinion of her was still the most important thing in her life.

"Ah, so a doctor finally did show up." Heath Starling handed Piper the bottle of water he had gotten her and began his rant. "We've been here for almost two hours. Are you here to take her to get this X-ray? You do know who my daughter is, right?"

"I know who your daughter is, sir." The doctor rose and offered his hand. "I'm Dr. Michaels."

Her father had no time for niceties. "We're on a tight schedule today. If her ankle is broken, we have to know so we can make adjustments sooner than later. Why do hospitals have to be so inefficient?"

The doctor was about to respond when Piper slid off the table and gingerly put some weight on her foot. "No X-ray, Dad. I'm fine. The doctor was just explaining to me that he's sure it's a sprain and not broken."

"Shouldn't we check to make sure?" The concern in his voice made her feel guilty for not being completely honest, but all Piper wanted was to get out of here before someone let her current condition slip.

"It would hurt a lot more if it was broken. As long as I rest it, I should be fine for the awards show."

She wished she could tell her dad the truth. What she wouldn't give to hear him reassure her that everything would be fine, but she knew there was no chance of that happening. An out-of-wedlock pregnancy with a man her father had convinced her was the wrong choice had the potential to ruin everything.

Thankfully, Heath was not a fan of hospitals. "Great! Then we'll make it to the radio interview after all," he said.

"I'll get the discharge paperwork together," Dr. Michaels said. "I'll have some instructions and recommendations for follow-up put in there for you, Piper. Good luck…with everything."

Piper needed more than luck. She needed someone to come in and tell the doctor that the lab had made a terrible mistake.

How could this have happened? Until now, every move she'd made had been perfectly orchestrated. Her image was vital to her success, which was why she always did as she was told. Her father constantly emphasized how one misstep could ruin a career. Say or do the wrong thing and the world would know about it instantly, thanks to social media and smartphones. And for some reason, the public was always on the lookout for their idol's fatal flaw.

Piper struggled to stop herself from trembling. A few months ago, she had fallen for Sawyer and his soulful brown eyes. She had let him woo her with his clever quips and gentle touch, but what she felt wasn't real. She'd been tricked into thinking she was in love by the intense emotions that writing music together pulled out of her.

Thankfully, her dad had helped get her head out of the clouds without even knowing how serious things had become between her and Sawyer. It was the wrong time for Piper to invest in a romantic relationship given her current career goals. Of course, being someone's mother could rock her career in a whole different way.

A nurse came in to wrap her ankle before they wheeled her outside to the car. Her father put a hand on her forehead.

"Are you sure you're okay? You look a little peaked."

"I'm fine. Just worried about how to cover this up so people don't notice tonight."

"Piper, no one is going to give you grief about twisting your ankle," her father promised. "I think the fans will forgive you for getting knocked over by that idiot."

Would everyone forgive her for getting knocked up by him, though? She wasn't so sure. Piper's heart ached as much as her stomach.

THE K104 STUDIOS were in the heart of downtown Nashville. Piper's ankle throbbed but was still the least of her problems. Her assistant, Lana, offered her a hand out of the limo.

"After your radio interview, you have about an hour and a half before you need to get to hair and makeup," Lana said as they made their way inside. "Your dinner reservations with Dean and his fiancée are at five. Luckily, the restaurant is near the Bridgestone Arena since the best time to get the most red carpet exposure is around six thirty."

The thought of being on display all night made Piper want to cry. Surely someone would know she was carrying around the secret of all secrets. She placed a hand on her stomach. Did she already have a baby bump? It was way too early for that. She was being paranoid. Pregnant and paranoid. The tension in her shoulders increased tenfold.

A representative from the radio station met them in the lobby. The young woman was tall and slender. She pushed her horn-rimmed glasses up her nose. "Piper Starling, welcome to K104! We're so excited to have you and Sawyer here."

Sawyer's here?

Piper felt her cheeks flush. She'd known she would have to face him tonight but had hoped the few hours she had before then would help her figure out what to do. She had to tell him. Not that he'd be very excited. When she had told him they couldn't be together, he had accused her of caring more about her career than the people in her life.

But quickly after that, he had acted like it was a relief they weren't going to be a couple. She glanced at her father, who apparently hadn't expected Sawyer Stratton to be there, either, given the way he scowled at Lana before dialing someone on his phone.

"You made it!" Dean Presley, the head of Grace Note Records, turned the corner. He pulled Piper in for a hug. "I'm so glad you're okay. We can deal with a sprain, right? A sprain won't hurt the tour, and I have a very good feeling everyone will want to see Piper Starling live after hearing you tonight."

Piper wasn't nominated for a Country Artist Award this year but had two proudly displayed at home on her mantel. She was here to promote the new album she'd written over the summer with Sawyer's help. He may have been a newbie to the country music scene, but he was also an excellent songwriter. Piper had spent too many years singing other people's music and it had been Sawyer's job to teach her how to write her own.

Tonight's performance would be crucial in setting the stage for her break into mainstream pop music. The new album had great crossover potential thanks to Sawyer's help.

Of course, all of that was in jeopardy now. Her stomach rolled and her head ached.

Heath slipped his phone back in his pocket. "This is your doing, Dean? Hasn't my daughter shared the headlines with this boy enough? She's a platinum recording artist while he just released his first album."

"Together, the two of them are magic. Their song's success is proof of that. The more we showcase them together, the better for both of them. I think Nashville deserves a preview of Sawyer and Piper before the rest of America hears them at the CAAs."

Her chest constricted at the thought of Dean's disappointment as well as her father's when they learned shc had ruined her perfect image. She trusted Dean's business sense and knew he believed in her, even if his trust had been misplaced. Keeping the facade up as long as possible, until she could figure out how to break the news to everyone, was her only option. There had to be a way to save her career from disaster.

Piper took a deep breath before she had a panic attack. "It was a great idea, Dean," she said, putting her smile back in place. "We're here to sell records. Mine and Sawyer's."

The radio station rep's relief was evident.

The earlier tension had not been lost on her. "Let me show you to our hospitality room."

Heart pounding, Piper followed the woman down the hall, into the elevator and up three floors. She could do this. She could sit next to Sawyer and answer questions about music. They could sing together like they did while writing songs and recording her album. Singing with him was the easy part. Avoiding his brown eyes, resisting his charm, ignoring the way he made her feel when he was near—those things might prove more difficult. Especially now.

It suddenly felt very warm. Piper was thankful she had dressed in layers. She peeled off her sweater and handed it to Lana for safekeeping.

Sawyer's voice reached her in the hallway. His playfulness was infectious as he sang and strummed a guitar. It was his lightheartedness that had gotten her in this trouble in the first place.

She steeled herself as she entered the hospitality room. Sawyer Stratton had accepted there wasn't a future for the two of them. How would he feel when he found out they'd be forever connected?

CHAPTER TWO

"YOU HAVE GOT to be kidding me," Sawyer said, setting his guitar down. "You are un-believable!"

His friend and bandmate Hunter pushed the last grape between his lips. His cheeks were puffed out like a chipmunk's. He had somehow managed to get an entire bowl of grapes in his mouth. Hunter's enormous cheek capacity was about to cost Sawyer ten dollars, and he was not a fan of parting with his hard-earned money.

"Impressive, but I can do better. If I can eat one of those sandwiches over there in one bite, you have to give me ten bucks," Sawyer said, making his way to the counter full of snacks.

Hunter shook his head, unable to speak. He held up two fingers before slashing the air with both hands.

"Double or nothing?" Sawyer clarified. Hunter nodded. "You think you can eat this whole sandwich right after swallowing all those grapes?"

Hunter nodded again and picked up a water bottle. After a quick swig, he wiped his mouth with the back of his hand. "If I do, you have to give me twenty bucks."

The turkey sandwich wasn't quite six inches long, but it was stuffed with all the trimmings and wouldn't go down easy. Better Hunter fail than him. "Go for it."

Hunter picked up the sub and took a breath before attempting to shove it all in his mouth. Sawyer couldn't help but bust out laughing.

"We have some snacks and beverages for you," a voice said from the doorway.

Sawyer turned, and there she was. Piper was always a sight for sore eyes. Her sunglasses rested on top of her head and her blond hair was pulled back into a ponytail. Even though she wore the same pale pink blouse and skinny white jeans he'd seen her in at rehearsal, the woman managed to take his breath away.

"Are you okay? Can you breathe?" The radio assistant came running at him.

How could she tell? It had only been a second. "I'm fine," he protested. He had known

Piper was coming—he just hadn't expected her to affect him the way she always seemed to.

The woman pushed past him and wrapped her arms around Hunter's chest. Two seconds later, a chewed-up wad of Italian bread shot across the room.

Hunter coughed and gratefully took the water offered to him by his rescuer. "Thank you," he choked out.

Sawyer shook off his embarrassment at misreading the situation and glanced at Piper. Her bright blue eyes were wide with shock, but her lips soon curled in amusement. Her father, however, stood behind her with his usual scowl.

"Perhaps Piper could have her own space to relax before the interview. These two—" Heath paused and glowered at Sawyer "—*gentlemen* seem to need some supervision we'd rather not be responsible for providing."

"It was a bet," Sawyer explained. "He lost. We're done now. No supervision required. Hey, Piper. How's the ankle? I'm so sorry about bumping into you."

He went in for the awkward hug and kiss on the cheek. She felt stiff in his arms but returned the innocent kiss.

"It's still a little sore. But I should be fine

by showtime." Her voice sounded different, colder if that was possible.

It had been awkward seeing her earlier today. Almost two months ago, he had followed his heart instead of listening to what his head had been telling him, which was that Piper would always put her career first.

He'd overreacted initially, but tried to cover up the humiliation he'd felt by pretending to be unaffected. They'd parted as friends, so why did Piper appear as if she'd rather be anywhere but in his company at the moment?

"Guess we get to perform our song two more times before we put it out to pasture," she said. Her neck was as flushed as her cheeks. He couldn't help but wonder if she was feeling all right.

Sawyer grabbed her a water bottle. "You saying we aren't going to tour together the rest of our lives so we can sing it five nights a week?"

"Oh, we haven't decided on an opening act yet." Piper seemed to panic. "We were thinking about going in a different direction, though. You weren't on our list. Our brands aren't the same."

Ouch. There was definitely no love there.

Everything was always about her career, her brand. "Well, we wouldn't want anything to tarnish your image, now would we?"

Clearly, Piper's feelings for him had soured, but it was for the best. Her daddy already hated him for no good reason. If he ever found about that night on the farm, heads would roll—Sawyer's and most likely Dean's, since he was the reason the two of them had met in the first place.

"How about we move things along? Piper has places to be," Heath said, placing himself between his darling daughter and the scoundrel he believed Sawyer to be.

"Great idea, Heath." Sawyer's use of his first name obviously irked the old man. That was as good a reason as any to make sure he used it all the time.

The radio assistant and Heimlich maneuver expert went to find out if the DJ was ready for them. Sawyer's whole body was tingling with excitement. This was the first time Dean had invited him to do something like this. K104 was the most popular country station in Nashville, and this kind of exposure meant the world to a new singer's career.

"Would it be okay if Sawyer and Piper signed some of our promo and took a couple pictures with Kelly first?" the woman asked when she returned.

"That's perfect, Nancy." Leave it to Piper to know her name. She probably knew if the radio station assistant was married or had children, where she'd gone to high school and college, and how she was spending the holidays this year. Piper was that kind of person—more interested in hearing about others than she was in talking about herself.

Sawyer followed them into another room and autographed everything they placed in front of him. He didn't think he'd ever get used to the fact that someone would want his signature. This was just the beginning, too. Kelly Bonner, the afternoon DJ on K104, came out of the studio and introduced herself. Sawyer knew who she was. She had jet-black hair and crystal-blue eyes that grabbed everyone's attention when they drove by the billboard along I-65. He had also listened to K104 for years, never imagining one day they'd play his songs across the airwaves.

"Thanks so much for coming in, you two," Kelly said. "I'm a huge fan."

Sawyer had *fans*. His chest puffed out. He wanted to soak this all in.

"Piper's on a tight schedule," her father reminded everyone.

Clearly, Heath and Piper were not among those fans. In fact, Piper's mission in life suddenly seemed to be to keep her distance from Sawyer. When they took a picture, she insisted Kelly stand between them. She nonchalantly moved her stool a few inches away from his when they got settled in the studio, and her eyes never left Kelly, even when Sawyer spoke.

"I heard that you two have spent quite a bit of time together the last few months. So, Sawyer, what was it like working with Piper not only on the duet for your album but on Piper's new album, as well?" Kelly asked.

"I am so grateful to Piper for giving me the opportunity to work on some songs with her. I think we both learned a lot. I mean, for me, writing songs is a very personal experience. You leave a part of yourself on the page and then add some more later when you sing."

Kelly raised a brow. "So, what did you learn about Piper?"

Piper finally glanced in his direction. Her face blanched.

Sawyer leaned in to the microphone. "I

learned that Piper is one of the hardest-working people I've ever met. And I grew up on a horse farm, so that's saying something."

He'd chosen something true and completely unobjectionable. There was no way Heath or Piper could take offense.

"What about you, Piper? What did you learn about Sawyer?"

Piper swallowed hard and bit down on her bottom lip. "That's a really good question," she replied.

The way she fidgeted in her seat, one would have thought this was the most difficult question anyone had ever asked her. Sawyer began to fear what she might say.

"Why do I get the feeling she's trying to come up with something really embarrassing?" he asked, hoping she wouldn't share some of her less than positive thoughts about him.

PIPER'S MIND WAS WHIRLING. What did she really know about the man sitting next to her? He was going to be the father of her child, and she barely knew anything about who he was. He had a sister and a dog. His father had passed away a few years ago. She didn't know anything about his mother. He had to have a mother.

"Come on, there must be something you can tell us about Sawyer. He's worried you're going to embarrass him. Does he have any annoying habits?" Kelly asked.

Radio interviews were so nerve-racking. Piper always feared she'd say the wrong thing. One comment could be spun a thousand different ways on Twitter. Sitting next to father of her unborn child wasn't easing her anxiety.

Sawyer flashed her one of his magical grins, his dimples in full effect. "Go ahead, tell Nashville what irks you about me."

"He smiles," Piper answered. "All the time. I know that seems harmless, but sometimes when you're having a terrible day and Sawyer's smiling like he doesn't have a care in the world, it can be annoying."

Like right now. Piper was carrying the weight of the world on her shoulders and he was thoroughly enjoying his first radio appearance. He had no cares...*yet*. He would feel differently once he knew what Piper knew.

"Can you blame me for smiling every time I'm around her?" Sawyer asked Kelly.

Kelly sighed. "You guys are so adorable. It's killing me." She let the listeners know Piper and Sawyer would sing after the commercial break.

Sawyer leaned over when the On Air sign was turned off. He brushed her knee with his hand. "Are we good?"

She froze. *Not good at all.* "We're fine," Piper lied.

Hunter brought Sawyer his guitar and they did a quick sound check. They got a thumbs-up from the producer on the other side of the glass.

Piper closed her eyes and tried to shut off her brain. *Don't look at him. Sing,* she told herself. She did just that. Kelly whistled and clapped for them when they finished.

"I love that song. I really do," she said. "I've got one more request before you two head out today."

"Request away," Sawyer said.

"You're performing tonight at the Country Artist Awards. Like I said, I love 'You Don't Need Me,' but I think I speak for everyone listening when I say we also love the chemistry between you two. I have watched that music video a hundred times. There is something so crazy good about the two of you together. Please tell me there's a hidden romance going on that you want to make official right now, here on K104."

Piper's heart stopped. She was speechless. Had she even been asked a question? Kelly smiled, as if waiting for a reply. Piper's entire face burned. She looked at Sawyer, who also seemed stunned by the insinuation.

There was nothing worse than dead air on the radio. Kelly was quick to end it. "I'm not going to let them answer so I can continue believing it's true, but if all you shippers could see the way both of them are blushing right now, there would be no doubts."

The panic cut off all the air to her lungs. Piper wanted to scream that there was no chance she and Sawyer would ever be together. Not the way she had once imagined.

"Thank you so much for stopping by," Kelly continued. "Please drop in the next time you're in town."

Never again.

"Absolutely," Piper said, finally finding her voice. All she wanted and needed was for this interview to end.

Sawyer simply nodded.

"All right. I've got a treat for y'all today," Kelly continued. "We've got the first single from Piper's new album that comes out at the end of the month. Sit back, enjoy the song and be sure to catch these two possible love-birds tonight on the Country Artist Awards."

As the song started, Piper took off her headphones. She noticed Sawyer's furrowed brow. "I think Sawyer might be mad at you for spreading rumors that he's anything other than single," she told Kelly.

"I'm not mad," he said. "I was caught off guard. You're probably mad."

"I'm not mad," Piper argued. She wasn't the only one who hadn't wanted to pursue a relationship. "I just thought you were going to set the record straight, so I didn't say anything."

"I didn't mean to put you two on the spot." Kelly slid her headphones off her head and let them hang around her neck. "There's something so heartbreaking about that song. The way you sing it makes me want to believe love will win in the end, even though you're saying goodbye. Does that even make sense?"

"Boone Williams knows how to write a song," Sawyer said, giving credit where credit was due.

Last summer, Dean had asked Boone to

mentor Piper so she could learn to write her own songs. Boone had tried, but the Grammy-award winner didn't have an abundance of patience, and writing songs had proved to be more difficult than Piper had hoped it would be.

He'd written most of "You Don't Need Me" and was kind enough to give Piper credit for the very little input she'd offered. Even after all his hard work on the song, he'd opted not to sing on the track. Boone had given that honor to Sawyer—as well as the job of helping her write songs for her new album.

"Boone once told me that a good song makes people feel," Piper said. "If our song made you feel like believing in love can win, then we did our job."

"You did an excellent job." Kelly smiled and saw them out. Heath and Lana were ready to leave as soon as the interview was over. Piper was ushered out of the station and back into the limo without a chance to say anything to Sawyer.

"Lana, make a note that the next time we go to K104, I'll need to approve all the questions ahead of time." Her father's peeved expression left no question he was unhappy with the insinuation that Piper and Sawyer were a couple. He was not going to take the news of this pregnancy well. "This is all Boone's fault. If he hadn't backed out of the arrangement I made with Dean, we wouldn't have to deal with this slander."

Piper wished she could blame someone other than herself, but she was the only one responsible for this entire mess. "Hoping Sawyer and I are dating is hardly slander."

"When the new album comes out, everyone will move on," Lana said. "People see them sing a love song together and it makes them want the feelings to be real. When you go your separate ways, the fans will forget about it."

"We can hope," her father replied.

The sinking feeling was back. He could hope all he wanted. Sawyer would forever be a part of their lives. There was a baby on the way, and Piper needed to figure out how to break the news to her father and Sawyer. Sooner than later.

CHAPTER THREE

SAWYER BOUNCED ON the balls of his feet as he shook out his arms and rolled his head from side to side like a boxer psyching himself up for his prizefight. Bridgestone Arena was where Sawyer had attended his very first concert back when he was sixteen. His sister, Faith, had driven him and two friends up to Nashville to see Kenny Chesney. Even from their nosebleed seats, he had felt the energy coming off the stage.

Now he was only a few minutes away from performing on that very stage. Not in front of thousands of screaming fans but hundreds of country music's elite. That was somehow more intimidating than the millions of people who would be watching him on their televisions at home.

"Is Piper ready?" Sawyer asked as Dean entered the dressing room, followed by Faith. "We're supposed to go on in a few minutes." Dean's eyes were glued to his phone. He hadn't stopped looking at that thing since they'd arrived at the arena.

"She'll be ready. Goodness, Facebook and Twitter are all over this."

"All over what?" Sawyer tried to sneak a peek over Dean's shoulder.

Dean spun around. "I think I have a way to make you a household name, little brother."

Sawyer's sister put her hand over her heart. "Aw, that's the first time I've heard you refer to him as your brother."

"Let's not call each other brother yet. You two aren't even married." Sawyer didn't mind that Dean would soon be his brother-in-law, but it wasn't something he wanted anyone to focus on too much. He feared people would accuse him of only getting ahead in this business because he was family. "What's happening on social media?"

"Ever since the radio interview, you and Piper have been trending on Twitter in Nashville with the hashtag #PipermakesSawyersmile."

Sawyer choked on the water he was drinking. It could not possibly be a good thing for anyone to think there was a romance going on between him and Piper. Not when she had made it clear they were better off as friends.

He ran a nervous hand through his hair. "Exactly how is that going to make me more famous? Piper and I are friends, but not even good friends. Barely friends. We're more like coworkers. Acquaintances maybe. Nothing more than singers on the same label. What will people think next? That I'm in love with Boone Williams?" Sawyer tried to laugh the whole thing off.

"Wow, from friends to only singers on the same label? Way to downplay your relationship. You act like it's inconceivable. You'd be lucky to date someone like Piper," Faith said. "She's beautiful, talented, ambitious and sweet on top of it all."

"Sounds like you're in love," Sawyer replied.

"Piper still hasn't signed off on an opening act for her first set of tour dates. You also have an album to promote," Dean said as his grin widened.

"And we've been talking about me doing a small-venue tour across the South this winter."

"Which was a great idea until another great idea came along."

Sawyer knew exactly where this was headed. "What? That I join Piper's tour?"

What Dean couldn't know was that when Piper had squashed the idea of being a couple, her support of his career had probably gone right along with it. She'd been mortified earlier when he suggested this not be the last performance they'd ever do together.

"I'm going to run it by Piper first, but I think if we play this right, we could create a buzz that sends you both to the top of the charts." Dean's excitement would have been contagious if it wasn't for the fact that he thought he could convince a woman who didn't even want to sit by Sawyer to let him open for her.

"What if Piper says no?" There was no if, only when. Piper wouldn't go for it. Most importantly, her father would *never* go for it, and he called all the shots in her career.

"She likes you. I saw how you two were on the farm. You helped her write the songs for this album. She owes you one."

Sawyer tugged at the collar of his shirt. He had ruined his chances of getting a hand up from Piper by getting too close. Dean could try to sweet-talk her, but the chances of her giving him a spot on her tour were slim. "Don't get your hopes up."

"Stop worrying. I'll make this work for

both of you. One more thing," Dean said, rubbing his hands together. "I think you should do something at the end of the performance tonight, but you can't tell Piper it's coming."

"Can I get you anything?" Lana asked from the other side of the bathroom door.

Piper wiped her mouth. "I'll be out in a second." How she wished she hadn't eaten dinner. She'd heard of morning sickness, but it was after seven o'clock in the evening. Why was she throwing up now?

"They're ready for you onstage. This thing is a well-oiled machine. They can't get backed up."

Piper washed her hands and checked her reflection in the mirror. She looked tired. Even with all the makeup magic her stylist had used to make her red-carpet ready tonight, she could see the exhaustion written all over her face.

No rest for the weary. Piper pulled open the door. "Let's go."

The anxious-looking stagehand behind Lana radioed to someone that they were on the move. All Piper had to do was sing "You Don't Need Me" one more time and then she could tell Sawyer about the baby. Once he knew the truth, maybe he would know what they were supposed to do.

Someone handed her an earpiece and a microphone as they approached the stage. Sawyer's hair was like spun gold under the glow of the stage lights. With a guitar strapped across his chest, he wore jeans and an oatmeal-colored henley, while she was tortured in a dress covered in red sequins. He had the shoulders of a man who had lifted hay bales his whole life. He was so strong and sturdy.

He reached for her hand when they were directed to head out during the commercial break. Like a stupid moth drawn to the flame that had no goal but to zap the life out of it, she took his hand and let him lead the way.

"I'm so nervous," he admitted. "Tell me everything's going to be all right."

Sawyer was usually so full of naive confidence. It always seemed like he had no idea whom he could disappoint. In front of this crowd, however, he was obviously humbled.

"Almost everyone out there has been on this stage and knows it's not easy. They're more forgiving than you'd expect. But we're going to be better than all right, so no worries," she assured him. At least she knew they would survive this performance. Afterward, things didn't look as promising.

"How's your sprain?"

She'd almost forgotten about her ankle. Had it not been for twisting it earlier today, she might not have figured out she was pregnant until much later. She wasn't sure if that was a good or a bad thing.

They had offered to let her sit on a stool for the performance, but she had refused. She would tough it out because she needed to knock this out of the park if she was going to have any hope saving her career from complete ruin.

The lights went down and the orchestra under the stage began to play. Commercial over. Piper felt her own set of butterflies, only they weren't flying—they were swimming some rough seas in her stomach. Closing her eyes, she prayed she wouldn't throw up onstage—on television—in front of millions of people.

One song. One last time pouring out her heart to a man who was about to find out their time together had major consequences. This song had brought them into each other's lives and yet was all about saying goodbye.

"I'm thrilled to present Piper Starling and

Sawyer Stratton!" country icon Sara Gilmore exclaimed as the lights came up and the music started to play.

Sawyer strummed his guitar and let what he did best guide him out of the fear. Piper reminded herself that the stage was home. Nothing could hurt her here. This was where she shone bright.

Piper sang the song, holding nothing back. She let her real emotions fuel the performance. The song was about fear—the fear of letting go. Piper was very much afraid, but this time of having to hold on.

As the song neared the end, their gazes locked. He sang about goodbye, and sadness tightened her throat. He stepped closer. Piper froze. At rehearsal, they had decided he would begin to back away as the music faded and the lights dimmed. He was clearly changing the plan here.

Piper's heart pounded as he stood in front of her. Sawyer pushed the guitar behind his back so there was nothing between them. He reached up and cradled her cheek in his hand. The blood thumped in her ears. She had no idea what he was doing. As the lights began to dim, he leaned forward, his lips inches from hers.

The crowd gasped and then exploded into thunderous applause. Piper blinked and everything went black.

CHAPTER FOUR

SAWYER TRIED NOT to panic as he scooped Piper up. The stage was dark, but there was little chance no one had noticed her faint. Her head fell back as she lay limp in his arms.

"Piper, wake up. Please wake up," he said as he carried her offstage. What was wrong with her? Fear mixed with the adrenaline coursing through his body was similar to what he'd felt when he found his father on the floor after his heart attack. "Piper, you need to wake up."

Hunter, drumsticks still in hand, was the first to join him. "I can't believe you made her pass out with one kiss."

"I didn't kiss her."

A bearded stage manager was waiting in the wings to help. He cleared a space for Sawyer to lay her down.

Sawyer put his face close to hers. He could feel her breath on his cheek, thank God. She felt warm to him, though, and her skin was covered in a light sheen of sweat.

"Come on, Piper. Wake up. Please, Piper."

"What happened out there?" Heath came barreling through the small crowd that had gathered.

"She passed out," Sawyer explained, although he knew that wasn't what Heath was curious about.

"Why were you in her personal space?" her father demanded. "What did you do to her?"

"I didn't do anything to her."

Piper's eyes fluttered open, her gaze landing on Sawyer first, then her father, then her surroundings. It was clear the moment she became aware she was lying on the ground instead of standing onstage. Her cheeks turned as red as the barn back at the Strattons' horse farm.

"What happened?" she asked as she tried to sit up. Both Sawyer and Heath reached out to help.

"You've done enough!" Heath's harsh tone was enough to get Sawyer to back off. "Can we keep the press away? I don't want any pictures of her like this."

Sawyer rolled his eyes. The only thing that

man seemed to care about was Piper's public image. God forbid she get sick or have a human moment in her life.

"Piper, are you okay?" Dean appeared over Heath's shoulder.

Sawyer wanted to shake Dean for coming up with the terrible idea of surprising her with what was supposed to look like a kiss. It had been nothing but a stupid publicity stunt. Why had he done it?

He'd done it because Dean had told him this was what the public wanted. Sawyer had to give people what they wanted if he was going to make it in this business.

It had also felt like the most natural thing in the world. Because when he'd listened to her sing, he had heard the pain in her words and wanted to take it away. Because when he'd looked at her, he had seen how vulnerable she allowed herself to be in front of not only everyone in the crowd and watching on television, but in front of him.

Sawyer got to his feet and took a couple steps back. Those were dangerous feelings. Piper had a way of drawing those out.

"I'm fine," she said, rubbing her forehead. "I don't know what happened."

"Let's get her to her dressing room." Heath

helped Piper to her feet, but she cried out when she tried to put weight on her bad foot.

Instinctively, Sawyer reached for her again. She steadied herself on one foot with his help. Their eyes met, and she bit down on her bottom lip. The desire to kiss her was immediately overwhelming. Sawyer picked her up instead and carried her to her dressing room.

Piper's arms stayed wrapped around his neck even after he set her back on her good foot. She wasn't helping him repress those feelings he was trying to avoid.

"You should sit," he suggested.

Her blue eyes stayed locked on his. "Why did you do that?" she asked.

"Because he's an idiot," Heath said, swooping in. He led her to the chaise lounge in the corner of the room. "Come lie down over here."

Piper's entourage, as well as several CAA employees, began to fill the room. Sawyer quickly became claustrophobic. He slipped out and found his sister and Hunter waiting outside.

"I can't believe you made Piper Starling pass out," Hunter teased. "Just the thought of having to kiss you knocked her out."

Sawyer shot him a look. "This isn't funny. She's hurt and obviously something is wrong."

"She's going to be fine," Faith promised him. "I heard Lana say she was sick before the performance. You know this really isn't your fault, right?"

"I know. I'm just worried." He tried to shake off the fear that still lingered. "When she started to go down, my heart stopped."

Faith patted him on the back. "It was a good thing you did what Dean told you to do. She could have been hurt much worse if you hadn't been there to catch her."

Dean came out and placed a hand on Sawyer's shoulder. "We're going to need you to talk to the press. Tell everyone Piper's fine. Don't confirm or deny anything between the two of you. Be as coy as possible."

"What? I don't know how to be coy. I'm a straight shooter. You know this."

"Trust me," Dean said. "If you play this right, you and Piper will be the headline story tomorrow."

Headlines were what the business of being famous was all about. This was Sawyer's chance to prove to Dean how much he wanted this.

"When they ask you if you're dating Piper, say something like, 'Wouldn't you like to know.' Then smile and they'll go nuts," Hunter suggested.

"Sawyer Stratton?" A frazzled-looking production assistant interrupted them. "We're ready for you in the pressroom. I need you to come with me now," he said.

Dean gave Sawyer a thumbs-up before slipping back into Piper's dressing room. How would she feel about Sawyer leading the world to believe there was something going on with them?

Full of reluctance, Sawyer shuffled behind the man, praying she wouldn't be angry with him for doing what was best for his career.

The assistant pushed open the door and held it so Sawyer could enter in front of him. "Just head on over to the microphone. They're pretty good about not all asking questions at once. I'll signal you when your time is up."

"Wish me luck," Sawyer said over his shoulder as he hesitantly made his way to the mic.

The clicking and flashing of the cameras overwhelmed his senses, quickly overriding the quiet murmurs of the reporters. Before

Sawyer had a chance to adjust the microphone to his height, the questions started coming. And no one was taking turns.

"What happened onstage tonight?"

"How's Piper doing?"

"Does this have anything to do with why she was at the hospital this morning?"

"Are you announcing that you and Piper are a couple?"

"Was fainting part of the performance?"

"How long have you and Piper been together?"

All the blood rushed to Sawyer's face. His hands began to shake, so he clasped them behind his back. He leaned forward toward the microphone and reminded himself that he only had to answer the questions he wanted to answer.

"Piper's fine. It's been a crazy day. She sprained her ankle at rehearsals this morning. With all the commotion, she didn't eat much today and got a little light-headed up there onstage. She wanted me to pass on to everyone that she'll be good as gold in no time. She's ready to get out and tour her new album."

The flashes from the cameras somehow seemed brighter. It was like standing in front of a strobe light. His answer had only sparked more questions about his relationship with Piper and the kiss that didn't happen.

Sawyer waited for something he could answer. From the back he heard, "What are your plans for touring?"

He pointed at the young female reporter. "Thanks for asking. I plan on touring this winter. I don't have all the details, but I am hoping to get out there and share my music with as much of America as I can."

"Will you join Piper's tour since you two seem to get along so well?" the reporter asked as a follow-up.

Of course he couldn't dodge the Piper bullet. It was always going to come back to her. He could hear Dean's voice in his head— *be coy*—but all he really wanted to do was set the record straight. There was no Sawyer and Piper. There would never be a Sawyer and Piper. For a moment two months ago, he'd thought he could let someone into his heart, but she'd quickly reminded him why he should stay single.

"If I was offered the chance, there's no one else I'd rather tour with. Can you blame me?"

The crowd again exploded in questions

about his relationship with Piper. Coy definitely got everyone talking and speculating the way Dean wanted.

Thankfully, the production assistant signaled to Sawyer that his time was up. He waved to the unsatisfied reporters and got the heck out of there.

He needed to check on Piper and let Dean know mission accomplished. Everyone would be talking about him and Piper tomorrow. He'd have to make sure he kept doing as he was told so his name stayed on their lips.

"WE NEED TO get a statement out before the press puts its own spin on this." Piper's father had not stopped pacing since they got in the dressing room.

Piper wanted this day to be over. She needed to get out of this arena and back to the hotel where she could hide. The press was sure to speculate about why she had fainted onstage, and none of their guesses would be helpful.

Lana handed her another bottle of apple juice. She couldn't bear to drink any more. They had been pushing cookies and juice on her so much that her body tingled from the excessive amounts of sugar.

"Sawyer let everyone know she's fine," Dean said. "Social media is lighting up about it, but it's all good."

"Good? My daughter fainted onstage. We're supposed to go on tour in a few weeks. People are going to question her stamina before she even begins touring."

"No one is focused on her not being well," Dean explained.

"What else would they be focused on?"

"Sawyer carrying her offstage. Everyone thinks it was part of the act, and they're loving it. They love Piper and Sawyer together."

Piper let that soak in. People loved her and Sawyer together. Everyone was thrilled at the simple idea of it. Except her father, of course.

"Ridiculous!" Heath scoured his own social media accounts to verify Dean's claims.

"I think we should take advantage of this. You could have Sawyer join Piper's tour as the opening act. As long as we don't deny the possibility of a relationship, people will be scrambling to buy tickets to see for themselves if they're a couple or not. It's a win-win for both of them."

"We were leaning more toward crossover

performers for opening acts. Artists who aren't only country."

"I think Sawyer's songs have a wide appeal, as well," Dean argued.

Heath wouldn't give in. "We were also considering female artists to avoid exactly what you're suggesting we promote—rumors about my daughter and her love life."

Piper saw it differently than her father for one very important reason. The baby wasn't going to be a secret forever. Eventually, she would have to not only come clean to her father and Dean but also the world. Maybe Dean was giving her the answer she had been looking for since this morning. Maybe the feelings she'd had for him were more real than she'd thought.

Piper let her head fall into her hands. Her thoughts drifted back to right before she'd passed out. Instead of walking away at the end of the song, Sawyer had been drawn to her. He was going to kiss her. Maybe his feelings had changed. Her father would have to come around. Sawyer would always be part of their lives.

"I need to talk to Sawyer," she announced. Everyone exchanged curious glances. "Now. I have to ask him something."

Dean went to find him. Her father sat beside her on the couch. "Do we need to go back to the hospital? I know you were sick before the performance, but maybe it's more than a stomach bug."

The sincere concern in his voice made Piper's guilt for keeping the secret resurge. Sawyer needed to hear the news first, however. "I'll be fine. It's nothing. Maybe I was more anxious about performing than I thought I was. I feel much better now, I swear."

"We don't have to include the Stratton boy in any of this. You know we can't let him distract us from your ultimate goal. It's not your job to sell his records, only yours."

"The rumors have already started. I need to talk to him about what's going on. I'm fully committed to making the crossover into popular music. I know what I have to do, and if Sawyer joins the tour, that's not going to change."

Piper couldn't let her father down. He had given up his career to be her manager, to help her make her dreams of being a country-western music star come true. The pressure of supporting her family was plenty of motivation, and now their family would be expanding.

Dean and Sawyer entered the room with equally worried expressions on their faces. Sawyer tried to smile, but it didn't reach his eyes.

"I need to talk to Sawyer alone," Piper said. Although they looked confused, Lana and Dean left the room. Her father needed an additional push. "I'll explain everything, I promise. Please give me a minute with Sawyer."

Reluctantly, Heath followed the rest out.

"How are you feeling?" Sawyer asked, taking her father's spot on the couch. He placed a warm hand on her knee. "You really gave me a scare there."

Piper's heart thumped double-time. Maybe everything was going to work out better than she'd imagined. "I'll be okay. Thank you for holding me up and getting me offstage."

"Anytime." His trademark smile was back.

"I wanted to talk to you about what happened. About what was about to happen *before* I fainted." Her stomach was in knots, but she had to know how he felt. If he had feelings for her, everything would truly be okay.

Sawyer stood up and rubbed the nape of his neck. "I am so sorry about that, Piper."

She could feel her hope rising. "Don't be sorry."

"Dean thought it would be a more dramatic ending if you didn't know it was coming. I wasn't so sure about it, but I'm the new guy around here. I'm just trying to make a good impression."

Piper's heart sank. "Dean told you to kiss me?"

"He told me to make it *look* like I was going to kiss you. Obviously he doesn't know about what happened between us, but he thought since Kelly Bonner was all about you and me being a secret item, we could really add fuel to the gossip fire."

So it had all been for show. Not real. There were no hidden feelings being revealed. Piper felt a strange amount of anger build in her chest. "So, whatever someone tells you will help your career, you'll do it. No questions asked, huh?"

Sawyer grimaced. He had basically accused her of the same thing a few months ago. "I should have clued you in on what was going to happen. Given the stuff that's gone on between us, I should have told you," Sawyer replied.

The *stuff.* Piper felt like a fool all over

again. This didn't change what needed to happen, though. In the end, there was only one solution to her problem.

With her heart in her throat, she stood up to look him straight in the eye. "Sawyer, I'm pregnant."

CHAPTER FIVE

"Excuse me?" There was no way Sawyer could have heard Piper correctly. The word pregnant could not have come out of her mouth. She had the stomach flu. Maybe she was delirious.

"The fans want us to be together, Dean said that going on tour together is the right thing to do for both of us, and the smartest move we can make is to give people what they want."

Sawyer's eyes couldn't get any wider. His mouth snapped shut. What in the world was she talking about? He could have sworn she'd told him she was pregnant, but now she was talking about what was best for their careers?

"Did you just say you're pregnant?" he finally managed to get out.

Piper began to flit around the room. Her arms flailed as she spoke. "I found out this morning at the hospital. Did you know they test for pregnancy without even asking? If you need an X-ray, they run a pregnancy test. Just like that. Then, the doctor walks in and drops the bomb—'You're pregnant!'—and you're supposed to take that all in and leave with your prescription for prenatal vitamins like it's no big deal. But let me tell you, it is a very big deal. It's the biggest deal ever."

"You're pregnant." Sawyer didn't know what else to say. He needed to sit down. His mind was racing. He plopped down on the couch and stared straight ahead. Piper was pregnant and he was the father.

How were the two of them going to raise a baby? Sawyer didn't have time to take care of his dog in this new life; how was he supposed to be a parent?

Piper kept moving like some sort of out-of-control Energizer Bunny. "I need to tell my father, but I thought you should hear it first. We need to convince him that this won't ruin everything. He'll know what to do so our careers stay on track."

Sawyer's brows pinched together. He didn't need Heath Starling telling him what to do about his child. Heath might control Piper, but he was not going to control Sawyer, and he *definitely* wouldn't be in charge of this child.

"This is our baby." He pointed to her flat stomach, trying to picture it round and swollen. "*We* get to decide what happens. Not your dad."

"I feel sick. I think I had too much sugar." Piper sat down next to him. "My dad can help protect my image."

"How can you think about your image right now?"

Piper didn't flinch. "How can I not? I am financially responsible for my entire family, Sawyer. My career pays for everything, including my brother's enormous medical bills. My family depends on me to uphold the image I've sold to the world." She placed a hand on her stomach. "And I am thinking about this baby. This baby is going to depend on it, as well."

Sawyer took a deep breath. "How is being pregnant going to ruin your image?"

Piper picked at the sequins on her dress. "Trust me. I've been at this longer than you have. I know how the business works. Country music is way more conservative than pop. I may be looking to cross over but my base is still country. Not to mention that my brand is good girl, girl-next-door, girl you can bring home to your mom. Good girls don't get themselves in this situation. Good girls get married and then have babies. There are mothers out there who would not want their daughters listening to my music if they thought I promoted anything other than a clean lifestyle."

Sawyer had issues with this logic but couldn't deny he'd seen other celebrities take a fall when a scandal hit. A baby and a wife weren't exactly part of his branding, either. He shook his head. How was *he* able to think about his image and career right now?

"Can I have a little more time to wrap my head around this before I have to deal with your father, who is probably going to kill me?"

"We have to tell him before I go meet with the tour promoters tomorrow to sign the contract. There's no way I can go on a yearlong tour when I'm going to have a baby in less than nine months."

The tour would have to be cut short. Sawyer hadn't thought about that. Heath really was going to kill him.

They agreed to meet in the morning for breakfast. They would tell Heath together.

Sawyer left Bridgestone Arena feeling much less confident about his future than he had coming in.

"THE MORE I think about it, the more I can't believe you're okay with the world thinking you and Piper have a thing going," Hunter said as they walked into their hotel. "Anyone who knows you is never going to believe it, and everyone who doesn't, will. So much for me being wingman to the most eligible bachelor on tour."

"I can't talk about this right now." Pretending to be dating Piper was the least of Sawyer's concerns.

"Poor Hunter is going to have to find his own dates," Faith teased. "And I'll say it again, there are worse things than dating Piper Starling."

Sawyer wasn't about to let himself truly fall for someone like Piper. He'd been avoiding women like her his entire adult life. Why had he let his guard down? Piper had made it clear back then and tonight that her career was her number one priority. She reminded him of women like his mother, who'd left her husband and children without ever looking back.

Sawyer wanted to be like his father—a strong provider who put his family first. But how was he going to manage raising a child while building a career in music? How difficult would Piper and Heath make it for him to be part of their child's life? He knew one thing for sure—he didn't want his child raised by nannies.

"I need a minute with my brother," Faith said, hooking her arm in his and pulling him in the direction of the stairs instead of the elevator. "We'll meet you upstairs."

She pushed the door open and motioned for him to lead the way. He might have grown up without a mother, but he had a Faith, and she knew him better than anyone.

"What's going on in that head of yours? Ever since you got done talking to Piper, you look like your favorite horse just ran away."

"It's been a pretty stressful day."

"Tell me what's really going on. Is there something wrong with Piper? Does she not want you to go on tour with her? What did she need to talk to you about?"

Lying to his sister was impossible, and right now he needed someone to talk to more than ever. "What if I told you it's not so far-fetched that Piper and I could be together?

What if we were together a couple months ago?"

Faith didn't buy it for a second. "I was there when you two were working on her album. You were living under my roof. You might have been flirtatious, but there's no way you were sneaking around having a secret romance. I would have noticed."

Sawyer side-eyed her as they made their way up the stairs. She was one to talk. Faith and Dean had carried on a secret romance for an entire summer over a dozen years ago when she was only eighteen.

"Right, because no one has ever gotten away with a secret relationship on our farm before."

"That's where you're wrong. Dad knew about me and Dean. I didn't know he knew, but he did. He told the Presleys about us." She was quiet, probably thinking back to when things were starting between Piper and Sawyer. "I'll admit, I noticed she looked at you like you hung the moon for a long time. I also noticed you were kind of loving all the attention. But those last couple weeks, it was different. It was almost like you were avoiding each other."

They had been avoiding each other, but

that was no longer a possibility. Piper would be a part of Sawyer's life forever. "What if we were in love? Or thought we were."

Faith laughed. "If you were in love, I would know, because it would change you. And you have been the same ol' Sawyer since she left Grass Lake."

"Well, I'm not the same Sawyer I was a couple hours ago."

"What's that supposed to mean?" she asked, trying to keep up with him. "What is going on? If you want me to tell Dean to back off this idea of you and Piper leading the rest of the world on, I will. I don't want you to feel like you have to lie about who you love or don't love."

"What if I don't have a choice?"

"What?" She tugged on his shirt to get him to stop. "Why wouldn't you have a choice?"

Sawyer pressed his back against the wall and pulled at the front of his hair. "I messed up, Faith. I messed up big-time."

"She's not sick." Faith stopped. He could imagine the gears turning in her head as she put everything together. She grasped the railing. "She's pregnant, isn't she?"

Sawyer nodded.

"Oh, my… Sawyer." She wrapped her

arms around him. He dropped his head on her shoulder. "We have to tell Dean," she said.

Sawyer straightened. "We can't. You can't tell Dean until Piper is ready to tell him. She is freaking out right now."

"How far along is she?"

"I would say about six weeks."

"When I was in Memphis for that horse show," she said, shaking her head. "Okay, six weeks. Has she made plans to see a doctor? She fainted today. Someone needs to make sure everything is okay with the baby."

"I don't think so. I think she's so over-whelmed, she doesn't know what to do."

"I know a midwife here in Nashville who would definitely be discreet."

Faith always knew what to do. Her level head had kept him out of trouble more times than he could count. "We can talk to her about it in the morning, when we tell her dad."

"I still think we should tell Dean."

"We can tell Dean when we tell Heath. Maybe the more people in the room, the less likely I'll end up dead. Heath is going to hate me."

"Don't worry about that. You're taking responsibility. That's all he can ask of you right now."

"What does being responsible mean? Do I marry her? Send her a check to help pay for expenses? I have no idea what to do. She thinks this is going to ruin her career. Is it going to ruin mine?" Sawyer was about to hyperventilate.

"Relax. Calm down."

"Faith, I found out I'm going to be a dad a few hours ago. I'm pretty sure when I wake up tomorrow, I'm going to need you to remind me this wasn't all a bad dream."

Faith frowned. "I hate that neither of you is thinking of a baby as a blessing." She placed a hand on her brother's cheek. "I know the timing sucks, but you're going to be a dad. That's the most important job you're ever going to have."

"Dad would be so disappointed in me for getting in this situation."

"Dad would be ecstatic about becoming a grandpa. He never would have judged you. You're both twenty-five years old. Our parents were younger than you when they had me."

"Yeah, but we're terrible parents already. Piper's freaking out. I'm terrified."

"If that makes people terrible parents, then everyone is a terrible parent. It's going to be okay," Faith assured him. "We'll figure it out. That's what family does."

Sawyer took a deep breath. He wanted to believe his sister, but who knew what Piper would think in the morning…or the lengths Heath would go to keep Piper's career on track.

CHAPTER SIX

PIPER'S HANDS TREMBLED. She sat on them to keep them still. Waiting for Sawyer to show up was torture. All she wanted to do was tell her dad what was wrong and let him fix it.

"Dean wasn't kidding," her dad said, lifting his eyes from his phone screen for a second. Heath had the country music TV station on in their suite while he scrolled through his social media feeds. "Everyone is talking about you right now. I haven't seen buzz like this since you met Prince Harry."

Sawyer wasn't the first guy the world had wanted Piper to date. A year ago, a very vocal group of fans had desperately wanted her to become a princess. At the time, she'd thought it was ridiculous. How she'd love to go back to laughing off the silly whims of some teenagers.

Piper jumped at the knock on the door. Her nerves were completely shot. "Remember to be nice, Daddy."

He smirked. "I'm always nice."

"If by 'always' you mean 'never,' I concur."

"Lana, I can be nice, can't I?"

Poor Lana froze as she arranged the room service breakfast they had ordered. "Of course, Mr. Starling."

Piper shook her head. There was no way Lana could answer that question honestly even if she wanted to. They all knew if there was one person who took the most of her father's abuse, it was poor Lana. "You're *too* nice, Lana."

She opened the door for Sawyer. Behind him stood Faith and Dean. Sawyer had texted her last night to tell her his sister had interrogated him until he broke. Faith was well aware of what was about to be discussed, but Dean was not.

"You ready for this?" Sawyer whispered as he greeted her with a hug.

"As ready as I'll ever be. You?"

"Let's do this," he replied.

The presidential suite at the Berkshire Hotel had two bedrooms, a spacious living room and an adjoining dining room. The living room had two sitting areas filled with plush couches and wingback chairs. A large flat-screen television hung on the wall above the fireplace.

"I figured we'd eat while we talked," Piper said. The table was covered in pastries and family-size portions of scrambled eggs, sausage, bacon and potatoes. There was a large platter of fresh fruit in the center.

They all sat down and everyone dug in except for Piper and Sawyer. Piper inhaled deeply. She'd never done anything to make her father angry with her. Growing up, she was the kid who did what she was told and never stepped out of line. Her brother's illness had given their parents enough grief.

Sawyer took her hand and held it under the table. The contact made her stomach flip and her skin tingle. As much as she appreciated the support, it was more distracting than anything else.

"So, Sawyer and I talked last night. We are both completely on board with touring together."

"That's great," Dean said. "I think it's a really solid business decision. You two are meeting with the tour promoters today?"

"This afternoon. Are you sure about this? We talked about a lot of other options," her father reminded her.

"There's a reason why I think it's a better idea to take Sawyer on tour," Piper replied.

Faith folded her hands in front of her. Her engagement ring caught the light and sparkled. Piper wished it was Faith and Dean making this announcement rather than her.

Everyone stared, waiting for Piper to go on. Surely they could all hear her heart thundering inside her chest.

"Do you plan to share?" Heath asked.

"When Sawyer and I were writing the songs for my album, we…thought we were in love. And foolishly, we acted on those feelings and—" Her voice cracked as her eyes darted from person to person. She didn't want to make eye contact with any one of them for too long.

"Piper is pregnant," Sawyer said. "We found out yesterday. We weren't sure how everyone would take the news, so we waited until this morning to tell everyone. Especially you, Mr. Starling."

Piper's father dropped his fork with a clang. "You have to be kidding me. Tell me he's kidding, Piper."

"I'm sorry, Daddy. I know this isn't what you want to hear right now, but I swear to you, I will do whatever it takes to make this okay."

Her stomach clenched as she waited for him to say something, anything to give her a clue as to what he was thinking.

"I suspected something was going on when I had to leave to help your mother with Matthew," he finally said. "I trusted you to not to do anything stupid, but I guess that trust was misplaced."

Piper squeezed Sawyer's hand as her shoulders stiffened.

"I don't think falling in love with my brother is stupid," Faith said, jumping to her brother's defense.

"Love?" Heath scoffed. "They were not and are not in love. They barely know one another."

"Okay, everybody needs to take a breath," Dean said. "Piper's pregnant. It's not the end of the world."

"Not the end of the world?" Heath's voice shook. "She has a reputation to uphold. She's about to start a yearlong tour across the US. This is a public relations nightmare."

"You've been drooling over all the positive press about me and Sawyer today even after I fainted on national television. Last night should have been a complete public relations nightmare, but we have everyone rooting for us to be together instead. Maybe there's a way to salvage this," Piper said.

Her father covered his eyes with one hand. His chest rose and fell with frustrated breaths. He dropped his hand, and his glare zeroed in on Sawyer. "There's only one way to salvage this. You will marry my daughter."

MARRY PIPER? SAWYER felt nauseous. The only Stratton getting married anytime soon was Faith. He glanced at Piper and those baby blue eyes. She had this sweetness about her that sucked him in. Maybe he had believed for half of a second that Piper could be the person he wanted to spend the rest of his life with, but she'd quickly proved she was not. She wasn't as innocent as she looked. She was as conniving as her father.

"I won't make Piper do any of this alone because this baby is my responsibility, too, but I can't get married. To me, people should only get married when they plan to stay married."

"I don't really care what your feelings on marriage are. You will make an honest woman out of my daughter before the press finds out."

Dean interrupted, "Heath, you can't force him to get married. Let's be reasonable about this."

"I am being reasonable! Aren't you the one who wanted to force my daughter to pretend she was in love with this boy? How is my request any less reasonable?"

Dean had no comeback.

Piper spoke up instead. "I know you're not in love with me," she told Sawyer, letting go of his hand. "I know you don't want to spend the rest of your life with me, but we are having a baby. We are going to be parents. My image can survive a divorce from the father of my child. I'm not sure it could withstand the beating it will take if the truth comes out."

There were a million things he would do for her, but marriage was off the table. "I can't marry you. We have to come up with another plan. What if being honest won't be as bad as you think? Our time together wasn't as meaningless as your father is acting like it was. I care about you."

"It will be just as bad as, if not worse than,

I think it will be. You say you care about me. I care about you, too. Isn't that enough?"

Sawyer couldn't believe she was this afraid of hurting her career. A loveless marriage was not worth all the success in the world. "Marriage should be based on love. I'm not *in love*. I like you, and I respect you too much to marry you knowing we're going to get divorced a couple months later."

Piper's shoulders slumped. "Do you really believe I want to marry someone who doesn't love me? This isn't about what I want, it's about what I need. I need you to do this for me, for the baby."

Faith pounded the table with her fist. The plates clattered and everyone's eyes turned on her. "My brother is not getting married. Period. You need to come up with a different plan. I don't care what it is as long as it does not include my brother making a vow in front of God that he does not intend to uphold. That is not the way we were raised."

"Well, I am pretty sure that God would take issue with him getting my daughter pregnant before making those vows." Heath raised his voice.

Sawyer had to stop himself from storming out. This was getting them nowhere and people were going to start saying things they didn't mean.

"Can we find a compromise?" he asked. "Can we say we're dating? Heck, I'll even go along with a fake engagement. I won't go through with a fake marriage, though. That's the line I won't cross."

"Engaged. Publicly?" Piper clarified.

Sawyer took a deep breath and nodded. "Publicly. And once enough time has passed, we call the engagement off."

"Are you sure about this, Sawyer?" Faith asked. "You don't have to agree to anything. We can think about it. Give everyone time to cool off."

"An engagement would be better than dating," Heath mused aloud without any apparent concern for Sawyer's certainty or lack thereof.

"Everyone on social media already thinks we're together," Piper added. "They've handed this to us on a silver platter. No one will doubt it."

Sawyer stared across the table at his sister. She had to know what he was thinking. He was just about to embark on a new life. One without any responsibilities tying him down. He was going to spread his wings and focus on himself. He'd spent his life working on the family's therapy farm, doing what his dad wanted and then helping his sister run Helping Hooves after their dad died. This was supposed to be his time.

He couldn't think like that. He had been raised by a father who was the rock to their mother's roll. A father who always put his children first despite their mother's selfish desire to be free.

He would never be his mother. "You're right. The ball is already rolling in that direction. Let's go with it."

"It works in your favor, really," Piper said. "In return for going along with this, you get to go on tour with me, get your music in front of more people than you could on your own. You can take advantage of the love my fans have for me, fans who will surely melt for the guy I tell them I want to marry."

He couldn't deny the positives that would come from being connected to her a little longer. Ever since Dean had suggested it, he couldn't stop thinking about how much exposure he'd get joining her tour. Raising a child was a lifelong commitment. But maybe he wouldn't lose every part of the new life he'd been building for himself.

"Don't do it unless you're absolutely sure," Faith said, trying her best to throw Sawyer a lifeline.

"It's not a bad plan," Dean said. Faith frowned. "I mean, it's not good that they have to lie, but it will help them both professionally. The better they do, the better they'll be able to support the baby. The sales will be off the charts. People are going to listen to every song on Piper's album, trying to figure out which ones are about you falling in love with one another. Then, they'll all turn around and buy a ticket to the show to see the lovebirds up close and in person."

Leave it to Dean to be able to put a positive spin on this whole thing. Sawyer wished he had his optimism.

"We'll need to come up with a story," Heath said, switching into business mode. "How you met, how you fell in love, how he proposed. All of that needs to be consistent whenever you talk to anyone."

"Sawyer and I will work out the details," Piper said. "We'll keep it simple so we don't get tripped up."

"I have a couple of conditions, as well," Heath said, raising two fingers in the air. "No one else can know the engagement isn't real, including Piper's mother." He fixed his gaze on Sawyer. "That means you will not flirt with any other women. You will appear completely devoted to Piper at all times, but public displays of affection will be kept to a minimum. Second, when the time comes to call it off, you will break the engagement, not Piper."

"Why does it matter who breaks it off?" Faith asked.

"Because if he does it, it makes Piper more sympathetic. We can't have her come off like an insensitive heartbreaker. Sawyer's much more appropriate for that role."

Sawyer tried hard not to roll his eyes. "Make me the bad guy. I really don't care."

"Well," Dean said, taking the napkin off his lap and setting it beside his half-eaten plate of food, "I guess all that's left to say is congratulations."

He stood up and walked around the table to give Piper a hug.

"Thank you, Dean," Piper whispered.

"Marriage or no marriage, this baby makes you family," he said. "And the Stratton family is a good one, I promise."

Piper's eyes watered. "Thank you."

"I think it's time everyone goes," Heath

said. "Piper and I have some things to discuss before we meet with the tour company and inform them we will only be signing on for a six-month tour. She also needs to call her mother and tell her the...news."

Piper's face paled. She had so many more people to answer to than Sawyer did. He stood and took her by the hand.

"It's going to be okay. And in the end, you'll have plenty of material for a great song about the jerk who broke off your engagement."

She managed to crack a smile for the first time since he'd arrived. "That's one way to look at it."

Sawyer reached up and brushed her cheek with his thumb. She leaned into his touch.

Heath cleared his throat. "I believe I said we have things to do."

Sawyer dropped his hand to his side. When the time came, it would not be difficult to convince the world they'd broken off their engagement because of her overbearing father.

"See you soon, Heath. Betcha can't wait. Maybe I can start calling you Dad. Yes? No?"

Heath pointed at the door. Dean grabbed

Sawyer by the elbow and guided him out into the hall.

"Let's not poke the bear, okay?"

"I can't believe you are okay with this," Faith said to Dean as they entered the elevator.

"I don't think anyone was really that interested in my opinion in the first place," he said, showing his palms.

Sawyer rubbed his forehead. "Don't be so hard on him. It's not like he knew we were going to drop a bomb on him."

"Well…" Faith cringed. "That's not totally true."

"I may have been informed last night," Dean confessed.

"You promised me you wouldn't tell him! What if Piper hadn't been okay with you two coming to breakfast this morning?"

"This is how I know you aren't ready to be married," Faith said, stepping forward. "The first rule of a good marriage is don't keep secrets. I think Heath is wrong to keep this from his wife. Honesty is the best and only policy. Lying by omission is still lying."

Sawyer should have expected his sister wouldn't be able to stay quiet all night. She and Dean had been through enough because of secrets and lies. It had been wrong of him to ask her to keep him out of the loop.

She was also right about him not being ready to get married. Hopefully he'd be able to pull off playing the doting fiancé. Everyone back home would be a tough sell.

As they exited the hotel, a handful of paparazzi appeared out of nowhere. The rumors had begun and the press was dying for more to the story. Cameras were rolling and the questions were, too.

"Secret rendezvous with your girlfriend?"

"How's Piper doing?"

"How long have you two been together?"

"Why have you been keeping this romance a secret?"

Sawyer ducked his head as the three of them ran for the car. He kept his mouth shut and could already imagine the look of dread on Piper's face when she found out reporters were circling the place like vultures.

"What does Heath Starling think about the two of you together?" someone shouted.

Even the paps knew who was in charge of Piper's life. Sawyer opened the passenger door for his sister and climbed into the back seat. Heath was going to do everything he could to control this situation. Sawyer needed to rise to the challenge.

CHAPTER SEVEN

"MY ANKLE IS a little black-and-blue, but it doesn't hurt to walk around."

Telling her father that she was pregnant had somehow been less daunting than sharing the same news with her mother. Maybe it was the impersonal nature of a phone call. Maybe it was the fact that Piper in no way felt like she would ever be as good at being a mom as hers was.

"Good. I wasn't expecting to hear from you so soon after we spoke last night. Is everything else all right?"

Piper glanced at her father's bedroom door. He hadn't said a word to her after everyone had left. He had had Lana run out and buy a home pregnancy test to be sure Piper hadn't been misdiagnosed. When it came back positive, he had gone into his bedroom and shut the door, leaving Piper to stew about the future and obsess over the way it felt when Sawyer held her hand.

"There was one thing I needed to tell you. I should have told you last night, but I was a little bit overwhelmed."

"Oh, sweetheart. That's understandable. You had a crazy day yesterday. What's going on?"

Piper crossed and uncrossed her legs. She was like the princess who could feel the pea under a hundred mattresses. No matter what she did, she could not get comfortable.

"When I was at the hospital yesterday, they had to do some blood tests before they could give me an X-ray." The other end of the line went dead silent. "Mom, are you there?"

"I'm here. Please tell me you're well. There's nothing wrong, is there?"

"Oh, no, I mean, yes. I'm fine. No problems. But I did find out something I wasn't exactly prepared for. They told me…I'm pregnant."

Her mom was quiet again before bursting with laughter. "That's a good one! I can picture your father's face when he heard that. What kind of hospital was this? How could they have messed that up so badly?"

Piper put her mom on speaker and pressed her palms over her eyes to stop the tears. Her throat was so tight, she wasn't sure she could get the words out.

"They didn't mess up, Mom. I did."

"What is that supposed to mean?"

"It means that I fell in love with Sawyer Stratton and we shared a moment of weakness six weeks ago, and in less than nine months, I'll be having a baby."

Her hands were no match for the tears that leaked out anyway. It was horrible to have to break the news this way. She couldn't imagine how disappointed her mother was.

"You're pregnant? For real?"

"For real. Dad had me take a second test to be sure."

Her mom was quiet another moment, which was a bad sign.

"How is your dad handling it?" she finally asked.

"He's disappointed and not talking to me."

Piper waited for her mom to repeat the same sentiments her dad had spewed before Sawyer and his family left. She had to be devastated.

"I know this comes as a surprise," Piper said to end the silence. "This is not the way I wanted to start a family, but here we are and I am ready to do whatever it takes to make it right."

"My baby is going to have a baby? Oh, Piper, this is so exciting!"

Exciting? That was not the word her dad had used. Piper's mouth fell open.

"You're happy for me?"

"Well, I realize I just called you my baby, but you're a grown woman. I know this isn't how you imagined your first pregnancy would go, but it is what it is. I'm going to be a grandma. Am I old enough to be a grandma? Your brother is going to freak out."

Piper was so stunned that her mom wasn't angry with her, she didn't know what to say.

"Matty's been a little frustrated lately. He said something yesterday about feeling like he's missing part of his life. Hearing he's going to be an uncle is going to put the biggest smile on his face."

"What do you mean, he feels like he's missing part of his life? Was he speaking literally about the seizures?"

"He's had a few absence seizures the last few weeks, but I think it's more about not having the independence he wants. I worry about him being depressed. I have a call in to the doctors."

Piper's stomach dropped. Matthew's seizures had begun when he was three. He was ten when they considered surgery, only to find he wasn't a good candidate because the seizures were happening all over his brain. Throughout adolescence, Matthew struggled with significant learning disabilities and behavior problems. His language was impaired as was his memory.

"I wish there was something I could do to help him." His illness made everyone in the family feel helpless.

Piper's career and success had become her father's primary focus in life at the same time the family had come to terms with the fact that Matthew was never going to have a normal life. Since then, Piper had always felt that because Heath couldn't make things better for Matty, he was committed to making sure she was a star instead.

"We all do, honey. But I am telling you, the baby news is going to cheer him up. I can't wait to tell him. When are we going to meet this Sawyer fellow?"

"Soon, I guess. We're planning on getting married."

"Married? Are you in love with him or are you getting married because of the baby?"

This was the part she hated the most. The lie was like a noose around her neck, tightening so she couldn't breathe. "Of course we're in love, Mom. We fell in love writing the album. We were scared to say anything, because you know how Dad is."

"Your father is going to have a terrible time. When a woman gets married, her father is no longer the most important man in her life. Always put your husband first, Piper. Even if it's going to be a tough pill for your father to swallow."

Well, he wouldn't have to swallow it anytime soon. There would be no marriage, no vows to make her and Sawyer man and wife.

They were saying their goodbyes just as her father's bedroom door opened.

"Mom says hi."

"Tell her I'll call her later."

"Did you hear that?" Piper asked her mom.

"Tell him I said to go easy on you. You're with child. He needs to pamper you."

Piper hung up and put her phone on the coffee table.

"She said she's excited about the baby. She hopes you and I can figure out how to be happy about it, too."

Heath exhaled a sigh. "Your mother has

always been able to see the glass as half-full even when it was empty. I'm not sure how she does it."

Piper's phone chimed with a text from Sawyer.

Call when you can talk

She tensed. Had he changed his mind already? The fear that he might back out was real. She got to her feet and retreated to her bedroom, closing the door behind her.

As the phone rang, she paced back and forth in front of the four-poster bed while trying to control her breathing.

"Hey, I hope I'm not bothering you," Sawyer said when he answered.

"No, it's fine. What's up?"

"My sister wants to know if you have plans to see a doctor."

"I can't see a doctor right now," Piper said, sitting on the edge of the bed. "We're meeting with the tour promoter today. I'm doing television promotion for the next week. I go home for Thanksgiving and then have rehearsals until the tour starts."

"Piper, you're pregnant. You need to see

a doctor. My sister knows a midwife here in Nashville."

"I'm sure the paparazzi would love to get a picture of me walking into a midwife's office. That would be super helpful."

"What if I told you all you had to do was visit Boone Williams?"

"Boone Williams is a midwife?"

"No," Sawyer said with a breathy laugh. "But he is dating one."

SAWYER HAD MET Ruby Wynn a handful of times when she'd brought her daughter, Violet, to Helping Hooves to work with Faith and the social worker on staff last summer. Her relationship with Boone had started while he was staying on the farm, writing his new album.

"You're sure Faith made it clear that no one else could know about the baby?" Piper asked as they pulled up to Boone's gated estate.

"Boone and Ruby are sworn to secrecy."

"But they think we're a real couple?" she asked as she tugged at the hem of her dress.

Sawyer threw his truck into Park. "We are in full fake-engagement mode."

Boone's mansion was something out of

Sawyer's dreams. Set in the middle of a cou
ple acres on the outskirts of Nashville, the
house was an all-brick beauty. Being rich
wasn't Sawyer's reason for going into music,
but it sure wasn't something he'd complain
about if he managed the success Boone had.

"Well, if it isn't the talk of the town,"
Boone said when he opened the door. "I
knew you'd make some amazing music together, but I gotta say, you surprised me with
the baby making." The megastar shook Sawyer's hand. "Congratulations."

"We really appreciate your help," Piper
said, accepting a hug from him.

"I'm happy to give it. I know all too well
what it's like to have my personal business
splashed across the magazines and internet.
You two deserve to keep this to yourselves
for as long as you want."

Boone was no stranger to scandal. He was
preparing a big comeback next year now that
he was clean and sober and a million times
happier than he had been when Sawyer first
met him. That probably had a lot to do with
the redheaded woman standing behind him.

Boone introduced Ruby even though they
had both met her in the summer. She had
kind eyes, which was important to Sawyer.

He believed he could tell quite a bit about someone by looking them straight in the eye.

"Dinner is supposed to be delivered in about an hour. If you want, we can take care of business before we eat. It's completely up to you," Ruby said.

Piper fiddled with her bracelets. "That would be great. Thank you."

Ruby led them all down the hall and into an office off the family room. Concert photographs decorated the walls. Boone had performed for millions of people all over the world during his career. He was a big reason Piper had gotten into the business and someone Sawyer admired as a musician and songwriter.

There was an ache in Sawyer's chest as he looked at the photos. Two days ago, he had been filled with the anticipation of getting out on the road and standing on stages like the ones Boone performed on. He glanced back at Piper, who had taken a seat across from Ruby. The thrill of touring had quickly been replaced by fear and anxiety. How was he going to convince the world he was happily engaged when he was currently miserable? All his hopes and dreams had to be put on hold once again. And then there was the fear of parenthood. What kind of dad would he be? What kind of dad would Heath *let* him be?

Ruby explained she'd be gathering a family history, drawing some blood and doing a thorough physical.

"Here?" Sawyer asked.

"The nice thing about a midwife is that we do house calls. It's not unusual for me to check on a patient in their home. I came prepared." She pointed to the medical bag by the chaise lounge. "Almost everything we need to do, I can do here, except for an ultrasound. I have a machine at my office, but we don't need to do one this early in the pregnancy. In a couple months, you should definitely have one done, though."

"I'm going to go set the table for dinner," Boone said, excusing himself. He gave Ruby a kiss on the cheek. "I'm leaving you two in capable hands, I promise."

This probably wasn't how Piper had imagined her first prenatal appointment. She spun her bracelets around her wrist.

"We're going on tour in a month. Is that going to be a problem?" Sawyer asked, taking the seat next to Piper.

"I don't know if I can answer that right

now. If she's in good health, she should be fine. You guys will have to keep up with regular checkups, though."

"We'll figure something out," Sawyer said since Piper remained quiet.

"How have you been feeling so far?" Ruby asked her.

"Fine, I guess. A little nauseous sometimes. Mostly tired, but that could be from my crazy schedule."

"She fainted onstage yesterday," Sawyer interjected. "That can't be good."

Ruby frowned. "That is definitely not good." She asked Piper a bunch of follow-up questions, jotting down notes as they spoke.

As hard as Sawyer was fighting not to feel overwhelmed, everything about this made him anxious. There was so much to worry about before the baby was even born. Piper worked harder than most people he knew. How was she going to take care of herself and this baby? How was he supposed to help when they weren't really a couple?

Ruby asked questions about their family history. Piper pulled a sheet of paper out of her purse. She was more prepared than Sawyer.

"My brother has epilepsy. Is that hereditary?" Piper asked, handing over a list of family medical concerns.

"Genetics play a role in epilepsy, but just because your brother has it doesn't mean your child will. The baby would be slightly more at risk, but that risk is small." Her smile seemed to reassure Piper. "What about you, Sawyer? Any significant family medical history?"

"My dad died of a heart attack at fifty. I don't really know anything about my mom. She could be dead, too, for all I know."

Piper gasped. "You don't know if your mom is alive?"

Sawyer's least favorite subject in the world was his mother. "She left when I was four. I think we got letters for a little while, but it ended pretty quick. My sister is more of a mom to me than she ever was."

"I'm so sorry. That's terrible," Piper whispered.

Sawyer didn't need anyone's sympathy. He'd dealt with his feelings about his mother's abandonment a long time ago. "Hey. Some people aren't meant to be parents. Unlike us," he said, touching Piper's knee. He could tell she needed the reassurance more than anything. No matter how afraid he was, he needed to make her feel confident that all would be okay. "We're going to be awesome."

Her forehead was still creased with worry. "Right," she said with a sigh.

"It's okay if you don't know everything," Ruby said. "We're simply trying to identify any possible concerns sooner than later. But there are a lot of ways for us to get information about the baby."

Ruby asked a few more questions before asking Sawyer to leave so she could examine Piper. He wandered out into the kitchen, where Boone was pulling some drinking glasses out of the cupboard.

"I'd offer you a beer, but I don't have any alcohol in the house. I've learned the hard way that the only way to resist temptation is to kick temptation to the curb."

Boone was an excellent reminder that everyone had their own issues.

"No worries. I'll take a Coke if you have one." Sawyer pulled out a stool from around the large island and sat down.

Boone went to the refrigerator and grabbed a can of soda. He slid both the can and a glass to Sawyer.

"So, you and Piper." Boone waggled his

brow and popped open his own can. "How's Heath dealing with all of this?"

That seemed to be a popular question for anyone who knew anything about Piper. "Heath sure does love his daughter and has lots of opinions about how she should live her life."

Boone chuckled. "You're a brave man. I only spent one month writing one song with that girl while her father breathed down my neck, and I barely survived. You're signing up for a lifetime of hovering. Good luck with that."

Sawyer would always have to deal with Heath, but hopefully not to the same extent he would if this relationship was real. In truth, he wasn't sure what would happen once the baby was born and they ended this ruse.

"I'm sure Piper is worth it," Boone said, scratching at his five o'clock shadow.

Sawyer dropped his eyes to the counter. "Right."

"Keep focused on the love, man. Without the love, all the other stuff gets in the way real fast. I learned that the hard way, too."

Sawyer's throat tightened as he nodded in agreement. He'd found that the less he said, the better when forced to lie to everyone around him.

"And you haven't even experienced what it's like to love a kid. That's a whole other level. Being a dad is life changing. Hard as heck but more rewarding than anything else you'll do."

"You can do both, right? Have a music career and be a dad? I mean, I want both. I want to be responsible for my child, but I really want this life. I want to go on tour and make music. It's been a dream, and the dream is this close to being a reality. Tell me I don't have to give that all up."

If anyone had the answers to these questions, it had to be Boone. He had lived it.

Boone set down his drink and placed his hands on his hips. He took a deep breath. "I'm not going to lie to you. It's hard. I didn't succeed at doing both. I missed a lot while Emmy was growing up. It's taken me until now to realize that I have to be willing to walk away from some things in order to put her first. Luckily for my daughter, my ex was willing to step away from the spotlight for a while to take care of her the way she deserved."

"So, it can be done?" Boone's ex-wife was

the one who had introduced him and Piper onstage last night. "Sara's still popular."

Boone shrugged. "The music business is tough. We've talked about this before. It chews people up and spits them out. You've got to be willing to work harder than everyone else. Especially in the beginning."

"I'm used to hard work. You know what the farm is like."

One side of Boone's mouth went up. "Yeah, I know what the farm is like, but in the music business, all eyes are on you. The farm can replace you and go on. The country artist Sawyer Stratton doesn't exist unless you're there every day making him relevant. Sara had more experience under her belt before taking a hiatus. She also had a husband who was selling millions of records to keep her in the style she was accustomed to."

"She chose family and you chose career."

"Yeah, but I wouldn't call that a recipe for success. We have an amazing kid, but we divorced and I nearly ruined my relationship with my daughter. I truly hope you and Piper figure out a better way."

"What if Piper and I choose both career and family?"

"I don't know. It's going to be harder with

both of you in this business. I mean, someone has to take care of the kid. Piper's more established like Sara was, so she can afford to be away longer before people forget about her. At the same time, the Piper Starling brand employs a lot of people, more than the Sawyer Stratton brand does. That's a ton of pressure. Everyone, from the bus drivers to the musicians who tour with her, depends on her. Everyone on the crew, her dad, even Dean, need her to work hard every day because their livelihoods depend on it."

Piper had basically said the same thing. It was why she was so protective of her brand and image. "I know we could get a nanny, but I don't want someone else raising my kid full-time. I know some people have to—even prefer to—do it that way, but I was hoping we could find a way to be more hands on while still working. Can people in this business make it work?"

"I have no idea what you two can accomplish. Maybe if you always tour together or take turns so one is home while the other is away. That's rough on a marriage, though. Like I said, it's all about balance, and figuring out the perfect balance is going to be up to you. The good news is you fell in love with an amazing woman. If you two hold on to that love and let it guide you, you'll be fine."

Sawyer didn't love that answer. He wanted it all without having to ask Piper to make sacrifices to get it.

"It's all about priorities. Look at my situation," Boone continued. "I've been away fixing myself, and I have no guarantee that the fans will welcome me back when this album drops. Hopefully they will, but if they don't, I'm okay with that. It was important to me to reconnect with the people I love. My relationships with Ruby and our daughters matter way more than how many albums I sell."

"Emmy and Violet will be happy to hear that," Ruby said, joining them around the island. Piper followed her.

"Everything good?" Sawyer asked, hoping for some good news. Boone's answers had only served to overwhelm him more. There was so much to think about, and not having to worry about how Piper was doing would help immensely.

"We'll have to wait for the blood tests to come back, but Ruby said I seem in tip-top shape."

"We still need to talk about eating right, foods you need to avoid and the inevitable weight gain that's coming. I hope you have a good seamstress going on tour with you."

"I have the best and a huge wardrobe budget."

While they chatted about tour budgets and the benefits of a good crew, Sawyer tried to wrap his head around what Boone had said. He made it sound even more difficult than Sawyer had anticipated to juggle this career and a family. Sawyer had grown up watching his father do it all. He had run his own business, coached Little League, made dinner for the family every night. Faith and Sawyer never felt like they were a burden. Big John had made it look so easy. Too easy. How was Sawyer going to pull that off? Boone was also under the assumption that Sawyer and Piper were in love and had that on their side to get through all this.

Love wasn't on their side, only deception. There was no telling how this was going to end.

CHAPTER EIGHT

"AFTER THE INTERVIEW, we need to hurry back downtown to meet up with the perfume people so you can choose from the scents they've narrowed down for you. I also confirmed your seven o'clock reservations at La Cage so you and Sawyer can make your first public appearance." Lana had a hard time keeping up as they made their way through the lobby of the Los Angeles Four Seasons.

Thanksgiving was next week, and Piper and Sawyer—and her team, of course—had successfully put everything they needed in place to make the big relationship reveal. Piper was scheduled to appear on the *Whitney Hansen Show* to talk about the new album and tour. What Whitney didn't know was that she was getting the scoop of the century.

Sawyer pulled his baseball cap down. He was about to become Whitney's surprise guest. He walked out to the limo first to make it appear as if they were trying to hide the fact that they were a couple.

A minute later, Heath held the door open for his daughter. Piper smiled and waved at the mob of fans who had given up their morning to wait outside the hotel in hopes of getting a glimpse of her. Two brawny security guards stood in front of the metal barricades that lined the entrance.

Everyone began shouting at once.

"Piper! You're the best!"

"We love you!"

"Was that Sawyer?"

"Piper, can you sign this?"

"Piper, can I get a pic?"

Everyone wanted their piece of her, but there wasn't time to greet them all. She smiled for some selfies and autographed glossy prints of herself. Near the end of the line, the most adorable little girl with big brown eyes and sandy-blond pigtails held out a magazine with Piper's face on the cover.

"How are you today, sweetheart?" Piper asked as she scrawled her name across the bottom of the photo.

"Good," the little girl replied. "I love you." Her fans, big and small, warmed Piper's heart in ways they would never understand.

Piper handed back the magazine. "You are so sweet. I love you, too."

"Can she please get a picture with you?" a woman standing beside the girl asked. Her phone was out and ready. "We traveled all the way from Vegas to meet you."

"That's so far! Thank you for coming to see me," Piper said before her dad grabbed her by the elbow.

"We're on a tight schedule. No more pictures." He tugged her toward the limo and away.

The look of confusion on the child's face was heartbreaking. Piper hated disappointing anyone, but a child was the worst.

She slid into the back of the limo as a familiar unease settled in the pit of her stomach. It wasn't like her to challenge her father, but something made her speak up this time. "It only would have taken a second to pose for a photo. Those people came a long way."

Heath didn't bother looking up from his phone. "That woman filmed the whole exchange between you and her little girl. Trust me, she got what she came for and then some."

There was no arguing with her father. He

was not one to admit he was wrong. Ever. Not that Piper tested those waters very often.

"Lana, next time we're in town, let's make sure not to leak the hotel online. I think we're past the need for all that. Incognito is the way to go," Heath said, slipping his phone into his breast pocket and fixing his tie.

Lana added that to the list she'd made on her phone. "Are we still tweeting where she eats dinner tonight?"

"Of course, we want everyone to see the *happy* couple. Hopefully Sawyer will learn how to smile by the time they go eat. Otherwise, the media is going to think he's a miserable piece of garbage who somehow got lucky enough to be with my daughter."

"Wow, Heath. Here I thought you and I were finally becoming buddies."

"Dad, please don't start. We *all* need to appear like a happy soon-to-be family this afternoon." Piper spun the diamond she had picked out to play the part of her engagement ring around her finger. There was no turning back now. Once they made the engagement public, the pregnancy would be next. Hopefully both pieces of news would be well received by the fans.

The ride to the Burbank studio was short.

Inside, they were greeted by Whitney's assistant, whose badge identified her as Casey. Casey was tall, slender and impeccably dressed. She gushed and couldn't thank Piper enough for coming.

"Thank you for having me," Piper replied. "I love Whitney."

"Well, she loves you, too. Let's get you settled backstage in your dressing room."

Casey left them alone, and Piper paced around the tiny room. She was about to lie to millions of people on national television.

"What are you so nervous about? You've been on this show before," her father said.

Before Piper could answer, there was a knock on the door and Whitney Hansen popped her curly-haired head in. "Hi, everyone!"

Whitney was one of America's most beloved talk show hosts. She had been a child star through her teens before disappearing from Hollywood for a while. When she tried to make a comeback about ten years ago, she'd struggled to find work on another sitcom, so instead of acting, she went into the talk show business. Her humor and charisma had won viewers over immediately.

"I am so excited to hear your new song

today. I've been waiting for the new Piper Starling album to come out ever since the last one was released!"

"That's what we like to hear," Heath said.

Piper introduced Whitney to everyone in the room, saving Sawyer for last.

"Sawyer Stratton? Why do I feel like this confirms the rumors are true?"

"Rumors? What rumors have you been hearing?" Piper purposely held up her left hand to show off her ring.

"Oh my goodness! Is that what I think it is?" Whitney grabbed her hand and gave the ring a closer look. "Are you—you are! Can we tell everyone?"

"I was hoping you'd be okay with me making a small announcement on your show today."

Whitney grabbed her tight brown curls with both hands. "Oh my, oh my! This is amazing! I am so honored that you want to do this on my show. We have to bring you out, Sawyer. I want the world to see this happy couple."

Sawyer seemed extremely displeased with that idea. Piper knew it was because it meant they would really have to sell the romance.

Everyone was already watching them to see how they acted around each other.

"Do I have to? My hair is not really TV ready." He took off his hat to prove his point.

"Oh, come on. The ladies love a guy in a baseball hat. We'll mention you're here and maybe have you standing stage left. I can invite you to join us, and you two can play it cool for a little bit before you tell the world the truth!"

The truth. Yeah, that was not happening. Piper gave Sawyer a pointed look. He needed to do this.

"Sounds perfect, Whitney," he said, probably cringing inside. "Can't wait."

Sawyer had gone along with this plan to announce their engagement on the *Whitney Hansen Show*, but he hadn't banked on having to help do the announcing.

Almost worse than having to go on television and lie was hearing Heath lecture him on all the ways he had better not screw this up for Piper. The man acted like Sawyer intended to walk out there and admit to being part of a hoax.

"Let's practice looking natural," Heath said once all of the show's people had left them alone. He had Piper and Sawyer sit on the couch next to one another in the dressing room. "Pretend Lana is Whitney."

"There's been a lot of talk about you two being a couple. True or not?" Lana asked.

"I guess you could say that our fans figured out our secret before we were ready to tell it," Sawyer replied. "Piper and I are together. We're a couple. We're in love."

"With each other," Piper added in case it wasn't obvious. She rested her head on his shoulder. He reached up and patted the side of her face. The awkwardness was epic. He could feel the heat of her cheeks as they turned a vibrant shade of red.

Heath's eyes were bulging from his head. "You two are trying to convince the world you're actually in love. Not convince me that you can't pull this charade off! No touching. She's not a pet, she's your fiancée."

"Maybe you should do the talking and I'll just smile and nod," Sawyer suggested.

"So how did you know Sawyer was the one?" Lana asked.

Piper straightened up. "I fell in love with Sawyer while we were writing songs for my album. He was charming and hilarious. He made me think about how I feel and what

I wanted to say. It was kind of refreshing. Plus, you should see this guy ride a horse wearing a cowboy hat." She fanned herself with her hand.

Sawyer's chest tightened. She sounded so sincere. Heath frowned as he glared at Sawyer. "Better," he said. "Piper should definitely do the talking."

"Now, THERE'S BEEN a lot of talk lately about you and a certain someone," Whitney said to Piper almost as soon as the interview started.

"Has there?"

Much to Sawyer's embarrassment, pictures of him shirtless flashed on the big screen behind them. "Do you recognize this man?"

Piper glanced over her shoulder and her smile widened. She was getting better at this game. "He looks vaguely familiar. What's his name again?"

The couple hundred people in the audience were eating this up. Whitney and Piper shared a laugh.

"Ah, I think you know. I believe you brought him with you today. In fact, can I get a camera over there on stage left?"

That was Sawyer's cue. He stepped out and waved to the screaming crowd. This was not the way he'd imagined his first television interview would go. He joined Piper on the guest couch.

"Well, well. Look who's here! Hello, Sawyer. Piper, have you met? This is Sawyer Stratton. Sawyer, this is Piper Starling."

The two of them shook hands and pretended to be surprised. "Nice to meet you," Sawyer said.

"Aren't they adorable. Come on now, Sawyer. I have to ask," Whitney continued. "What brings you backstage at my show today?"

"I heard you had that dancing dog on today, and I'm a big fan, so…"

"You're a big fan of the dancing dog, huh?" Whitney turned to her audience. Several of them shook their heads and shouted their disbelief. "They don't believe you, Sawyer. They know why you're really here."

He reached for the mug of water on the oval-shaped coffee table in front of them. He took a couple sips to kill some time.

"Okay, okay," Piper said, joining in the fun. "He came with me. I brought him to LA because he needed a little break before we head out on tour together in a couple weeks."

"You two are going on tour together. How

interesting." Whitney gave her audience a knowing look.

"Yep, I just thought since Sawyer's been so busy rehearsing and buying me coffee and an engagement ring, he deserved a vacation."

The audience immediately began to freak out. It was mass hysteria. Women were cheering like they had just won the lottery. Many were wide-eyed in disbelief.

"I'm sorry, I think I misheard you on that last one. He's been busy rehearsing, buying you coffee and doing what else?" Whitney asked over the din of the crowd.

Piper held up her left hand to show off the ring she'd purchased online a week ago. Sawyer felt kind of bad that she had to buy her own fake engagement ring, but not bad enough to part with the amount of money she'd spent on it.

It didn't seem possible for the audience to get any louder, but they somehow managed. Sawyer realized in that moment how popular his fake-fiancée truly was. Whitney pretended this was the first she'd heard of this news and threw to commercial break before hugging both of them.

"Great job, you two. That was perfect!" she said as they group-hugged.

The two people assigned to crowd control attempted to settle the audience and remind them to follow their cues. The show's director called for the next segment to start. The spectators managed to follow directions, clapping and quieting when told.

Whitney stared into the camera. "We're back, and in case you're just joining us, I'm here with my guests Piper Starling and Sawyer Stratton, who nearly gave this poor woman in the front row a heart attack. Are you okay, ma'am?"

One of the cameras turned to get her in the shot. The woman nodded and assured Whitney she was fine. She was still wiping tears and breathing heavily. "I'm just so happy for them. I'm the biggest Piper Starling fan. I knew after the Country Artist Awards that they were together, but I wasn't expecting this."

Sawyer was shocked at how emotional complete strangers could become over this. It made little sense that people would get so invested in two people they didn't even know.

"I wasn't, either, my friend! Did that really happen? Did you just announce on my show that you're engaged?" Whitney asked.

"We are," Piper confirmed.

Sawyer put his arm around her, hoping it made them look more like a real couple. The audience cheered for them again but quieted quickly.

"Oh my goodness, I am so happy for you two, but I feel like you just met. Are you sure you know each other well enough to take the plunge?"

Sawyer noticed a tic in Piper's jaw.

"I sure hope so," Sawyer answered, garnering a laugh.

"When you meet the right person, you don't need a lot of time to know he's the one for you," Piper said. "I think I knew it almost as soon as I met him. We just clicked."

"I am a huge believer in love at first sight," Whitney said. "At the end of their very first date, my father told my mother he was going to marry her. He said he just knew."

"Did she feel the same way?" Sawyer asked, his curiosity piqued.

"Oh, heck no. She told him he was nuts and asked her roommate to screen all her calls after that. Lucky for him, the roommate never did as she was asked and my mother gave him a second chance. They were married six months later."

"Sawyer wasn't so sure at first, either,"

Piper said after the audience stopped clapping for Mr. and Mrs. Hansen's love story. "But apparently I wore him down."

Piper gave his knee a squeeze. He pretended to laugh and pulled her closer. "She's lying. Who *wouldn't* fall head over heels for this woman?"

"No one," Whitney agreed. "I think it might be fun to test you two, make sure you're ready to take this next step in your relationship. How do you feel about playing a little game with me? It's a bit like *The Newlywed Game* but with a Whitney Hansen twist. Are you two up for it?"

Piper stiffened but kept the smile she was wearing firmly in place. "I guess so. What do you think, babe?" she asked Sawyer.

Every fiber of his body wanted to scream no, but he was in full fake-engagement mode, so he threw his arm over her shoulders and pulled her closer. "Let's do it."

Whitney had a member of her staff run out with two Ping-Pong paddles, "Piper" written on one side and "Sawyer" on the other. While they waited for Whitney to scan her game cards, Piper fidgeted with the paddle and her bracelets.

Sawyer needed to calm her down. He leaned over and whispered, "We got this."

She nodded, but the worry in her blue eyes didn't fade. Without thinking, he gave her a quick kiss on the lips.

Whitney sighed. "You two are so darn cute. I can't stand it."

She went on to explain the game. The object was to show the name of the person who most closely resembled whatever was asked. To get a point, they both had to show the same name.

"Okay, here we go. This person will kill all the spiders in your house."

Sawyer had no idea how Piper felt about spiders, but he had lived with a sister who once duct-taped the bathroom door closed because she had seen one in there and no one else was home. He raised the paddle with his name showing. Leaning forward, he could see Piper had done the same.

"Oh, one point! Good job. Who is likely to steal all the covers at night?"

Sawyer lifted the side with Piper's name on it for the laugh.

"He's always complaining he's hot, so it has to be me," Piper said.

"He's hot, all right," Whitney added with a wink. "Two points. Who's the better driver?"

Sawyer raised his name and felt the need to explain. "She never drives herself anywhere. I bet she doesn't even have a license."

Glancing at Piper's sign, they matched again. Piper cringed. "I don't. I never got it," she admitted with a shrug.

"Seriously?" Whitney shook her head and flipped to the next question. "Oh, I love this game. This one could get ugly. Who…is the better singer?"

Sawyer held up the side with Piper's name on it. He was nothing if not a gentleman.

"Did you all see how quick she was to raise her own name?" Whitney asked the audience with a laugh.

Sawyer nudged her with his elbow. "Thanks a lot, hon."

Piper's face flushed. "Honestly, I'm just trying to win, and I knew you would pick me."

"Aw, so sweet. You two are proving that you know quite a bit about each other. Let's see if you can get a perfect score. Last question. Get this right and you win. This one is almost too easy. I'll forgive my writers since they had to throw these questions together last minute." Sawyer relaxed, thankful for a simple one. "Who said 'I love you' first?"

Sawyer hesitated. If they were a real couple, this would have been the easiest question. Only, they had never said those words to one another. Sawyer had never said them to any woman. He held up his sign, hoping they had both picked the same sign.

Leaning forward, he saw Piper had chosen herself. He had picked himself. His stomach dropped.

"Okay, hold on a second. One of you forgot who said 'I love you' first?"

Piper pretended to hit him with the paddle. He held his hands up to protect himself. Trying to save face, he asked, "Wait, what was the question again? I thought you asked who fell in love first."

"Who *said* 'I love you' first?" Whitney repeated.

"Oh," Sawyer said, playing dumb. He turned his paddle around. "She said it first, but I was *in* love first."

"I'll give it to them. Perfect score. You have my blessing to get married," Whitney said before thanking them for coming on and congratulating them once more on their engagement.

They cut to commercial break and announced they would be filming out of sequence so Piper could be done for the day. She would perform before Whitney's next guest instead of at the end of the show.

"Good save," Piper said to Sawyer as they waited for the crew to set up the stage. "I know you were worried, but I think we fumbled through that pretty well."

"I was worried? You were worried. I could tell. You fidget with your jewelry when you're nervous."

Piper tilted her head. "I do?"

Sawyer nodded. "I'm very observant. I guess I know you better than we thought."

A stagehand came over and handed Piper a microphone. Sawyer told her to break a leg and headed backstage, where he watched her perform on the monitors. She really was the better singer.

Piper was a lot of things—beautiful, talented, funny, generous. He hadn't been lying when he said any guy would fall head over heels for her. Someone would fall for her and sweep her off her feet in the process. Some guy would tell her he loved her and marry her for real, without any hesitation. For some reason, that was as troublesome to him as the fact that this same man would also be another father to Sawyer's child.

A strange sensation came over him. He was jealous. Jealous that he couldn't be that guy because Piper's father hadn't deemed him good enough, and Piper never did anything without her father's consent. Sawyer had to pretend they were perfect for one another, knowing Piper had never really felt that way about him. But she would eventually feel that way about someone else. How ridiculous, to be jealous of some guy who didn't even exist yet.

Of course, someday he would.

CHAPTER NINE

"Do not touch those cookies, Sawyer, or I will chop off your hands after I finish chopping these onions." Faith held up her knife like someone out of a horror movie.

Sawyer put his hands behind his back. His chocolate Lab, Scout, gave them a sniff like he might be hiding something back there. "Someone should taste one to make sure they're acceptable for Heath Starling."

Thanksgiving was usually one of Sawyer's favorite holidays, mainly because he loved to eat and his sister was an incredible cook. The farmhouse smelled like warm apple pie, savory turkey that had been roasting all morning and her famous salted whiskey chocolate chip cookies.

Dean waltzed in, looking like he'd just rolled out of bed. He snatched one of the cookies right off the cooling rack. It was in his mouth before Sawyer could protest.

"Mmm-mmm. Heath will definitely approve." Dean gave Faith a kiss on the lips.

"How come I get threatened with bodily harm and he gets a cookie and a kiss?" Sawyer complained, grabbing a banana and taking a seat at the kitchen table. Scout lay at his feet.

"Advantages of being her soon-to-be husband, little brother," Dean said. "Too bad it doesn't work that way in a fake engagement. Bummer for you."

Sawyer rubbed the back of his neck. This year he was dreading Thanksgiving because of the lies he had to tell. He had invited the Starling family to Grass Lake for the holiday with the plan being to convince his friends this engagement was real.

"What time are our guests of honor arriving?" Dean asked, taking another cookie off the rack. This time Faith took it away and set it back down.

The Starlings had two estates in a town about twenty minutes north of Nashville while Grass Lake was a little over an hour south of the city. "I told Piper to come on over around two o'clock."

"Then I better jump in the shower and make myself presentable." Dean started to leave but sneaked back to grab another cookie and ran.

"You ready for today?" Faith asked.

"I cannot wait to lie to all my friends, deceive Piper's mother and brother, and listen to Heath tell me I'm not good enough for his daughter."

"I really don't like him," Faith said. "And I usually like everyone."

"He's so condescending. He treats us like we're two kids who don't know what we're doing. He thinks he needs to throw in his two cents all the time. Maybe when Piper has the baby, he'll accept that we're capable of handling this on our own."

Faith pressed her lips together and her eyebrows shot up.

"What? You don't think so?"

"I think you're being very optimistic that he's going to loosen his hold over Piper once the baby is born."

Maybe she was right. Heath's behavior during this entire ordeal was exactly why he hadn't fought her about wanting to end the relationship. Piper was completely under her father's thumb and too willing to put her career before everything else in her life.

Even if she truly had entertained the idea

of being in a relationship back then, Sawyer would have regretted it in the end. He wanted to be like his father without having to make the same mistakes. Falling in love with someone who wouldn't stick it out in the long run was one he absolutely wanted to avoid.

"I don't know what's going to happen," Sawyer said. "I only know I hate being disingenuous. It makes me feel like my emotions are everywhere and nowhere at the same time. I don't even know how I really feel about anything, because I'm so busy trying to make sure I act like I feel the way I am supposed to feel."

Faith stopped cooking and sat down next to her brother. "I hate that. I am all for telling the whole truth and nothing but the truth. We both know that lying has never gotten me what I wanted. What do you want?"

"I want to go on tour and play music."

"You're going to do that."

"I want to have fun and not have to constantly think about whether or not what I do is going to ruin someone's brand."

Faith frowned. "Piper's brand."

"Piper's brand, my brand, Grace Note's brand. I didn't realize this business was so complicated. I thought I was finally getting the chance to be me. Not the me Dad wanted me to be or the me you wanted me to be, but the me *I* wanted to be. Now I have to be the me Piper wants me to be so no one finds out who she really is."

"And who is that?"

"I don't even know!" Sawyer threw his hands up. "I'm not sure I've even met the real Piper. I've only caught glimpses of her. Everything about her is so calculated. She has to be this, that and everything else to keep everyone else happy."

"She seems so sweet and genuine."

"I'm not saying she's not a good person. She cares about people. But she also cares too much about what they think. Sometimes I just want her to tell me what's going on inside her head. She must have opinions that are only hers."

Faith put her hand on his. "She thought you two should be together while her dad was away. That was all her. She saw something in you."

Piper saw something in him, that's for sure. Sawyer felt so naive for thinking he had been with the real Piper a couple months ago. It hadn't taken her long to show him all he was good for were a few lyrics and mel-

odies. Whatever boosted the Piper Starling
brand was all that mattered. Faith propped
her chin up on her hand. "I wish I knew what
to tell you, but I'm just as lost as you are. I'm
here for you whenever you need me, though.
If you want to vent or scream or just be your
weird self, you can always do that with me."

She warmed his heart. "Have I told you
lately that you are my favorite sister ever?"

"That would probably make me feel more
special if I wasn't your only sister, but I'll
take it." Faith's smile lit up her whole face as
she went back to the kitchen island to finish
chopping onions. "Maybe you should talk to
Harriet tonight about the baby on the way,"
she suggested. "She might have some words
of wisdom."

Harriet was a dear family friend who had
acted as a surrogate mother to the Stratton
siblings after theirs left. She was big on personality and always willing to help without
being intrusive.

"That's a good idea. I'm sure she'll have
some interesting opinions about all this."

Faith chuckled. "Oh, for sure."

PIPER SLID THE charm on her necklace back
and forth along the chain. By the end of the

day, she needed to convince Sawyer's friends she had won his heart. Her stomach was in knots as she rode in the back of the town car to the Strattons' farm.

Matthew squeezed just above her knee. "You okay?"

"I'm fine," she assured him. "I can't wait for you to see all of Sawyer's horses. They are so beautiful."

"I wish I could ride," he said, staring out the window at the rolling hills.

"We can feed them apples," Piper said to console him. Sawyer had taken her to the stables to feed them when she was working on her album. He had kissed her for the first time in those stables. His lips had made her promises his heart couldn't keep.

The driver turned onto the dusty road that led to the farmhouse. The house where the baby growing in her belly had been conceived. It was also the place where Sawyer had rejected her. She touched her stomach. How different things would be if she had gone back to the bed-and-breakfast that night.

"I hope they like pecan pie," her mom said as they got out of the car. She wrapped an arm around Piper's back. "I figured if I made your dad's favorite, he'd stay through dessert."

Claudia was as smart as she was beautiful. Piper had always looked up to her mom as the epitome of patience and strength—besides being Matthew's full-time caregiver, she wasn't married to the most easygoing man. They had the same blond hair and blue eyes, but Piper couldn't ever imagine being as fierce as her mother.

"I hope I'm half the wife and mother you are someday," Piper said, taking the pie from her. "Though I know I don't have a prayer in the baking department."

Sawyer opened the front door before they even got to the porch. He wore jeans and an untucked forest green button-down shirt that was sure to irk her father, who thought holidays were formal affairs. His big dog barked at his side. Sawyer pushed the dog back into the house. He didn't wait for an introduction, instead wrapping her mom in a big hug and welcoming her to his family farm.

"It is so good to finally meet you," he said. "Piper talks about you all the time, but she failed to mention that you could pass for her sister."

Claudia waved him off with a huge smile. "Oh, stop."

"You stop. You must hear that all the time."

Piper and Sawyer had talked about strategy and she'd told him winning over her mother was imperative. He had obviously listened. The charm was turned up to ten.

"And you must be Matthew."

Matthew climbed the stairs and shook Sawyer's hand. "Hurt my sister and I'll hurt you."

Sawyer fumbled for something to say.

Matthew patted him on the back, laughing. "I'm kidding. I'm a pacifist. I would never hurt anyone."

"That's good," Sawyer said with a sigh of relief.

"Plus, she pays her huge security guys to handle that kind of stuff." Matthew winked over his shoulder at his sister.

"Don't listen to him," Piper said, handing him the pie. "He thinks he's hilarious. We brought a pecan pie."

"I love pecan pie, so thank you."

Heath trailed behind his family. Sawyer wished him a happy Thanksgiving, but Heath wasn't in the mood for niceties. "When someone tells you not to hurt Piper or else, you say you would never think about hurting her. That's what a devoted fiancé would say."

Her dad had relentlessly corrected Sawyer for the last few weeks. She could tell Sawyer was only going to tolerate so much more of that.

They entered the house, which was filled with the sounds of people talking and laughing. Sawyer had warned her that their family friends with no other place to go on the holidays came to the Strattons' house every year. Sawyer's dog gave them all a sniff before accepting that the Starlings were welcomed by the humans and therefore allowed to be there.

They moved through the farmhouse, meeting the other guests as they went. Jesse Keyes and Lily Peters were sitting in the front room. They both worked for Faith, Jesse as the therapy farm's social worker and Lily as a teen volunteer. Sawyer had strongly suggested Piper not get too talkative with Jesse. He was scary good at getting people to tell him their secrets.

Dean and his father, Ted, were filling the water glasses on the enormous dining room table that they had moved into the great room. Ted Presley was a supersized version of his son with blue eyes instead of green.

In the kitchen, Faith was busy cooking with the help of several of the guests. The woman dressed in an olive tweed riding jacket and a burnt-orange beret embellished with a flowery appliqué was Harriet Windsor. They had met a couple of times when Piper was working on the album here, and Sawyer had made it clear she was one Piper needed to win over.

"Can you imagine what Big John would say about all these famous people hanging around here these days? First Boone Williams, now Piper Starling. It's nice to see you again, dear."

"You, too. Did you do the flowers out there?" Piper motioned toward the great room, where the table was decorated with the loveliest bouquets of bright yellow sunflowers, orange lilies and rusty roses.

Harriet owned the flower shop in town and was very close to Sawyer and his sister. "Of course, I did. I might have overdone it a bit to impress a certain bride-to-be," she mock whispered.

Bride-not-to-be anytime soon was more like it. As lovely as the flowers were, it was unlikely that Sawyer's family friend would agree to do the flowers for Piper's wedding to someone else. If there ever was a someone else.

"They're gorgeous. You're very talented. I can't imagine Sawyer would want anyone other than you to do the flowers for his wedding."

"Sawyer's wedding," Hunter mused from the kitchen table, where he was putting the finishing touches on a black forest cake. "I can't even believe we're allowed to say those two words in the same sentence. Remember when you used to say you were never getting married, Sawyer?"

He had said that? Piper was surprised.

Sawyer drew in a long breath. "I know I said that in the past, but that was before I met Piper. Weren't you one of the people who always told me that once I met the right woman, I would change my mind? Well, Piper is the right woman."

Faith's friend Josie slid the sweet potatoes into the top section of the double oven. Josie Peters owned the Sundown Bar and Grill in town. She was also Lily's mother. "You have to tell us how and when you proposed. I love a good proposal story."

Sawyer and Piper had practiced answering all of these questions, but he seemed flustered. Lying to a camera was one thing; lying to his family and friends was another.

"His proposal was a little bit spontaneous," Piper replied. "It was after the CAAs. We hadn't seen each other for a bit between recording the album and the show."

"Seeing her and performing with her onstage just made me realize I never wanted to be apart from her again," Sawyer jumped in. "I asked her to marry me backstage. I didn't even have a ring."

Hunter's creased brow was full of skepticism. "You're telling me you were in love with her the whole time but never once let on there was something going on between you two?"

"Guess he's not the only Stratton who likes dating in secret," Marilee Presley said. She was Dean's mom. Dean and Faith had known each other most of their lives. They had secretly dated for a summer after Faith graduated from high school.

"At least Sawyer didn't wait twelve years to figure out she was the one. Unlike *some* people," Josie said as Dean emerged from the great room.

"What are we talking about?" he asked.

"How Sawyer and Piper are moving at the speed of light with this engagement," Hunter said. Piper hadn't expected him to be the tough sell. "I thought I was your best friend, bro."

Sawyer squared up to Hunter. "What is your problem all of a sudden?"

"How could you not tell me?"

It was clear Sawyer had no answer for that.

"That was probably because of me," Piper's dad said to help out. "They were apparently hiding from me. The less people who knew, the less likely I was to find out."

"Do you think they're moving too fast?" Harriet asked Heath.

"Why did this become an interrogation?" Dean asked. "Piper and Sawyer are in love. They want to get married. They are adults capable of making their own choices."

"Let's get everything on the table," Faith said. "Who's hungry?"

Much to Piper's relief, that was all it took to shift everyone's attention. Dean led the way into the other room. Sawyer and Piper hung back.

"Sorry about that," he said. "I didn't realize we were walking into an inquisition."

"Hunter is your best friend. He was with us at the awards show. Of course he's going to question how you could go from never wanting to get married to being engaged to someone he didn't even know you were interested in. Because you weren't."

It was disappointing that at no time when they were working on the album together had Sawyer spoken to his best friend about having any feelings for her. The way it had felt was so different from what it had apparently really been.

"I hate lying," he said.

She hated it, too, but Piper needed this facade to hold strong. Once they announced her pregnancy, more people were going to question the romance. They had to be as convincing as possible to squash as many rumors as they could when the time came to tell the world about their baby.

THE THANKSGIVING MEAL was served, which thankfully distracted everyone from asking questions Sawyer didn't want to answer. Instead, they were all busy devouring every last bite.

Sawyer was happy to see Piper and her family fitting in with this quirky little makeshift family of his own. Harriet and Claudia chatted all through the meal. Dean and his dad kept Heath occupied. Josie and Faith helped make Piper feel welcome.

Matthew didn't say much, but he seemed to be enjoying the food. Sawyer had been told it was hard for her brother to follow what people were saying when there were multiple conversations going on at once. He also had word-retrieval issues, which embarrassed him in front of strangers.

"Have you talked to Boone lately?" Jesse asked Sawyer as the meal was coming to an end. He wiped his mouth and set his napkin on the table. Boone and Jesse had spent a lot of quality time together when Boone was on the farm last summer.

"Piper and I had dinner with him a couple days after the CAAs. He's looking good. He seems very happy."

Jesse smiled. "You think Ruby has something to do with that?"

"I would say she probably has a lot to do with that."

"Love changes a person. Of course, I'm preaching to the choir. You know all about that, don't you?"

Sawyer thought he knew what love felt

like, but obviously he had been wrong. He glanced over at Piper sitting on his other side. She laughed at something Josie said. Her head fell back and her eyes closed. It had been a long time since he'd seen her laugh like that. Lately, all she did was frown or bite her lip with worry.

"Is he okay?" Jesse asked. The concern in his voice got Sawyer's attention. He looked back at Jesse, who was staring at Matthew.

Piper and her mother took notice, as well. Matthew sat rigid in his seat. His eyes were fixed on the wall behind Faith's head. He didn't blink or move.

"He's okay," his mother said. "He's having a seizure. He'll be okay."

Piper wrestled the fork out of her brother's hand. The whole table went silent as everyone waited for the seizure to pass. Heath froze in his spot. After a minute or so, Matthew began to blink. Claudia kept asking him if he could hear her, but he didn't respond.

Sawyer hated feeling helpless. He didn't know what to do or say, so he sat by and watched. The joy he had seen on Piper's face a moment ago was completely erased by worry and fear.

"Matthew has epilepsy," Piper explained

without making eye contact with anyone. Her voice was tight. "He's having what we call an absence seizure. He's going to be very embarrassed when he comes out of this. If you all could please keep eating and talking, it would help a lot."

Everyone did their best to go back to normal. Matthew eyes began to dart around. His breathing changed, quickening as he regained consciousness.

"You're okay," his mom said. "We're at Thanksgiving dinner with Piper and her fiancé. We're in Grass Lake. You're okay."

Piper started to hum "You Are My Sunshine" and Matthew's body relaxed. She ran her fingers through the hair above his ear.

"You're okay," Claudia continued to repeat. "We're eating Thanksgiving dinner at Sawyer's. Does your head hurt?"

Matthew nodded. "It hurts."

"On a scale of one to ten, how bad does it hurt?"

Matthew's eyes roamed around the table. His face was flushed and dripping with perspiration. His mouth began to move as he tried to form the word, but nothing came out.

Faith offered a place for him to lie down. Piper and her mother helped him to his feet and followed her out of the room. Harriet went after them. Heath looked as though he had been holding his breath until the entire episode was over. Sawyer could see his frustration and discomfort.

"Do you want to check on them?" Sawyer asked him.

Heath shook his head. "Would you show me where the bathroom is?"

Dean offered to show him, leaving Sawyer once again with nothing to do except sit with the rest of the mortified group.

"Sorry about that, everyone," he said, not knowing what else to do but apologize.

"Don't be sorry. That poor young man," Marilee said. "What a horrible disorder."

Faith returned with a dessert platter full of cookies. "I think we all need a little sweetness after that."

Sawyer and Josie jumped up to help clear the table for dessert. After dropping some bowls in the kitchen, Sawyer went into the front room, where Matthew was resting on the couch.

"How are we doing out here?" he asked. Piper turned to face him. Her eyes were watery.

"He'll be fine. He needs a few minutes for the headache to pass."

"Can I get you anything?"

"A cure for epilepsy?"

Sawyer didn't think about how he was supposed to act or what a devoted fiancé would do. He did what felt natural. He put his arms around Piper and pulled her close.

"You are a really good sister."

She linked her hands behind his back and pressed her cheek to his chest. "I pay all this money for doctors and medicines and nothing helps. It's so frustrating." She lowered her voice. "My mom wants to get him into this experimental medication study she found in Pennsylvania. It's going to cost more than I'd planned to get them out there and set them up with a place to live while he's in treatment."

Everything Piper had been saying about why she needed to protect her image was making perfect sense when Sawyer saw her brother's illness up close and personal. There was no room to wiggle out of this fake engagement. Piper's reputation needed protecting so Matthew could get the treatment he needed. Maybe she cared so much about her image because of the people she loved after all. Sawyer just wasn't one of them.

"I'm here for you," he said, but she stiffened and pulled back.

"We've got this. Don't worry about me."

Sawyer couldn't hide his confusion. She had this way of running away from him even when they were in the same room.

"Come help me get started on the dishes," Harriet said to Sawyer from the doorway. If he wasn't needed here, there was no reason to stay.

"Thanks for helping out," he said as they began sorting through the dirty dishes. "Piper was worried that he might get triggered."

"It's a shame what that young man has to deal with. His family is wonderful, though."

"Piper and her mom are great." Sawyer wasn't about to give Heath any credit.

"I could see how hard it was for his dad to watch that. It's no wonder he's so focused on Piper. At least he feels he can do some good there."

"Focused is a nice way to put it. I usually call that level of interest an obsession."

"You know, it's pretty normal for there to be friction between a man and his father-in-law, especially when the woman is the dad's only daughter. Your grandfather used to give your father a heck of a time."

"What?" Sawyer had never met his maternal grandfather, who had passed away before he was born. "Dad never mentioned that. He always spoke well of Grandpa."

Harriet laughed and bent over to retrieve the dishwashing liquid from under the sink. "Oh, my, your mother used to tell me stories!"

"Like what? What was Grandpa's issue?"

"Well, he thought they were too young to get married. Your father didn't have a college degree yet, and your mother…" She paused for a long beat. "Your mother had never committed herself to anything, let alone any*one*, in her entire life. He thought it was a big mistake."

Sawyer really couldn't argue with that. "I guess he was sort of right."

"What?" Harriet shrieked. "Because of that marriage, you and your sister were born. I don't think your parents would ever call that a mistake. I know I wouldn't."

"I know Dad never would have said that. He loved us. He wanted us. Mom, on the other hand—she clearly thought it was all a very big mistake."

"Is that what you think?"

"That's what I know. She left, Harriet. Never came back. Never called. Never cared. She's no one to me."

Harriet frowned and sighed. "I love you and I love your mom. I don't know why Gretchen thought her leaving was best for you all, but I have to believe she did it because she thought it was."

"I love you, too, but you cannot convince me that my mom left her amazing husband and two little kids because she thought it was better for them. If you said she left because she thought it was better for *her*, then I would believe you."

Sawyer could feel his blood beginning to boil. If there was someone who got under his skin worse than Heath Starling, it was Gretchen Stratton.

"How'd we get on the subject of your mother anyway? I thought we agreed not to go there."

Sawyer and Harriet had a long-standing agreement not to talk about his mother, because they were destined to disagree. There was nothing Harriet could say that would make him think Gretchen was anything other than selfish.

"You were supposed to be giving me some insight into my future father-in-law. Did Grandpa come around? He must have eventually figured out that Dad was a stand-up guy."

"He sure did. As soon as Faith was born. When he saw what kind of father your dad was, he came around. Your dad loved your mom and his kids with everything he was. So, if you're worried about Mr. Starling, my suggestion is just love your wife—and someday your children—with all your heart. Make it undeniable and he'll come around."

This felt a lot like the speech Boone had given him a couple weeks ago. Love, love, love. Would his father have loved his mother so much if he had known she was going to run away? Would he have tried so hard to give her everything she wanted if he had known their family would never be enough for her?

Piper wanted to be famous. To provide for her family by doing as she was told. She would always bend to her father's interpretation of what was right for her, because taking care of her family was the most important thing. Sawyer could love her with all his heart and in the end, Piper could still walk away. The fake engagement was about pleasing the masses. As soon as they lost interest, so could Piper.

Sawyer would not fall blindly in love like his dad did, trusting that someone would put him first, only to be disappointed. Love like that was a risk Sawyer wouldn't take, but he would emulate his father in another way.

The baby had already won his heart. Sawyer had no idea what Heath had in mind. Maybe he planned to have Piper raise the baby without Sawyer. Maybe Heath would encourage Piper to turn custody over to Sawyer once he saw what kind of father he could be.

When the baby was born, new rules would have to be established. Sawyer wouldn't lie to his child—or make his child live a lie. He certainly wouldn't walk away from the baby, no matter what Heath or Piper thought was best for her career. This was a conversation he and Piper needed to have, and soon.

CHAPTER TEN

"OH, PLEASE DON'T CRY!"

Piper threw her arms around the teenage girl who had dissolved into tears when it was her turn to meet the country singer. The girl could barely speak. Her equally emotional friend joined in the hug. It was the opening night of Piper's tour. The holidays were over and January was in full swing.

Performing and recording music were all Piper had wanted to do since she was knee-high. What she hadn't expected was the loneliness that would come hand in hand with celebrity.

Thankfully, the meet and greets backstage before the show gave her a chance to connect with her fans on a personal level. That was something she couldn't get when she was on-stage in front of tens of thousands of them.

"We just love you so much. We can't believe we're here," the first girl said.

More tears. More hugging. Piper thanked

them for coming to the show and for supporting her new album. Sawyer hung back, seemingly a bit afraid of the overwrought teenagers.

"I'm so happy for you two," the second girl said. "Hannah wanted you to marry Boone Williams, but I think he's too old for you. You and Sawyer are perfect."

"Oh my gosh, Sabrina! I do not want her to marry Boone! I said a long time ago that it would be cool if she got to marry her idol, but I've wanted Piper and Sawyer to get together since their song came out," Hannah defended herself. "You're adorable together."

"Well, thank you. It would have been very cool to marry Boone as well, but he is madly in love with someone else, so I am stuck with this guy," Piper joked, trying to ease the girl's embarrassment and her own.

There was one more round of hugging before Piper and Sawyer signed the girls' backstage passes. They posed for a picture, and Piper hoped this was a day the girls would never forget.

"Be sure to stop at the candy bar over there and fill up a bag with all the sugar you can handle."

The candy bar had been Piper's idea. Glass

jars filled with every colorful candy imaginable were lined up on tables along the back wall. Lollipops were displayed in huge, floral-like bouquets, and there was enough chocolate to make every man, woman and child backstage happy. Something sweet from America's sweetheart.

"You do a good job of making this moment magical," Sawyer said, leaning close. "I'm taking notes."

The smell of his cologne brought back memories of being in his arms. Memories Piper wished she could forget. His brown eyes melted her insides. She wondered if he knew how unfair it was for a man to have such beautiful eyelashes. She turned her gaze on the next fan waiting to meet them, wishing all these feelings Sawyer stirred in her would go far, far away.

Pretending to be in love was messing with her head. The pregnancy hormones weren't helping, either. Besides this new desire for something real to happen between her and Sawyer, Piper could easily eat every piece of milk chocolate on the back table. Resisting all forms of temptation when they were right in front of her was torture.

Last up at the meet and greet was a family brought backstage by the Wish Upon a Star charity group. Piper had been prepped ahead of time. Liam was a six-year-old with Stage IV neuroblastoma. The cancer that had started in the nerve tissue of his abdomen had spread to his lymph nodes and was now in his liver. His parents had told WUAS that Piper's music was the one thing that brought him comfort in the hospital when he went in for treatments and surgeries. He knew every word to every song.

He also only had a few months to live. Piper swallowed the lump in her throat as the brave little boy confidently strode up to them.

"I have a bone to pick with you, mister," he said, shaking a finger at Sawyer. His bald head was covered by a Carolina Panthers baseball cap, and his WUAS T-shirt was too big for his tiny frame.

Sawyer put his hands up like he was surrendering. "What did I do?"

"I was supposed to marry Piper when I get big and you stole her away." He folded his arms across his chest and glared at Sawyer.

Sawyer was quick to apologize. "I'm so sorry, man. I didn't know you were interested. She probably only said yes to me because I asked first."

"Liam actually wrote her a letter a year ago asking if she would marry him," his mother said.

"See? You stole her." Liam threw his hands up.

"Piper, we need to talk. You did not mention you were waiting for someone to get bigger when I asked you to marry me."

"Oh, Liam. This is all my fault," Piper said, getting down on one knee to be at his level. "I was so worried you would find a nice girl your own age that I accepted Sawyer's proposal instead."

"It's okay. Waiting for me to get big is gonna take a long time." Liam placed a hand on her shoulder. "You deserve to be happy, babe."

"Did he just call her babe?" Sawyer asked Liam's mom with a laugh.

"He's always had personality to spare," she replied.

Piper loved this kid. "You are too much. Can we be friends at least?"

"Friends." Liam offered to shake her hand, but she opened her arms for a hug instead.

He wrapped his little arms around Piper and hugged her with everything he had.

Piper cleared her throat and wiped her eyes discreetly as she stood back up.

"I have a couple questions for you," Liam said, pulling a piece of paper out of his front pocket. "I'm writing a blog post about meeting you, and I need some facts."

"Great. I love giving facts." Which was true. Piper much preferred telling the truth.

"First, if you could be any superhero, who would you be?"

Piper had to think about it for a second. "Tough question. I'm going to go with Wonder Woman, because her costume is pretty awesome."

Liam's giggle made Piper smile. "You can't pick her because of the costume!"

"I can't? But that's what us girls care about!" She winked.

Liam accepted her answer and moved on to Sawyer. "What about you?"

"I want to be you."

"Me?" Liam's brow furrowed.

"Yeah, you. I heard you've been very brave. Braver than any superhero I know."

Piper and Liam's mom exchanged a look, both clearly touched by that answer.

"Pretty good answer for a wife stealer." Liam looked over his list of questions. "Which would you rather be, a fish or a bird?"

"Bird. Who doesn't want to fly?" Sawyer answered first.

"Me," Piper said. "I would be a fish. I hate flying."

"You would make a lovely mermaid." Sawyer made her blush when he said things like that.

"Which cookie is the best—Oreos or chocolate chip?"

"Oh, come on, peanut butter is the best! You're not even going to make that a choice?" Piper had a peanut butter cookie obsession. They were the only thing on her tour rider that she actually ate.

"My sister makes these peanut butter and bourbon cookies for the Sundown that you would die for," Sawyer told her. "Remind me to text her later. I'll have her send some to one of the next stops on the tour."

Why did he have to be so nice? *He's playing the part of the devoted fiancé*, she had to remind herself.

Liam ran through the rest of his questions

and then announced he had one more important one.

"Lay it on me," Piper said.

"I know you probably give lots of money to charity, but I wanted to know if you would be willing to support my charity, the Super Liam Foundation, to fight childhood cancer?"

Piper didn't hesitate. "Of course I would."

"So you are a superhero. I knew it," Sawyer said.

Liam looked like he'd won the lottery. Liam's mom had brought several items that they planned to auction off at an event they were having for the Super Liam Foundation a couple weeks from now, and she asked Piper and Sawyer to sign them. Sawyer finished first and took Liam to fill up a candy bag.

"Thank you so much for doing this. It really does mean a lot to him," his mom said.

"We're happy to do it," Piper said as she signed some CDs. "He's awesome."

"You and Sawyer are really good with kids. You'll be great parents someday."

Piper's hand slipped and she smudged her signature. Would they? She'd spent so much time working out how they were going to convince the world their engagement was real, she hadn't thought to talk to Sawyer about how they'd parent their child once the engagement was called off. Maybe they'd parent tag-team style, one at a time. That wasn't very traditional.

"Hopefully," she said, wanting to talk about anything other than babies. "We're just looking forward to the wedding."

"I bet. The way he looked at you when you were talking with the fans was really sweet. You can tell how much he loves you."

Correction—Piper wanted to talk about anything other than babies or how well Sawyer was faking his feelings for her.

WHILE PIPER AND Liam's parents chatted about what else she could do to help, Liam hit the candy table with Sawyer.

"Piper definitely thinks I'm cuter than you," Liam said as he filled up his bag with gummy bears, which were supposedly his little sister's favorite.

Sawyer laughed. "You might be right."

"But she loves you, so you're pretty lucky."

"Very lucky." Sawyer scratched the nape of his neck.

"Maybe I can come to your wedding. I could be the ring boy."

The knot in Sawyer's stomach tightened. One, there was never going to be a wedding and two, even if there was, Liam probably wouldn't be alive to see it.

"I don't see why not," Sawyer answered. He swallowed hard, trying not to think about how this kid would never grow up to be the big man he wanted to be. He wouldn't fall in love and get that first kiss. He wouldn't get to go to prom or marry the girl of his dreams. Or hold his own child in his arms.

Lucky. Sawyer had been lucky enough to do many of those things, but he took others for granted. He was about to become a dad. It was one of those things he'd thought he wouldn't get to experience since he had sworn off marriage. Meeting Piper had changed all that. For the short time they'd been together, he'd started to believe marriage wasn't the dirty word he'd built it up to be. Of course, he'd never imagined those feelings would lead to them having to pretend to take the plunge. Now, he wasn't sure where he stood on the idea of spending his life with someone.

Liam ran back over to Piper. She was in her element tonight. She had walked into this room full of fans and lit it right up. She'd had no qualms about hugging whoever she could get her hands on.

The fans had been mildly interested in Sawyer, but they were definitely more excited to see Piper. She'd reminded him of his sister—Faith and Piper both had a way of making everyone feel welcome.

She'd had them under her spell. She was good at that. Sawyer couldn't afford to let himself get caught in her web, though. He needed to protect his heart. Piper treated everyone like they were special, but who really was? Sawyer wasn't about to fall for someone who held him in the same regard as she held a fan or a friend. He wanted someone who loved him back. Maybe he had more abandonment issues than he cared to admit, but he wanted someone who would choose him over everyone else. Piper wouldn't...or maybe *couldn't* do that.

"I can't tell you what it means to Liam that you guys are willing to support his foundation," Liam's dad said, joining him at the candy bar.

"He's a real inspiration," Sawyer said. "It's

hard to believe he's only six. He's wise beyond his years."

Tears welled in the man's eyes. "He's been through more than most people ten times his age. Two months ago, the doctors told us he only had about three months left. I wish he would get those sixty years. But every day is a gift at this point."

Sawyer's heart clenched. Liam was busy showing his mom and Piper everything he had in his bag and explaining all the people he wanted to share with. He was so generous when so much was being taken from him. Sawyer fought back his own tears at the thought of such a bright light being extinguished.

"I'm so sorry."

"Don't be sorry," Liam's dad said. "It would have been worse not to know him at all. These six years have been a roller coaster, but I wouldn't give them back for all the money in the world."

Sawyer couldn't help but admire the man's strength. Having been so caught up in his drama with Piper, Sawyer hadn't thought about what loving a child would be like. He'd assumed it would be easy. Yet this experience had shown him it was anything but. What horrible helplessness this man must feel day in and day out.

Piper, on the other hand, had firsthand experience with this kind of thing. Her family dealt with her brother's illness every day. She was willing to do anything to help Matty and would most likely go to any extreme for their child, as well. Maybe that was why she was so afraid. She knew bad things could happen and that this job they were about to take on would be full of challenges—even if their child was completely healthy.

Sawyer watched Liam's father rejoin his family. He put his arm around his wife and kissed her head. The burden the two of them carried was so heavy, but because they carried it together, they could still breathe. Sawyer's gaze fell on Piper. How much more could they accomplish together?

Lana announced the end of the meet and greet. Time to shift into performance mode. If this was how all these things were going to be, Sawyer was in trouble. The emotional toll was more than he'd ever expected.

"I have to go and you better get in your seats for the show," Piper said, trying to sound as upbeat as she could. "But I want to thank you for coming to see me today."

"You're welcome." Sweet Liam smiled from ear to ear. "Sawyer said I can be in your wedding. Just email my mom with all the details."

Sawyer's eyes went wide. He hadn't expected the kid to tell Piper. Her jaw was tight, but she managed a smile.

"I'll do that," she said and gave Liam a kiss on the cheek.

When Liam and his family left the room, the only ones left behind were Piper, Sawyer, Lana and a couple security guards. Piper pressed her back to the wall and covered her face with her hands.

"Hey." Sawyer had to control the emotion in his own voice. He wrapped his arms around her and pulled her against his chest. Piper cried on his shoulder as he rubbed her back.

Lana escorted the security guys out of the room and closed the door to give them some privacy. Wouldn't want anyone to know this whole thing was nothing but a giant fraud.

"Life is so unfair," she said as she cried. "He seems so full of life."

"I know."

"His mom said he—he—he isn't expected to make it to his seventh birthday. Why did you tell him he could be in our wedding?"

"I wanted to give him something no one else could."

"What?" she sobbed. "Another lie? Is that all we do now?"

Sawyer pulled back and held her wet face in his hands. "We gave that little boy hope. Hope that he might get to walk down the aisle at Piper Starling's wedding someday."

"What good is it to hope for something impossible?" Her eyes bored into his, begging for an answer.

"Without hope, all he's left with is fear. Hope keeps the fear of death at bay."

"Can you stop?" She pushed him away and took a couple steps back. "You're always making me feel things I don't want to feel."

"I'm sorry," Sawyer said, frustrated that they were in this situation. "I'm not trying to do anything but help you."

"Well, it's not helping. I get that this is all pretend. But when you treat me like you care about me behind closed doors, you give me this false hope. Hope doesn't make things better. It hurts."

Was that what he had been doing? And since when was Piper hoping there was something real going on between them?

"I'm not *acting* like I care about you, Piper. You were the one who told me we were moving too fast, that it was the wrong time to get into a relationship. Or did you forget about that?"

"Well, you didn't argue with me. You seemed to agree that the timing wasn't right, that we were caught up in something that wasn't real."

"Maybe you made me feel things I didn't want to feel. Maybe I let you go because I don't trust you. I definitely don't trust your dad."

"You don't trust my dad?" The tips of Piper's ears were bright red.

"You do whatever he says. Don't even deny it. You were happy in my arms until he showed back up and started filling your head with all these ideas about what you should and shouldn't do. Next thing I know, you're cutting me loose like I meant nothing to you."

"You didn't mean nothing. Maybe I was confused," she said with a little less fire.

Sawyer raked his fingers through his hair. "You sure confuse me. What do you want, Piper? Do you want me to care about you or not? I can't tell."

"I want you to be honest with me. I know we have to lie to everyone else, but can you please be honest with me?"

Did she have any idea how much easier things would be if he could tell her how he truly felt? If he could trust her, he'd happily give her his heart. They were going to be parents. Nothing would make him happier than to raise this baby with her. To be a family.

But every time he let himself believe it might be okay to let her in, she proved his needs and wants weren't a priority for her. Piper was committed to *her* family, *her* career, even to being good to her fans, but she was willing to walk away from Sawyer without a second thought.

"Honestly, I don't know how I feel—except sad that I can't completely trust you."

Piper's chin trembled before the anger re-ignited in her eyes. Whatever she'd been feeling a moment ago was gone.

"Well, you need to be onstage in a few minutes. I suggest you go get ready and I'll see you out there for our duet. Can *I* trust *you* not to mess this up?"

Piper stormed out of the room and left him alone with nothing but his thoughts. The rumors about trouble in paradise would soon be brewing. Why did that make him feel worse?

CHAPTER ELEVEN

"THANK YOU, CHARLOTTE! Good night!"

The crowd roared as Piper waved and ran offstage. Lana handed her a bottle of water and they raced back to the dressing room. Her body vibrated from the euphoria of performing.

Opening night was a success. Piper loved performing. She had loved it since she'd been able to put two words together. Singing for arenas full of adoring fans was a once-in-a-lifetime kind of experience that she was fortunate enough to get to do night after night. At least until the baby was born. All of this might change once she became a single mother.

Darla, the head of Piper's wardrobe department, was waiting for her along with her makeup artist, Trina. They were in charge of not only making her look good for the show but also deconstructing her afterward.

"Everything is set for dinner. People are

headed over there now," Lana said. It was tradition after the first show for Piper to treat the crew to dinner to celebrate the kickoff of the tour.

There was a knock on the door, and Heath popped his head in. "Great show, sweetheart. You were amazing."

Her father, Dean, Faith and Sawyer entered the room. They were full of praise and congratulations. But Piper went from elated to deflated the moment she locked eyes with Sawyer.

"Thanks," she said, forcing herself to look away. "There were a couple of transitions that didn't go as smoothly as I wanted."

"We'll talk about it later," her dad said. "I'm going to head over to the restaurant to make sure everything is in order. I'll take Dean and Faith with me. I'll leave your fiancé behind and send the car back to get you in an hour."

"Oh." Sawyer seemed hesitant. "I was going to head over with Hunter and the other guys from the band."

Clearly, he hadn't expected to be stuck with Piper.

"If you want to go ahead without me, you

can." Piper had a hard time hiding her annoyance. "I can get there on my own."

"No, it's fine. I can tell them to go on ahead. I only thought, given our conversation before the show, that it was better if I gave you some space." He said it like she might get the wrong idea if he went with her.

Piper started to wipe off the thick layer of stage makeup from her face. She was far from being confused at the moment. "It's a free country. You can do anything you want. Leave, stay. It's totally up to you."

He sat down on the couch like a defiant child. "I'll stay then."

Heath's displeasure in their unfriendly display was evident. "I'm confident you two will work out whatever is going on before we get to dinner. I expect happy faces when I see you next."

"Sure, Dad," Piper promised, knowing she had to plaster on a smile in front of the crew.

Staring at Sawyer through the mirror didn't make her want to smile, though. He glared back as the stylists finished taking off her makeup and hair extensions. What was he trying to prove?

Once Piper was ready for a shower, everyone left the room except for Sawyer and Lana.

"You two need to be careful," Lana said. "People are going to talk if you argue like that in front of them. The goal is to convince people that you love each other."

"He's the one who's acting like a child all of a sudden."

"Oh, I'm acting like a child? Don't you think it's so interesting, Lana, that Piper will tell me this is a free country where people can do whatever they want, but when her father tells her to do something, she does it without question?"

Piper turned to face him, her eyes narrowed in anger. "I do what he says because he's right. Do you think we should go into this dinner looking like we hate each other?"

"I don't hate you, Piper. I never have and I hopefully never will."

"But you don't trust me." His earlier words had hurt.

"You haven't given me much reason to."

She tilted her head. "What exactly have I done that makes you say that? You act like I've lied to you over and over again. I was confused by my feelings for you. Is that a crime?"

"No." Sawyer rose to his feet. "It's fine to be confused. But that's not what happened.

You turn your emotions off and on like a faucet. One minute, you're letting me in and the next, you're shutting me out. I guess your father decided having feelings wasn't going to make you a pop star."

Piper got out of her makeup chair and right up in his face. He was not going to make this about her. "How dare you? I am grateful that my father is always there to support me and what I want."

"What you want or what he wants you for you? Do you even know if there's a difference?"

"You love to make this about my dad, about me. You want me to believe you let me go because of my priorities. But the truth is, you were never confused. You're just mad I called things off first."

Sawyer dared to laugh. "What?"

"Hunter told me at Thanksgiving dinner that you haven't ever had a serious relationship, but you've never turned down a date with any of the pretty girls in Grass Lake, either. He said you were the love-'em-and-leave-'em type…until me."

"Hunter shouldn't have been talking to you about that stuff."

"Was he telling the truth?"

Sawyer turned his head and averted his eyes. That was all the answer she needed.

"Tell me who's more untrustworthy, Lana, me or Sawyer? Someone who was afraid things were moving too fast and that the timing was off, or someone who breaks hearts all over Tennessee?"

Lana didn't have to reply. Sawyer wasn't interested in commitment; he was only sore about being rejected.

"I'm going to jump in the shower and get ready," Piper said, leaving the two of them standing there in silence. "We'll leave in thirty minutes."

SAWYER ORDERED A drink at the bar. The aftershow party was in full swing by the time he and Piper arrived. They had walked in hand in hand for effect and quickly went their separate ways.

She had put him in his place tonight, and he was still sore about it. Piper wasn't wrong about him. He had issues. But she had issues, too, whether she wanted to believe it or not. It was both of their issues that were causing the trouble between them.

"You aren't making the rounds to say hello to everyone with the soon-to-be missus?"

Hunter asked, sidling up next to him and adding a beer for himself to the order.

"Nah, she's throwing this party, not me."

"Everything all right? I heard there's been some tension. The tour rumor mill says that the happy couple had their first fight today."

Just as Sawyer had suspected. People loved to gossip. Heath would have his head for this. "We're fine. It's been a stressful day. And it didn't help that you thought you should run your mouth to Piper about my previous dating habits at Thanksgiving."

"Is that what you were fighting about? I didn't tell her that to make her mad at you. If she's going to get all bent out of shape because you've dated a lot of women, maybe you need to rethink what you're doing."

Hunter had no idea what he was talking about, and if he kept this up, there would be nothing but trouble.

"I don't need to rethink anything. I need you to be quiet."

The bartender came over with their drinks. "Here you go, boys. Let me know if you need anything else," she said with a wink.

"We will, thanks," Hunter said, leaving her a couple dollars as a tip.

Sawyer grabbed his drink and turned

around to look over the crowd. Boone hadn't been kidding when he said Piper employed a lot of people. This wasn't even everyone. There was a whole crew back at the arena breaking down the stage and packing it up in the trucks.

Piper had rented out the entire restaurant for this soiree. A bunch of tables were pushed together to form a horseshoe for them to sit around. The staff was busy setting up a buffet-style meal along one wall while the guests mingled and hung around the bar.

"Did you see how she just looked at you?"

"Who?"

"The hot bartender. Man, I hate that you're so much better looking than I am." Hunter messed with his hair in a poor attempt to make it look tousled like Sawyer's.

"What are you talking about?" Sawyer glanced back and caught the bartender staring. She quickly looked away and poured a drink for someone else.

"You must really be in love to not notice when gorgeous women are practically throwing themselves at you."

Love, love, love. He was tired of that word.

"You're ridiculous. She was only doing her job." He peeked over his shoulder, and she smiled back at him from the other side of the bar. Sawyer's head snapped forward. Maybe Hunter wasn't totally off base.

"This would have been the first day of a very different experience if you hadn't gone and fallen for the headliner. You could have had no-strings-attached fun all across the country."

As much as he hated to admit it, Hunter was right. If Piper wasn't pregnant and they weren't pretending to be engaged, Sawyer most definitely would have been flirting with the bartender, and she would have only been the first of many. Every city would have presented new opportunities. But right now, only one woman had his attention. The woman carrying his child. Being a dad would soon take precedence over everything else, including his love life.

Piper hugged one of the sound techs before being pulled away by Darla. Even without the fake eyelashes and with her hair up in a simple bun, she was the prettiest woman in the room. She glowed, and it had nothing to do with being pregnant.

"Maybe you can still help me out," Hunter said, slapping him on the back. "Why don't you introduce me to whoever that is Piper's talking to? She's totally out of my league, but maybe she'll give me a shot if she knows I'm best friends with Piper's future husband." Hunter motioned for the bartender. "Let's bring them a drink. What's Piper's drink of choice?"

Another thing to add to the long list of things they didn't know about one another. It was good she couldn't have alcohol right now. "Piper only drinks water."

"Water? We're celebrating—let's get them some champagne."

The bartender wasted no time coming over. "Need me so soon or did you just miss me?" she asked with eyelashes fluttering.

"Can we get four glasses of champagne?" Hunter asked.

"Just two glasses of champagne and one glass of water," Sawyer corrected him, holding up his beer. "I don't need another drink."

"Come on, seriously?" Hunter smiled at the bartender. "He's fighting with his girl. Guess he doesn't want either one of them to have fun tonight."

Sawyer gave his bigmouthed friend a shove.

"Oh my gosh, you're Sawyer Stratton,

aren't you?" the bartender asked. "I didn't recognize you. You and Piper are in a fight?"

Great. This was exactly the opposite of what was supposed to happen when they were in public together. "I'm not fighting with anyone except this bozo. My fiancée needs water because she just ran around a stage for two hours doing what she does best," Sawyer said, trying to clean up Hunter's mess.

"Of course," she said with a chagrined smile. "Two champagnes, one water coming right up."

She walked away to get a bottle of champagne, stopping to whisper something to the other bartender. Paranoia exploded inside Sawyer like a bomb.

Leaning over Hunter, he whispered, "Can you please not talk about me and Piper fighting in front of other people?"

Hunter's face scrunched up. "What is your problem?"

Sawyer puffed his chest out. "I have no problems. I'm great. I just performed in front of nine thousand people. And I get to do that again and again for the next six months. I'm also engaged to Piper Starling. My life is great! What is *your* problem?"

A hand gripped his arm. "Everything okay over here?" Faith slipped in between her brother and Hunter.

The bartender came back with their drinks. Sawyer snatched the water off the bar. "Everything is great."

He marched over to Piper and apologized to Darla for interrupting. "I thought maybe you needed this," he said, handing her the glass of water.

Piper seemed a bit startled by his appearance. "Thanks," she said taking a sip and setting it on the table.

"Can I get everyone's attention for a minute?" he shouted over the din of conversation. The couple of dozen people quieted at his request. "Before we sit down to eat, I thought we should raise a glass to this amazing woman right here. Piper, you are an incredible talent. You are also the hardest-working and most generous person I know. I am so lucky to be along for this ride with you. To Piper!"

Sawyer held up his beer, and everyone followed suit.

While everyone clapped, Sawyer decided to make a real statement. He set down his drink next to her water and wrapped an arm around her waist. Pulling her close, he gently dragged his thumb down her cheek. Piper's breathing hitched, and his heart thumped in time with hers. Their eyes were locked until he closed his when their lips touched.

Something like an electrical shock ran through his entire body. The plan had been for this to be all show, a way to stop any of the rumors about them fighting dead in their tracks. He hadn't been prepared for the way this kiss would send his heart into overdrive or how hard it was to stop. Kissing her wasn't supposed to feel this way anymore. Yet it did.

The crowd cheered louder and Sawyer felt Piper's hand push against his shoulder. He opened his eyes to find her staring back and breathless. He pressed one more peck on her lips.

Sawyer watched as she struggled to control her expression. She blinked a few times and forced a smile. "We should really toast all of you guys. If it wasn't for everyone in this room, Sawyer and I wouldn't sound or look half as good. Let's eat!"

Heath appeared at Sawyer's side as everyone scrambled to find a seat. "Nice work, but the kiss was a little much, don't you think?" he murmured.

Sawyer threw an arm around his shoulders. "Smile, Heath. Nothing but happy faces, remember?"

DINNER WAS A BLUR. Piper struggled to focus. The roller-coaster ride that was her life had her head spinning. Sawyer acted like nothing she said today mattered. A kiss would have been no big deal. She would have given him a little kiss for saying those nice things about her, but that kiss was anything but little.

He had kissed her the way people kiss in movies. It was over-the-top and full of passion that she was sure didn't exist. She'd told him her heart couldn't take this. Did he have no regard for how something like that would make her feel?

"I need to speak to you," she said to Sawyer as they got into the elevator back at the hotel. "Can we talk in your room?"

"Are you sure that's a good idea?" her father asked in a tone that meant he didn't think so.

The way Sawyer looked at her was clearly a challenge. Would she or would she not do something her father didn't want her to do? She would show him she could make up her own mind about things.

"I'm sure," she replied.

"We can talk wherever you want to, Piper."

The elevator stopped on his floor, and the two of them exited. She followed him, trying to muster up the courage to confront him in the most productive way possible. She needed him to continue with this charade until it was safe to call things off.

"I'm sorry," he said as soon as they were behind closed doors.

His unexpected apology caused all her thoughts to scatter. "Sorry for what?"

"I'm not good at this, Piper. I don't know how to turn my feelings off and on. I don't know how to smile when I want to scream. I'm used to being straight with people."

Piper sat down on the bed. It had been a long and exhausting day, and they had to get up tomorrow and do it all over again.

"Are you saying you want to back out of our agreement?" she asked, afraid to hear the answer.

He sat next to her and placed his hand over hers, lacing their fingers together. "I don't know. Do you?"

"No. I need this."

"But do you want this?"

"A fake engagement? Of course not, but it's all I've got."

Sawyer shifted to face her. "You know what I was thinking about all through dinner tonight?"

Piper had no idea. She'd been thinking about that kiss, but it was unlikely that was where his head was. "What?"

"I was thinking about Liam. Liam is going to die. He's going to die before he knows what it's like to be seven years old. He's going to die before he knows what it's like to drive a car or buy a house. He's going to die without ever knowing what it means to fall in love."

Tears welled in his eyes, and Piper's heart broke open. "It's so tragic."

"It is. He's also going to die without ever knowing what it means to fall in love. And it made me realize I don't want to die without ever knowing what that feels like, either."

This was it. He had been lying when he said he didn't know what he wanted. He wanted the chance to fall in love, and he couldn't do that when he was fake engaged. She was holding him back.

Piper pulled her hand away and exhaled slowly so she wouldn't break down. "I get that, and I want that for you. I do. I just need a little more of your time."

"Piper," he said, lifting her chin and bringing her eyes back to his. "Let me finish. I want to fall in love, and I can't deny that when I'm with you, it feels a lot like what falling in love is supposed to feel like. But I need you to be less confused. I need you to tell me what you want. Not what your dad says you should want or what will best fit your brand. What do *you* want?"

Fat tears rolled down Piper's cheeks. Sawyer wiped her face and then his own.

"I want you to trust me because I think I'm falling in love with you, too."

He smiled so both dimples showed. "Then how do you feel about dating the guy you're fake engaged to?"

CHAPTER TWELVE

"SAWYER! PIPER! CAN we get a picture? Look this way!"

Sawyer put his arm around her waist and gave her a kiss on the temple. Piper smiled for all the cameras as they stood outside the auditorium hosting the Grammy Awards.

Smiling was a lot easier these days. When Sawyer kissed her, she didn't question if he wanted to or if he was doing it because he thought he should. He always wanted to.

"Why do they all shout at the same time? I can't look at all of them at the same time," Sawyer said as they posed.

"All I can think about is how everyone will be circling my baby bump when these shots hit the internet."

Piper had tried on a dozen dresses before deciding on what she wore: a body-hugging, baby blue column dress and a diamond necklace that was on loan from one of the biggest jewelers in Los Angeles.

Sawyer gave her a squeeze. "You look gorgeous. Don't worry about it."

They were finally ushered along. It was time to stop and talk to reporters. This was the part Piper had been most anxious about. It was time to tell the world they were expecting. Valentine's Day was around the corner, and she was officially twenty weeks pregnant. Hiding it would soon prove very hard to do.

It would be a relief to finally be done with the lies, but it was time for judgments to be made. Sawyer and Piper were engaged, not married. There was still a chance people would take issue with them doing things out of order.

There was also that little issue of them saying they were engaged when they were actually only dating. Sawyer had come a long way, but they had not professed their love for each other yet.

"You ready for this?" he asked as they waited in line to talk to the first reporter.

"I hope so."

Piper glanced over at Lana, who gave her the thumbs-up. She had been in charge of posting a picture to all of Piper's social media accounts of Sawyer's hands making the shape of a heart on Piper's stomach with a caption that read, "The three of us can't wait to attend the Grammys tonight! Did we say three? Yes, we did."

If everything went as planned, most of the reporters along the red carpet should be dying to talk to them about it. Piper's job was to be enthusiastic and to skirt any questions having to do with weddings or due dates.

"And it looks like we have country sensation Piper Starling and her fiancé, singer Sawyer Stratton, up next." Lia Jones was there representing *Good Morning USA*. Piper could tell by the look on her face that she'd been told about the post.

"So I know I am supposed to ask you about who you're wearing and how thrilled you are to be here, but I think you two have something a little more exciting to talk about. Maybe something to do with this Twitter post my producers are putting on the screen right now."

"We're very excited to announce we're expecting our first baby," Piper said, holding her stomach in a way that accentuated the little bump there.

Lia squealed and gave them both a hug. One down, dozens to go. Sawyer and Piper made their way through, accepting everyone's congratulations and keeping things focused on the tour. They were halfway through when someone finally asked a question Piper had hoped to avoid.

Colin Giser was a blogger for an entertainment news site. "So what will come first, the baby or the wedding?"

"Well, we still don't have a wedding date," Sawyer said, fielding the question for her. "Right now, we're so focused on the tour that we haven't really had time to plan a wedding. We'll see how things go."

"That's a bit nontraditional for someone like you, Piper. But I guess it goes hand in hand with the other changes we've been seeing from you. You wrote many of the songs on your new album, which sounds less country and more pop than your previous records. Would you say you're becoming a little more LA and a little less Nashville?"

Piper prayed her face didn't flush with embarrassment. "I'm a Nashville girl through and through. My fans know my heart and understand sometimes you live life a little out of order."

At least she hoped they would.

SAWYER MISSED THE days when he had no idea what social media was. The only reason he had an Instagram account was because Dean insisted he needed one in this business. He still thought the whole thing was silly.

Piper, on the other hand, was obsessed. Not as obsessed as her father, but pretty close. The two Starlings had been glued to their phones since they'd left the Grammy Awards and got back in the limo. They had to head straight to the airport to hop on a flight to Nashville for two nights of shows there.

"Anything new?" he asked, even though he really didn't care.

"Mostly congratulations. A couple trolls, but that was to be expected," Heath answered.

Sawyer took the phone out of Piper's hand and tossed it to Lana. "Hide that for a little bit, okay?"

Piper looked like she wanted to dive across the aisle and grab it back, but her dress would never allow it. "We need to stay on top of it so we're prepared."

"Your dad will keep us posted." He put his arm around her and pulled her close. She relented and rested her cheek against his chest. Sawyer kissed the top of her head. "I'm more worried about what everyone on tour is going to say when we get back."

They had decided not to announce to the crew before leaving for the Grammys for fear someone would leak the news.

"I think we need to nail down a wedding date. Saying you're too busy to pick a date is fishy—makes you seem like you aren't really committed," Heath said, setting his own phone down.

Sawyer's shoulders tensed. "I disagree. Setting a date before we're ready is pointless."

"Pick any day in the summer. It doesn't matter, you'll be calling it off after the baby is born anyway."

Heath was having a hard time accepting that even though the engagement was fake, the relationship was real. Sawyer hadn't been there when Piper explained it to him, but he trusted she had been clear.

"Dad, we aren't planning on a breakup anymore. We're slowing things down in our relationship, remember?"

"I'm not sure it's a good idea to veer from the original plan, Piper. The original plan is a good one."

This was a test. If Piper caved, Sawyer

would know for sure that this wasn't meant to be. He prayed she would back him and not give in to her father's demands for a fake wedding date.

"No, it's not," Sawyer said. "I'm not ready to get married or break up."

"But you're ready to become a parent? Because that's not something you can slow down, young man. That's happening. And the world is going to wonder why you're taking it slow when you seemed to have no problem going fast last September."

Sawyer pressed his lips together. Trying to win an argument with Heath was like sweeping a dirt floor. He didn't need to convince Heath of anything anyway. This was between him and Piper.

"Let's stay focused on more productive topics," Piper suggested. It wasn't exactly strong support for Sawyer's stance, but at least she hadn't agreed with Heath.

"We can go over the schedule for tomorrow," Lana said once it was clear they were done arguing. "You have a full day. Your appointment with Ruby is first thing in the morning. After that, you're both scheduled to appear on Kelly Bonner's radio show, then Piper has the appearance and signing at

Thornberry's to promote her perfume. Sound check for Sawyer begins at three. Piper needs to be there by four. Meet and greet starts at six. Show starts at seven thirty."

"I'm tired just listening to it." Piper yawned. The late nights and constant travel had been hard on her. At least they had two days in Nashville and then a short break before heading to the Midwest for two weeks. Sawyer was excited to go home for a few days, see the horses and his dog, but seeing his child for the first time was what he was most looking forward to doing in Nashville. He couldn't wait to count ten toes and ten fingers. Maybe they'd find out if it was a boy or a girl. He'd be thrilled with either.

He kissed Piper on top of the head again. He also had an extra-special Valentine's Day surprise for her in the works, thanks to Harriet.

Heath could hope for a breakup, but he wasn't going to get one if Sawyer had anything to say about it.

PIPER SLEPT MOST of the trip to Nashville. An hour after they landed, she was in her bed at the Berkshire. When her alarm went off a few hours later, it felt like she hadn't slept at all. But none of that mattered, because today she was going to see her baby.

"How have you been feeling?" Ruby asked as she wrapped the blood pressure cuff around her arm.

"Good. Tired. Touring had been a lot harder than I thought it would be. Sleeping on buses, planes and hotel beds isn't as pleasant when you're pregnant."

"Is it ever pleasant?" Ruby asked with a scrunched-up nose. "Well, the good news is that you're in the second trimester, which is usually considered the honeymoon phase of pregnancy. You should sleep better and have a little more energy than you did those first months."

Ruby did a normal checkup, commenting only on Piper's slow weight gain. She got a little lecture on making sure she was eating at least three meals a day. Sawyer promised to keep better watch.

"You two ready to see your baby?" Ruby asked, wheeling the ultrasound machine closer to the exam table.

Piper had never been more ready for anything in her life. Sawyer reached for her hand and gave it a gentle squeeze.

"Does this hurt the baby at all?" he asked.

"I mean, I'm dying to see this little guy, but this isn't going to make him or her radioactive or anything, is it?"

Ruby tried to hide her laughter. "No, an ultrasound is completely safe. There are no radioactive rays that can harm the baby. It's just sound waves that bounce off the baby. The echoes turn into an image on this screen."

Sawyer visibly relaxed. "Sound waves? That's cool. Let's do this. We've been waiting for this appointment since we scheduled it. Come on, now. Let's get these echoes going."

His excitement over this made it that much more special for Piper. This child had a real shot at a life with two parents who loved one another. She was optimistic that even though he wasn't ready to be married yet, he would be soon.

Piper expected the blue gel Ruby squirted on her stomach to be cold, but it was warm, like massage oil. She bit down on her bottom lip as she watched Ruby press the ultrasound wand to her belly.

"Bear with me," Ruby said. "I need to look at a bunch of things and take lots of measurements, but I promise to point out all the good stuff."

Piper stared at the black-and-white screen,

hoping to make sense of shapes that seemed to morph one into another. Ruby pushed the wand a little harder.

"Okay, here we go. Can you tell what this is?" She pointed to what clearly looked like the baby's profile. "Here's the baby's head, nose, lips." She moved the wand a little. "Oh, and there's an arm right above the face there."

Piper was completely mesmerized. Tears appeared in the corners of her eyes as her bottom lip quivered. There was her baby. *Their* baby. As scary as it had been to find out she was pregnant, seeing this living being inside her stirred up nothing but the anticipation of holding and caring for him or her.

"And there's a thumb. Looks like he or she is trying to get that in its mouth."

Sawyer was transfixed, as well. He asked questions and pointed out things he saw as Ruby moved the wand around. "What was that?" he asked. "Is that a foot?"

Ruby showed them their baby had ten toes. She gathered the information she needed and answered all of their questions. She stopped to zoom in on the baby's chest.

"Here's the heart." She took some measurements. "It looks good and strong."

The lump in Piper's throat made it impossible to speak. The baby's tiny heart pumped so fast, it was like her little one was running a marathon in there. Ruby assured them it was normal for the heartbeat to be much faster than an adult's.

"Can you tell if it's a boy or a girl?" Sawyer asked. They had agreed that if she could tell, they wanted to know.

Ruby had to move the wand around and press it into Piper's belly a bit. Piper couldn't tell what she was looking at. Ruby grinned as she froze the picture on the screen.

"I know it might be hard for you to tell, but we are clearly looking at a little boy right here."

"A boy?" Sawyer wiped his eyes and gave Piper a kiss. "We're having a boy."

A boy. Piper had been hoping for a boy. It meant he'd be the big brother to however many more came after him. She had always wanted an older brother, someone to look out for her the way she tried to look out for Matthew.

"Congratulations," Ruby said, wiping the gel off Piper's stomach. "What an exciting start to your family."

Ruby printed out some pictures for them.

Piper showed them off to Lana and her father, who had been in the waiting room. Piper flipped through the images when they got in the car, unable to stop staring at him. He was so tiny, only the size of a banana, according to Ruby, but he already sucked his thumb and got the hiccups. He was the perfect start to their family.

Sawyer had bounced all the way to the car, singing "Having My Baby" but changing the words to *you're having my baby boy.* "I don't know if I should call my sister or wait to tell her in person," Sawyer said.

"Tell her in person so you can see her face. She's going to be so happy for you."

"For us," he said, threading his fingers through hers. Piper's heart skipped a beat. "I'll have to call Harriet after I tell Faith."

He was so happy. This moment was the one she had dreamed about. It made all the heartache in the beginning worth it. Everything was going to work out better than she'd hoped.

Their driver took them straight from Ruby's office to the K104 studios for their interview. Nancy, the production assistant, set them up in a greenroom before they went on air. Heath and Lana left to go over the approved question list with Kelly while Piper and Sawyer stayed behind.

"You want to bet me ten dollars I can't shove a whole bagel in my mouth?" Piper joked, making light of the last time they had been here.

"That was the day you found out you were pregnant." Sawyer placed his hands on her hips. "And here we are after finding out we're having a boy. This place is always going to remind me of our little buddy in there."

Fourteen weeks ago, tensions were so high. Today, Piper had hope for the future.

"So, I've been thinking about what my dad said last night."

"I've been thinking about that, too. Is there a reason why he hates me so much?"

"He doesn't hate you."

"He still wants us to call off the engagement."

Piper ran her fingers along the pearls around her neck. "Well, what if it wasn't a fake engagement?" she whispered the last words. "What if we picked a date and made this a real engagement? We could tell Kelly the good news."

Sawyer's hands dropped to his sides. "Piper."

"What? I know you like to argue with my dad because you feel like he calls all the shots, but maybe he's right about this. Maybe we should set a date."

Instead of jumping at the chance to make this family legitimate, Sawyer stepped back. "Piper, I am having the time of my life and my feelings for you get stronger every day, but I'm not ready to say 'I do.'"

"I don't understand. For the last couple weeks, you've been talking about where we should live once the baby's born and how you can't wait to spend a quiet Sunday lounging around the house together, watching football."

"I am thinking about those things. I want to be in a normal relationship with you. I want to see what it's like to be together without all the people and chaos around us all the time. But that doesn't mean I'm ready to get married."

Feeling desperate, Piper tried to compromise. "I'm not saying the wedding has to be tomorrow. We can set a date for a year from now, for all I care."

Sawyer shook his head. "You're doing it again."

"Doing what?"

"Letting what your father wants carry more weight than what I want."

"What do you want?"

"I want you to stop pressuring me. I don't want there to be some kind of deadline hanging over us. Marriage is forever. I need to be sure—you need to be sure."

Piper felt the blood drain from her face. He didn't know if he wanted to be with her forever. There was nothing left to say.

Nancy came in with a smile on her face and Heath and Lana right behind her. "We'll be ready for you in the studio in five."

Piper couldn't do it. For the first time since she'd found out she was pregnant, she was going to use the baby to get out of something. "I'm so sorry, Nancy. But I'm suddenly not feeling well. I hate to do this to Kelly, but I think I should lie down and let Sawyer handle this on his own."

"What's wrong?" Her dad stepped forward, his face full of concern.

"It's probably nothing, but Ruby said it's important to pay attention to when my body is saying it needs a break."

"Should we call her?" Lana asked, pulling out her phone.

Piper's stomach hurt only because she was

causing them unnecessary worry. "No, I just need somewhere to rest."

"Piper…" Sawyer said with a heavy sigh.

"I'll see you at the show," she said without looking back at him. There was no way she would let those pretty brown eyes convince her to stay.

Once they made it to the car, Heath had the driver put on K104 so they could listen to Sawyer's interview.

"Is there something going on that I need to know about? When we got here, you two were celebrating parenthood and twenty minutes later, you're asking to leave. What happened?" her father asked.

"How did you know Mom was the one? Did you know right away? Or did you slowly figure it out over time?"

The corners of her father's lips curled up the way they always did when he thought about her mother.

"After my second date with your mom, I I felt pretty confident I was in love with her. Your mother is the most amazing woman I have ever met. But I decided I wouldn't tell her until we had been dating a month. I thought that sounded like a reasonable amount of time to wait. Of course, the next time I saw her, I blurted it out in the middle of dinner."

"What did she do? What did she say?"

"I believe she said, 'Can you pass the ketchup?'" His smile broadened at the memory.

Piper chuckled, picturing a younger version of her parents having a moment like that. They were once scared and awkward, too. Unsure of themselves and afraid of their feelings not being reciprocated.

"When I took her home that night, she kissed me goodbye and whispered that she loved me, too. Those were the best three words I have ever heard. I thought I'd blown it, but she loved me back. I'll never regret telling her when I did."

Maybe Sawyer was like her mom and she was like her dad. Perhaps there was still a chance. This wasn't her second date with Sawyer, though. She was having his baby. The entire world thought they were perfect for each other. If he still thought it was too soon to know how he felt, maybe he was waiting for a feeling that wasn't coming.

Maybe this fake engagement was doomed to end with a very real breakup.

The interview with Sawyer began on the radio. She listened to them chitchat.

"Well, I had a whole bunch of questions for Piper, but now that it's only you and me, we can toss those and get to the good stuff," Kelly said. The sound of crumpling paper could be heard in the background.

"Unbelievable," Heath groaned. "We are never going back there. She can't follow the rules."

"When's the big day? I want to make sure to clear my calendar in case you want to invite your favorite Sawyer-Piper shipper."

"You were definitely one of the fans who caught on early," Sawyer said, carefully sidestepping the question.

"So, when is it?"

"Honestly, I have no idea. I leave stuff like that up to Piper. Brides have way more say in the whole wedding planning thing than the groom does."

"Ha!" Piper let out a bitter laugh. He had asked her to tell him what she wanted and when she had, he'd shot her down and made her feel like she was her father's puppet.

She wanted to set a date. Piper pulled out her phone. Maybe she'd regret this, but she needed to tell Sawyer how she felt. The rest would be up to him.

CHAPTER THIRTEEN

"You've been on the road now for over a month now—how's the tour been going?" Kelly asked.

Sawyer was grateful for the easy topic. He began to tell her all about life on the road, but Kelly was busy checking things on her computer. Her eyebrows rose and a huge grin appeared.

"I don't mean to cut you off," she said. "But looks like your bride-to-be doesn't want to be left out of the interview after all. My producer is telling me we've got Piper Starling on the phone."

Sawyer's stomach knotted. What in the world was she doing?

Kelly flipped her dark hair over her shoulder. "Piper, Sawyer was telling us he's not too involved in the wedding planning. Is that true?"

"Well, he does leave a lot of things up to me. It's hard when we're juggling the demands of a tour at the same time as planning a wedding. But he's better at making decisions than he's saying."

"He told me you were picking the date," Kelly said. "So when is the big day, Piper?"

There was no way Piper had called to talk about a wedding date. Not after the argument they'd just had. Sawyer scratched the back of his neck.

"Well, I want a summer wedding," Piper said. Sawyer couldn't believe she was doing this. "We really want to be married before the baby comes. It's important to me...to us."

It was a good thing Kelly was focused on asking Piper questions, because he was speechless. She had drawn a line in the sand. The question was, would he cross it?

The rest of the interview was a blur. Sawyer would not stand by and let Piper back him into a corner. He'd thought she had more respect for him than that. Getting to the venue was the only thing on his mind when he finished with Kelly.

Outside the arena, Piper had eleven buses that carried around the 150-odd people who toured with her. Sawyer and his band had one. Piper's was in the middle of what she liked to call Bus City.

He waved to her driver to open up the door. He climbed aboard to find Heath and Lana sitting in the front living room section. Piper had to be in the back, hiding.

"She's resting before we have to head over to the perfume unveiling," Heath said, standing in Sawyer's way.

"I need to talk to her." Sawyer tried to muscle his way through. Heath held his ground.

"It's been an extremely stressful couple of days. She needs to rest. Let her be," Heath said.

Sawyer would not give up. She owed him an explanation at the very least. "Piper, I want to talk to you!"

Piper came out of her hiding space. She had changed into comfortable clothes and her hair was down. In her oversize T-shirt, her baby bump was barely noticeable.

"I'm writing a song. I could use your help," she said, as if she hadn't told everyone listening to K104 today that they'd be getting married before the baby was born. "Let him through, Dad."

She turned around and disappeared into the back of the bus. Heath puffed out his chest and fixed the collar on his shirt, which had flipped up in their tussle. He moved aside and motioned for Sawyer to pass.

The living space in the back of Piper's bus had a sectional couch that included a pullout full-size bed. The bed was open and Piper sat cross-legged in the center of it. With pencil in hand, she was hunched over a notebook.

"Can you explain to me why you would call in to the show and say that after I told you how I felt? If you don't care how I feel, then I know for a fact that we shouldn't get married, because caring about each other's feelings is a nonnegotiable must in a marriage."

Piper wrote something down, her pencil gliding across the page in haste. "What's another word that means the same thing as 'devoted'?" she asked as if he hadn't said a thing.

Frustrated, Sawyer sat on the bed and snatched the pencil from her hand. This was the emotional shutdown he couldn't handle from her. "I'm not kidding, Piper. You want me to trust you and then you go and do something like that? Did your dad tell you to do it? Was that the plan all along? I bet you chickened out when you realized you'd have to do it to my face. That's why you left."

Piper took her pencil back. "My father didn't tell me to do anything. I made a choice and now you have to make one."

"Marry you or what? Break up? You're giving me an ultimatum?"

"No, it's a fake wedding plan for a fake engagement. The plan was never to get married. You made it clear that was never your intention." She continued to write in her notebook, refusing to look at him.

"And when summer comes and we don't get married like everyone expects?"

Piper shrugged her shoulders. "You've made yourself clear and I think I've done the same. I won't play house. I'm not going to date you for the next ten years while you figure out how you feel about me. I won't do that to this baby. He deserves to know how his parents feel about each other."

"I never said it would take ten years. I'm asking for a little time to be with you before we make a once-in-a-lifetime commitment."

She put the pencil down and lifted her eyes to his. "I love you, Sawyer. I was falling in love with you while we were recording 'You Don't Need Me.' Maybe my dad talked me into walking away. Maybe I listened. But you have to understand, when I do something, I put my whole heart into it. I didn't think I could give you all of me, which is what you deserved. That's why I walked."

Sawyer was stuck on the first three words she'd said—*I love you*. How did she know? Why didn't he? What was wrong with him? What was he so afraid of?

"Now there's a baby and everything has changed," she continued. "I see us together as a family, Sawyer, but I can't make you feel the same way. Maybe you will, maybe you won't. I won't wait forever, though."

"Piper needs to get ready to go," Heath said, standing in the doorway with her hair-and-makeup team behind him. "We have to be at Thornberry's in forty minutes for the signing."

Someone always needed her for something. She was usually being pulled in ten different directions. Maybe that was what scared him the most. What if one of those things eventually pulled her away from him?

"Is your baby going to wear this perfume?" The preteen waiting for her signed poster picked up the display bottle of Starlit on the table.

Piper couldn't tell her the baby was a boy.

She wasn't ready to share that information with the world yet. "Well, not right away. I love the way babies smell. I wouldn't want to cover that up."

The young girl's face scrunched up. "My baby cousin does not smell great when he needs his diaper changed."

Piper handed her a signed Starlit poster and thanked her for the advice. The line ran all the way through the department store, and she only had ninety minutes to get as many fans' posters signed as possible.

Thornberry's was a large chain with stores all across the country. They were the biggest sponsor of Piper's tour and would exclusively sell the Piper Starling perfume brand.

The Nashville Thornberry's had rolled out the red carpet for Piper's arrival. There were Starlit banners hanging all over the store and bouquets of lavender roses, stalks of purple and lavender gillyflower, and bunches of fresh purple statice decorating the signing table to match the purple bottle of perfume.

"You look so pretty. Even prettier in person," the next girl said as she waited for her poster.

Piper appreciated the compliment. The purple off-the-shoulder dress she wore was a tad lighter than it had been when they'd bought it. All she could think about as she'd posed for pictures with the Starlit bottle before the signing was her baby bump.

"Thank you, sweetie." Piper handed her a poster and readied herself for the next fan.

A woman close to her mother's age approached the table. She had chestnut-brown hair that reminded Piper of the models in shampoo commercials. Her eye color matched her hair, and she seemed somehow familiar.

"Thank you for coming out today to support Starlit," Piper said. The woman stared at her without saying a word. "Can I make this out to someone in particular?"

"I needed to see you in person and this was the only way I could think to make it happen."

A chill went down Piper's spine. She glanced to her right, where Mitch, her security guard, stood. "Well, I'm so glad you did," she said, handing her a signed poster without any personalization.

"Is Sawyer here with you?" the woman asked.

Piper glanced at Mitch once more, her signal for him to come closer. "He's not, unfortunately. He's busy getting ready for the show tonight."

The woman set the poster down on the table. She spoke rapidly. "Is he happy? Is he getting married because there's a baby on the way? He shouldn't do that. He will regret that." She pounded the table with her fists.

Mitch stepped up and asked the woman to move along. Heath moved around to the other side of the table and looked ready to attack should the woman not comply. When she didn't step aside, the security guard took her by the arm and removed her as she continued to rant about Sawyer making a mistake.

Piper's heart felt like a jackhammer in her chest. She'd heard there were people out there who got attached to celebrities and stalked them. She wasn't sure if this woman was Sawyer's stalker, but she was awfully concerned about his intentions. Her outburst felt more intense than the usual fan freak-outs Piper had come to expect.

"Are you okay? Do you want to stop?" her father asked.

Piper placed a hand on her belly. Being with child made the encounter a thousand times scarier than it might have been otherwise. Her gaze drifted down the line of waiting fans. Who else could be here to intimidate her?

Her father crouched down. "You don't have to keep going. We can leave right now."

A little girl in the front of the line held on to her mother's hand. Piper remembered when her mom had taken her to see Boone Williams when she was little. They'd waited outside by the tour buses after the show, and when he came out, he'd stopped and signed her tour book. It was one of the best moments of her life.

Piper couldn't let one wacko keep her from her real fans. She took a deep breath to steady herself. "I'll be okay. Let's finish."

Heath stayed close the rest of the signing, as did her security guard. Piper tried to smile through the anxiety, signing as many posters as she could before time ran out.

"We need to be prepared for some backlash," Heath said when they were in the car. "I've seen it online, but it could continue to show up in person on the tour. Your little boyfriend has developed his own fan base, and not all of them are happy about him being off the market."

"Maybe we should cancel the meet and

greet before the show," Lana suggested. "Give you some time to rest and shake this off."

"No, I can't do that to the people who paid good money to meet me." Plus, there would be two security guards in the room as well as Sawyer. He might not be in love with her, but he would never let anyone hurt her or the baby.

WHEN SAWYER FINISHED sound check, he followed Hunter backstage. His best friend had made it pretty obvious that he was angry with him.

"Hunter, can we talk about this?" Sawyer asked, grabbing his arm and pulling him into his dressing room.

"What's there to talk about? I'm sure if there's anything you want me to know, I can read about it in the next edition of *People*."

Sawyer sighed. "I'm sorry. We didn't tell the media everything. We're having a boy. No one else knows that."

"Wow. Thanks for keeping me in the loop. Maybe I'll be invited to the wedding this summer, or maybe I'll just just have to read about it." Hunter wasn't making this easy.

"Come on, man. It's not like that."

Hunter flopped down on the couch and crossed his arms over his chest. "I thought I was your best friend. I thought that meant something."

"We had to keep it quiet so we could control when the news was made public," Sawyer said.

"Do you even hear yourself? You sound like Heath Starling. Were you worried about what a baby could do to your brand? Was there talk about how many records you might not sell if you told your best friend you were having a baby?"

"Don't ever compare me to Heath Starling." Sawyer couldn't keep the edge out of his voice. "I'm sorry I didn't tell you, but you do have a big mouth lately and I couldn't risk it."

"That's bull. This girl is changing you, man. She's turning you into someone I don't even know anymore. You used to be fun. Now all you seem to care about is how what you do or say is going to impact your social media following."

Sawyer felt like his friend had punched him in the gut. He didn't care about those things, but he knew Piper did. He was going along with things because he wanted her to be happy. He didn't want her stressed out when she was carrying their baby.

"She's not changing me. I am still the same guy."

"You're not. Heath tells you and Piper what to do and you do it. I bet he's the one who told you to marry her because she's pregnant. You're turning into a robot, just like her."

Hunter had no idea how hard Sawyer had been working to stand his ground. It was impossible to explain how difficult it was to manage all the things on his plate lately. If Hunter really was his best friend, he would try to be a bit more understanding.

"Sorry to interrupt." Piper stood in the doorway. Sawyer hadn't realized they had left the door open.

"You're back," he said, hoping she hadn't heard anything.

"When you have a minute, could you come to my dressing room?"

"Yeah, sure." There was something off. Sawyer had that sinking feeling she had heard part of his conversation with Hunter.

"I can leave. You probably have to tell him something I'm not allowed to know," Hunter grumbled, getting to his feet.

"No, don't. You clearly have a lot to say

and I know Sawyer could really use a friend right now."

Hunter had no comeback. She had most definitely heard what he'd said.

INSIDE HER DRESSING ROOM, Piper allowed herself to feel. Warm, wet tears ran down her face. She was no robot. She had feelings, and they could be hurt.

Piper quickly dried her face when there was knock at the door. "Come in," she said, turning her back to the door and rummaging through her clothes.

"Sorry it took me so long," Sawyer said.

Piper wiped her nose with the back of her hand. "No worries."

"I heard there was some drama at the signing. Some lady attacked you?"

"It wasn't *that* dramatic." She wondered who had told him. "Someone just wanted me to pass on a message to you."

"To me?"

Piper turned around, hoping he wouldn't be able to tell she'd been crying. "She said you'll regret marrying me, especially if you only marry me because I'm pregnant."

"Seriously? Someone said that to you?"

"I'm sure it's nothing you haven't already

heard," she said. Not only did some fan think she was wrong for him, but so did his best friend. She was doomed.

Sawyer took a step in her direction. His proximity made her want to fall into his arms, but she knew she couldn't.

"Hunter didn't know what he was saying," he said.

"It's fine." She moved away from him and toward the bathroom. "I'm having a bit of a bad day. I need to change so I can get to sound check."

Sawyer let her go and was gone when she came out. She should probably get used to that.

BY SIX O'CLOCK, Piper regretted agreeing to go on with the meet and greet. Today had started with so much promise and had turned into complete disaster, and she hadn't even taken the stage yet.

Security was doubled due to the incident at Thornberry's. Her father had a security guard in every corner of the greenroom. Even with the extra protection, Piper was on edge.

"We came all the way from Memphis to

see the show tonight. We are your biggest fans in the whole world."

The two young women were doing their best to turn Piper's day around. They wore handmade shirts with all their favorite Piper Starling song titles written on them. One of them had a tattoo of a line from her first song to make it on the country top 100 list.

"I am so happy you guys are here," Piper said. "I hope y'all enjoy the show tonight and never stop being the amazing women you are."

Piper posed for a couple of pictures and signed their tour books. Sawyer stepped in for some, as well.

"You better treat her right," one of the women said to him. "She deserves to be treated like a queen. Don't disappoint us."

"My goal is to never disappoint," Sawyer said. He glanced at Piper, who raised a brow. It was nice to hear someone defend her for once today.

As the girls made their way to the candy bar, there was a commotion at the door. A security guard argued with Faith, preventing her from entering the room.

"I have an all-access pass. He's my brother, for goodness' sake!"

"She's family, Kyle. Let her come on in," Piper said. These guards didn't even know the good guys from the bad guys.

Faith's face was flushed and her eyes focused on her brother. Sawyer stepped around Piper to meet Faith halfway. "What's wrong?"

"You need to come with me. Right now," she said, grabbing his arm.

"We're almost done. Can you wait a couple minutes? What's the matter?"

The door opened again and the woman from Thornberry's came in, dragging Dean behind her. "You all act like you're protecting the gosh darn president! Let me through!"

The hair stood up on the back of Piper's neck. She ran over to Sawyer and pulled him back. How in the world had she gotten backstage?

Sawyer's body went rigid. Piper watched as the bodyguards tackled the woman to the ground. Arena staff and security flooded the room. Hunter rushed in and stood beside Dean, but both did nothing but gape at the scene unfolding in front of them.

As the woman screamed, Faith tried to pull the men off her. "Let her go! Get your hands off her. Dean, tell them to stop!"

Piper's panic skyrocketed. Faith was trying to help the woman who was here to do heaven knew what. It was hard to breathe.

"That's the woman from Thornberry's," Piper gasped. "Why is your sister helping her?"

Sawyer was frozen. His eyes fixed on the thrashing woman on the ground. One of the guards lifted Faith off her feet and tried to carry her away from the melee. Dean snapped out of his stupor and demanded that Faith be released.

"Sawyer, do something. Tell them to stop," Faith pleaded.

"What is happening?" Piper asked as Heath shouted for someone to call 911.

Sawyer took Piper by the hand. A mix of confusion and horror contorted his features. His breathing was as labored as hers. He licked his lips and swallowed hard. Turning his head, he looked Piper in the eye.

"I think that's my mom."

CHAPTER FOURTEEN

THE LAST TIME Sawyer had seen his mother, he was four years old. He'd gone to bed like always, figuring in the morning she would be there to make him breakfast and read him his favorite stories about wild horses that no one could break.

Only that next morning, his mom had not been in the kitchen cooking up eggs and bacon. She hadn't been in the laundry room, folding his dad's flannel shirts and jeans. She hadn't been out in the barn, feeding the horses or mucking the stalls. She was gone and she never came back.

"Sawyer, tell them to let her go," Faith said again. "She's our mother."

Heath would have none of it. "Don't you dare let her go," he warned the guard pinning her on the floor. "Mitch, help me get Piper out of here."

Mitch and Heath stood on either side of her and led her out, leaving Sawyer standing in the center of the room with a sick feeling in the pit of his stomach. Faith got away from the bodyguard holding her and ran over to their mother. She pushed the guard away and helped the woman to her feet.

"We'll take her to Sawyer's dressing room," Faith said, putting an arm around her shoulders.

Sawyer's feet were cemented to the ground. He couldn't follow as they left the room with Dean. The small group of fans there for the meet and greet cowered in a corner. Lana tried to apologize to them, but it was clear she was at a complete loss for what to do beyond that.

Hunter came over and placed a hand on Sawyer's shoulder. "Come on, man. Let's go to your dressing room." He tugged on Sawyer's shirtsleeve.

"How did this happen? Where in the world did she come from and how did she get back here?" Sawyer asked as they walked down the hall.

"One of the dancers was walking around the outside of the arena and heard some woman arguing with security, telling them she was your mom. Everybody assumed it was a fan trying to get backstage. When word got to your sister, she thought she should check it out because they were talking about arresting the woman if she didn't leave. She knew Heath would be ticked if there was any more bad press, so she thought confronting the lady herself would end it without having to call the cops. Next thing I know, Faith's running around back here, looking for Dean like there was some sort of emergency. I guess she had him get your mom a backstage pass."

Sawyer stopped. He couldn't go into his dressing room. Not with that woman in there. How could Faith have let her back here? He shook his head. His sister had always held out hope their mom would come back. He'd thought she'd finally let that go when Gretchen didn't show up at their father's funeral. Sawyer had assumed he would never see her again. How he wished he had been right.

"Tell my sister to come out here."

Hunter exhaled loudly and went in without him. Faith came out a few seconds later.

"Why aren't you coming in?"

"Why did you let her back here?"

Faith's brow furrowed. "Because she's our mother."

"How can you be sure if that's really her? And even if she is our mother, why in the world did you think I would want to see or talk to her?"

Faith gave her brother a hug. "I know this has to be overwhelming."

He pushed Faith away. "It's not overwhelming. It's ridiculous. She left and now that I'm famous, she reappears, looking to talk to me. What a coincidence, wouldn't you say?"

"She doesn't want anything from you. We can't ignore her."

"Why not? She ignored us for the last twenty-plus years!"

"Oh, my, it's like this place went into lockdown. What's going on?" Harriet came around the corner with her backstage pass swinging around her neck. "I had to go through three checkpoints. It wasn't like that the last time."

"I'm so glad you're here," Faith said, throwing her arms around Harriet.

"I told Sawyer I would be here after I finished decorating the bus like we talked about." Harriet turned to Sawyer. "I hope your fiancée will be very pleased."

Given the insanity of the day, Sawyer had

forgotten all about the big pre–Valentine's Day surprise. Between the argument they'd had this morning and his mother's arrival, he wasn't sure Piper even wanted to date him anymore.

"You're never going to believe who's here," Faith said, acting like it was some gift that their mother had dared to show her face.

"Did you know she's the one who disrupted the signing at Thornberry's today?" he asked his sister before Harriet could answer. "She waited in line to see Piper and then proceeded to verbally attack her. I want nothing to do with her."

"Who are we talking about?"

As if on cue, Gretchen pulled open the door and stuck her head out. "Harriet Windsor, as I live and breathe."

It took a moment for Harriet to recognize her. "Gretchen? Oh my goodness, is that you?"

"I keep telling all these bodyguards it's me, but none of them want to listen." She stepped into the hall and Harriet wrapped her in an embrace like she really was a long-lost friend. But real friends didn't disappear off the face of the earth for twenty years. "My boy has gotten so popular they won't let anyone near him without a background check and a blood test."

He didn't appreciate the way she treated this whole thing like some sort of joke.

"I can't do this," Sawyer said. He took off in the direction of Piper's dressing room. He had to make sure she was okay.

Mitch and another bodyguard stood outside her room. He knocked on the door before pushing it open. Heath was right there, blocking him from entering.

"Can I come in please?"

"Is that woman really your mother?"

"Apparently," Sawyer said with a huff. "Can I please see Piper?"

"Is your *apparent* mother still here?"

"She's in my dressing room with my family."

"Then, no. You can't come in. You need to get rid of her or Piper will not be performing. Understand that if that maniac isn't out of this building by seven o'clock, you will have to explain to those thousands of people out there why you're the only one performing tonight." Heath shut the door.

Dean came down the hall with two more of the bodyguards from the meet and greet. "What do you want to do about this?" he asked Sawyer. "I should have had Faith talk to you before she let Gretchen backstage. That's on me."

"I want to send her back to wherever she came from, but Faith will have a fit."

Dean grimaced, knowing Sawyer was right. "Let's go talk to your sister."

"But you're going to support me on this, right? She can't stay if Heath is canceling Piper's performance."

"That's what I have these two guys for," Dean said, gesturing to the two dudes who looked like football linemen.

Sawyer braced himself as he walked into his dressing room. The lights around the makeup mirrors were on. Harriet and Gretchen sat on the couch to the right while Faith sat in a chair across from them.

"Faith, can we have a moment?" Dean asked.

Sawyer couldn't tear his eyes off his mother. She looked almost exactly the same as she did in his memories. Same long, dark hair. Same eccentric taste in clothes, like Harriet.

"I didn't mean to cause a ruckus, Sawyer. I really didn't," Gretchen said, getting to her feet.

Faith stood in between them. "Let me talk to him first, Mom."

"I don't need you to run interference, Faith. I want her to leave. She can choose to go on her own or I can have her escorted out. It's up to her."

"Sawyer…" Faith tried.

"He looks so much like his father," Gretchen said. "But he's definitely got my stubbornness. If he wants me to go, I'll go. I came because I felt like I had to reach out to you. I know that might seem selfish, but I couldn't sit back and watch you do this to yourself."

"Do what to myself?"

"Get married out of obligation," she answered plainly.

"How would you know anything about why I'm getting married?"

"Well, I'm not stupid. I also know from experience."

Faith's eyebrows shot up. It was news to them that their mother had gotten pregnant before marriage.

"You don't even know me or Piper. Are you concerned that Faith is getting married? Did you even know that Faith was getting married? Probably not, because you aren't part of our lives. Something you chose."

"And maybe I'm choosing to come back into your life so I can help stop you from making a terrible mistake."

Sawyer felt as if he'd just stepped off a spinning ride at an amusement park. There was nothing amusing about his mother, however. "It's not up to you anymore."

In Sawyer's mind she was no different from a bank robber who had decided she wanted to go back and open up an account at the bank she'd robbed. It was not happening. She was not welcome.

"I am going to visit your sister in Grass Lake for a couple weeks. If you change your mind, you know where to find me."

Sawyer threw his hands up. "Faith, what are you thinking? I'm coming home in two days. You can't let her stay with you, in Dad's house."

"It's my house," Faith said. "And maybe I want her to come."

"Gretchen can stay with me," Harriet offered. "I think that would be best anyway, especially if Sawyer is coming home."

Gretchen in Grass Lake. It was obviously the end of the world as they knew it.

"I CAN'T FOCUS." Piper sat in front of her mirror and stared at her reflection as her stylist put her extensions in. She held her hands in her lap to keep them from shaking.

"Lana, go make sure that woman is gone," Heath demanded. "I wasn't kidding when I said Piper won't perform tonight if she's anywhere in this building."

Piper wasn't sure that would help. It didn't matter if Sawyer's mom was in the building. It mattered that she wanted back into Sawyer's life and clearly did not want him to be with Piper. All the support she'd felt from Sawyer's side of the family seemed threatened by Mrs. Stratton's arrival.

Sawyer returned with Lana. Heath tried to keep him out, but Piper needed to see him. "Let him in, Daddy."

Sawyer sat in the makeup chair next to hers. He looked like she felt—mentally and physically exhausted. He slouched in his seat and pulled on the front of his hair.

"I can't believe she had the nerve to show up here," he said. "Or at Thornberry's. I am so sorry for what she put you through today."

"What did she want?" Piper asked, though she already knew his mom didn't want him to get married. She'd made that clear.

"I don't really care what she wanted. She comes here acting like she gets to have an opinion on how I live. Who does that? She abandoned us when we were kids, when we needed her opinions and guidance. Does she really think I need anything from her?"

Piper felt horrible for him. She'd been so busy worrying about what that woman's appearance meant to her that she had failed to realize what it meant to Sawyer.

"I'm sorry she's causing you so much pain." Piper reached over and touched his hand.

"Dean warned me that when you become famous, people crawl out of the woodwork. You suddenly have something they want, which is usually money. I don't know if that's her ultimate goal, but I wouldn't put it past her. Right now, she's claiming she's only here to stop me from ruining my life."

Piper twisted her stud earring. His mother thought Piper was going to ruin his life.

"Because of me and the baby?"

Sawyer turned his head toward her. "You and the baby are not going to ruin my life."

"I'm glad you think so."

"I know so," he said firmly.

Piper's shoulders relaxed. "I'm sorry I

pressured you today. I wish I could go back in time and not call in to Kelly's show. That was stupid."

"Hey." He stopped her. "Let's not look back. Let's move forward. I need to focus on the show we're about to put on tonight, and you need to do the same."

She nodded. One thing at a time. The past was the past and there was no predicting the future.

He placed his hand on her belly. "How's my boy doing?"

As soon as he asked, the baby kicked. Sawyer's and Piper's eyes widened. "Did you feel that?" she asked.

"It's like he knew I was talking about him." The smile on Sawyer's face was as big as the one he'd worn this morning during the ultrasound.

The baby kicked again. He was definitely letting them know he was there. He was the one who mattered. Piper needed to take care of herself so the baby wouldn't feel her stress. She wanted her child to have two parents who loved one another, and nothing would stop her from getting her goal. Not unsupportive best friends. Not well-intentioned fathers. Not long-lost mothers, either.

"GOOD NIGHT, NASHVILLE!" Piper shouted over the screaming crowd. She stood on the trapdoor of the stage and disappeared in a cloud of smoke.

Under the stage, her people were waiting to take her back to the dressing room. The show had gone off without a hitch. That was a huge relief given the events of the day.

Sawyer was noticeably missing from the backstage area. He usually waited for her when she got offstage, but wasn't anywhere to be seen. That awful feeling of dread resurfaced. What if his mom had reappeared?

She didn't bother with a shower at the arena, opting to go straight to the hotel instead. She made it out to the bus in record time and knew something was up immediately.

The inside of her bus had been transformed into a flower garden. Bouquets of her favorites covered every flat surface. Fuchsia roses, pink gerbera daisies and cream calla lilies exploded from vases. Garlands of fresh, pale pink peonies, white hydrangeas and branches of boxwood ran from the front to the back of the bus. Strands of twinkling lights were twirled around the garlands.

"Happy Valentine's Day," Sawyer said, coming out of the back room.

Piper almost burst into tears. No one had ever made this kind of grand gesture for her before. "You did this for me?"

"I certainly didn't do it for your dad," he said with a wink.

Piper turned around and noticed her dad and Lana had not followed her onto the bus. After everything that had happened today, this was the perfect way to end the night. She ran into his arms.

"Was my dad in on this?"

"Just Lana. She sure knows a lot about you. She's my go-to person if I need to find out what your favorite color, food, animal, flower or television show is."

"I'm not going to want to sleep in the hotel tonight!"

"We can hang out here all night if you want."

She hugged him tightly around the neck until she got a whiff of herself. She pulled back. "On second thought, I think we better go to the hotel so I can shower."

"There's one thing I need to do before we let your dad back on the bus." Sawyer stepped back. "I know I said a lot of things today about not being sure and not wanting to rush things. I know I hurt you by being so indecisive. I need to prove to you that I'm not going to run out on you and the baby. Ever."

He bent down on one knee. Piper was positively choked by emotion. He took her hand.

"Marry me."

CHAPTER FIFTEEN

"You did what?" Faith stood in the farm-house kitchen with an apron tied around her waist.

Sawyer grabbed a peanut butter–bourbon cookie off the cooling rack. He'd gotten home too late last night to tell her the news. Scout looked up at him as if to say, "Feel free to drop one of those on the ground. I'll pick it up."

"I asked her to marry me, and we want to do it while we're on break. We went to the county clerk's office in Nashville before our second show yesterday and got a marriage license."

He had done it. He had jumped all in and Piper had said yes. Heath wasn't ecstatic, but Sawyer didn't care. Their parents could call them reckless. They could say they were making a huge mistake. Sawyer didn't care one bit. Piper had said yes even though her dad didn't want her to go through with it. That had to count for something.

"You were the one who said there was no reason to rush into this. What could have possibly changed your mind?" She didn't let him answer before answering herself. "Mom."

"I couldn't care less what Gretchen thinks. I am marrying Piper because it's the right thing to do."

Faith threw her hands up. "It's the right thing to do? That's a terrible answer! You're supposed to marry someone because you're in love with her."

"And...that," Sawyer said, fumbling his words. "That's a given."

"Love is a given? You've told her you love her? You feel it in your heart that you love her?" Faith pressed.

He wasn't going to answer that. "I need to know if you're all right with us getting married here on the farm. I'll call Pastor Kline and see if he'll officiate. I want to do it outside with family only."

"Sawyer..." Faith moved toward him.

"Faith, yes or no? Can we get married here this week?"

"I would never tell you no. This is your

home, but I'm not going to lie, I think this is too much, too fast."

Maybe it was, but Sawyer couldn't stop now. Piper had already told her mother and was happier than he'd ever seen her. It would all work out in the end.

"Thank you for your concern. I am going to check with Pastor Kline and visit Harriet to see what she can do on short notice for flowers." He grabbed one more cookie. "Oh, and Gretchen is *not* invited. Don't even ask."

He took off and ran outside. Piper's bus was parked in the lot. Instead of going home, she'd come with him to make arrangements.

"We're all clear to have the wedding here," he said when he got on the bus.

"My dad has sent me thirty-seven texts and called me fifteen times." Her phone beeped. "Thirty-eight texts."

Heath, who had demanded in the beginning that they marry, was suddenly unhappy about this turn of events. He refused to give his blessing until his lawyer had a chance to put together a prenuptial agreement.

"How long does it take to draft a prenup?" Sawyer asked, taking a seat next to his bride-to-be.

Piper flinched at the word. "I don't want

to make you sign a prenup. That's like saying we know we're going to get a divorce so we'd better figure out who gets what ahead of time."

"If it makes your dad feel better, I'll sign anything. I don't want your money." He kissed her cheek, making her blush. "All I want are those smiles."

"Are you sure about all this? I don't want you to do this just because it's what I want. I want you to be as sure as I am."

Sawyer felt a twinge of doubt but pushed it down. "I'm sure."

"I want both my parents to be here. I need my dad to walk me down the aisle or I'll regret it."

"Then call him and tell him to bring his prenup and a pen. Your husband isn't afraid to sign it." He cupped her cheek and planted a kiss on her forehead. "I have to call the pastor and our florist."

"Why don't you ask her if we could take all the flowers in here and reuse them?"

Sawyer gave her another kiss. "Good thinking, honey. I like that idea, because these are already paid for."

He left her to deal with her father while he went back in the house to call Pastor Kline.

He was halfway up the stairs when he heard Faith's voice. She was talking to someone in her room with the door closed.

Sawyer crept up the remaining steps and stood outside her door. She must have been on the phone, because she was the only one he could hear.

"I have a bad feeling about this. I feel like this is more about Mom than it is about Piper." She paused. "I know. But how do I tell him that? How do I convince him of that?"

Sawyer pushed open the door. There was nothing she could say to convince him not to go through with this. He was marrying Piper because he wanted to. This had nothing to do with Gretchen. Why would he care what Gretchen had to say?

"Who are you talking to?"

Faith spun around and her face flamed. "I have to go," she said into the phone before hanging up. "Sawyer…"

"Who was on the phone?"

"It was Dean." She fidgeted with her phone before setting it down on the dresser. "I'm worried about you and he's my person."

"What are you so worried about?"

"You're so angry. Look…when Mom left,

you blamed yourself. Dad tried his best to reassure you, but I know you took it personally."

"What?" Maybe he'd felt that way when he was four, but he wasn't a kid anymore. "That was a long time ago, Faith. I think I've gotten over it."

"You say that, but I think until you sit down and talk to her about why she left, you're never going to heal."

Sit down with Gretchen? *No, thanks.* Sawyer didn't blame himself for her leaving. She left because she was a terrible mom. She left because she was selfish, and she'd returned for the same reason. It wouldn't take long for her to show her true colors. She'd be asking for money in no time.

He didn't want to waste another minute listening to his sister act like an armchair psychologist. There was nothing wrong with him. He wasn't suffering from any ridiculous childhood trauma. His life was better because Gretchen wasn't in it. His dad had made sure he had everything he needed. And what his father couldn't do, Harriet and Faith had taken care of for him. They still did.

"Think what you want. I don't need to have a sit-down with someone who isn't relevant in my life." Sawyer ducked into his room and grabbed his phone off the bed. Instead of calling Pastor Kline, he called Harriet first. He'd show them all that this had nothing to do with Gretchen by going over to Harriet's without a care in the world.

PIPER DIDN'T WANT to hear her father complain anymore. "Dad, this is what you wanted the day I told you we were having a baby. You said you wanted Sawyer to make an honest woman out of me. Not only is he going to do that, but he wants to do it. We don't have to fake anything."

"There's no reason to get married in two days' time. I've got Benjamin working on a prenup, but I'll need to review it, Sawyer should have a lawyer review it, and—"

"What about me? Shouldn't I review it?" she asked.

"I'm reviewing it for you."

"Okay, but I'm the one signing it. Shouldn't I read it so I know what I'm agreeing to?"

"Do you read your record contracts? Do you read your touring contracts? Or do you trust me to look out for your best interests?"

She did let him take care of those other things. Piper had always figured he understood it better than she could. Plus, they paid their lawyer a lot of money to make sure they were getting the best deals possible, but it was time for her to step up. To handle things like an adult. She was going to be a parent. What kind of example would she be setting if she didn't have any agency in her own career?

"Well, I understand that, but I'm getting married. I need to take a more hands-on role in my business dealings, and this is a business deal between me and my husband. We both need to read it."

"Fine—another reason you need more time. You, Sawyer, his lawyer... A lot of people need to review it before anyone signs off."

"We don't have any more time, Dad. The prenup should be simple. If we ever get divorced, which we won't, I keep my money and he keeps his."

"What about the baby?" Heath asked. "You're going to have to address the custody issues, as well."

Piper didn't have to think about it. "Joint custody, of course. There's no question about that."

"I'm not sure you should be so quick to split custody."

He was beyond infuriating. "We won't be getting divorced, so it's not going to matter."

"I'm not going to argue with you. Benjamin will send me the draft when he's finished and I will email it to you. Please think about what I said about slowing things down. I feel like you're caught up in a lot of emotion and following your heart, not your head."

"Maybe you need to follow your heart a little more and your head a little less," Piper proposed.

"I always follow my heart where you're concerned."

He had a way of disarming her at the most unexpected moments.

"I love you, Daddy, and I'll see you in a couple days."

Piper hung up the phone and placed both hands on her belly. "Don't worry, little buddy. Your dad and I have everything under control. We're going to be the family you deserve."

She meant it. Even if all this felt a bit surreal. There was a lot to do and very little time to do it. Of course, all that mattered was that they said "I do." Whether she had the perfect dress or not wouldn't impact the outcome of the day. All she needed was for

Sawyer to stand before her and promise to love her forever.

The baby kicked, and an overwhelming sense of fear ran through her. Sawyer had never used that word. Not even when he'd asked her to marry him. He must love her, though. It was one of his conditions to marry her. He'd said he wanted to be in love before he took the plunge.

She pushed those feelings of fear aside. They would not sidetrack her from the things she needed to get done today. First up, finding a dress. Hopefully Faith would be willing to take her shopping.

SAWYER CLIMBED OUT of his pickup truck. Main Street was looking a bit less festive now that the winter holidays were over and spring was still a bit off. A few store windows were decorated for Valentine's Day, but it was nothing like it had been a couple months ago when the Christmas lights lit up the whole street.

"Sawyer Stratton, is that you?" Pastor Kline had a box of doughnuts in his hands.

Sawyer couldn't believe his luck. This wedding was meant to be. Why else would the good Lord put the pastor right outside

Harriet's flower shop so he could kill two birds with one stone?

"It is, sir. How are you this morning?"

"I'm good. I've been following you in the news. You seem to be having quite the adventure."

"I am, sir. It's been very exciting traveling the country, meeting a ton of people and getting to sing my songs almost every night. I'm truly blessed."

"Well, make sure you remember who to thank for that," Pastor Kline said, making his way to his car.

"Pastor, I was actually going to call you today," Sawyer said, jogging up alongside him. "I'm sure if you've been following the news about me, you've heard I'm engaged."

"I have. Congratulations, son."

"Thanks, but I was going to call you, because Piper and I were hoping you would officiate at our wedding."

"Me? Well, I'd be honored. Why don't you call me when you have a chance and we can schedule a meeting so I can get to know your fiancée? From there, we can talk about setting a wedding date and get you enrolled in the Prepare and Enrich program we run for couples looking to marry at the church."

"Oh, we already have a date and we're planning to get married at my family farm, not the church. Is that a problem?"

Pastor Kline shook his head. "If you want to get married at home, we can definitely make that work. Like I said, you give me a call and we'll set up that first meeting."

"Well, sir. There's just one other thing. We were hoping you would marry us two days from now. We're heading back out on tour at the end of the week, and we were really hoping to get this all done quickly."

The pastor's eyes nearly popped out of his head. "Two days? Sawyer, that's awfully soon. I know you've been engaged for a bit, but have you done anything to prepare for marriage?"

Sawyer contemplated lying for about half a second. The last thing he wanted was to curse the marriage by deceiving a man of God.

"We haven't had any formal preparation. We would absolutely be willing to meet with you in the future, but we really want to get married as soon as possible."

Pastor Kline's forehead was creased and his mouth was in a straight line. "I'm a huge proponent of having these conversations before the wedding, before you've said your vows and made the commitment before God."

"I'm only getting married once, sir. You know me. You know how seriously I take my commitments. I promise you that Piper and I are on the same page about a lot of things. We've spent hours talking about what's important to us, especially with the baby on the way. The baby is another big reason we'd like to do this sooner rather than later."

"I heard about the baby, as well." Pastor Kline set his box of doughnuts on the roof of his car and pulled his keys out of his pocket. "If you promise me that the two of you will come in and do some faith sharing with me in the near future, I will perform the ceremony in two days."

Sawyer exhaled in relief. "Thank you so much, sir."

"You must really love this woman," he said, opening his car door.

Sawyer felt his smile falter. He nodded rather than say anything out loud. "Thank you again. We'll be in touch."

One down, one to go. He hurried back to Harriet's. The bell above the door rang as he entered. Only it wasn't Harriet standing behind the cash register—it was Gretchen. She had the money drawer open and a stack of bills in her hand.

"Faith does the books here. She makes sure Harriet knows where every nickel and dime goes. You might want to think about that before you do something you regret."

Gretchen set the bills back in the register with an annoying grin on her face. "I think there's only one of us at risk of having some major regrets soon."

"I need to talk to Harriet. Is she upstairs?" Harriet lived in the apartment above the shop.

"I know you're mad at me, and you have every right to be." Her expression softened. "I'm not here looking for your forgiveness, because I haven't earned that. I'm here because I see you and you're so much like me. You deserve to be young and free. I'd hate to see you make the same mistakes I made."

Though she'd sounded sincere at first, Sawyer's anger started in his toes and crawled up the entire length of his body until it felt like flames were shooting out the top of his head. "I'm nothing like you. I'm like my father, a man whose first instinct is to take care of his family and do what's right for them above everything else. Don't think for a second that you know me. You gave up that privilege long ago."

"Hello there, sugarplum." Harriet came down the stairs wearing a bright red dress and a wide-brimmed red church hat with red feathers and a giant flower on the side. "Why don't we take a walk down to the Cup and Spoon Diner and you can buy me a coffee while we chat."

"We don't have to leave on account of her," Sawyer said, waving a hand in Gretchen's direction. "I am not afraid to say what I have to say with her standing right there."

"He's not like me at all, Harriet," Gretchen said with obvious sarcasm. "He's got *no* angst."

"You don't need to get him any more fired up than he already is," Harriet chided.

"I'm getting married," Sawyer announced.

Harriet didn't flinch. "I know. I'm happy for you."

"I'm not," Gretchen threw out.

"Hush," Harriet said. "Are you here to officially ask me to do the flowers? Because you know I will. It would be my honor and it will be my gift."

"I'm getting married in two days," he said

dropping the real bomb. "I need to know if you think we can use the flowers from the bus to make some bouquets and center-pieces."

"Are you nuts?" Gretchen shouted as Harriet's jaw dropped. "What are you thinking? You can't marry that girl in two days. This is not the 1950s. You don't have to have a shotgun wedding because someone tells you to. You can raise a child together without being married."

"Oh, because that worked out real well for you, didn't it?" Sawyer said. "You were a big help to Dad all those years. Oh, wait. That was *Harriet*. My bad." He turned back to Harriet. "What do you think? Can you make it work?"

"I don't see why not," she replied, having regained her composure.

"Great. Feel free to stop by anytime to re-purpose the flowers however you see fit. The bus is at the farm. It's going to be a small wedding. Only family and close friends. I don't think you'll need to make more than two bouquets and a couple centerpieces."

"I'll make it work."

"Gretchen is not invited, in case you

were wondering. She's neither family nor a friend," he added.

"You know what's a great reason to get married, Harriet?" Gretchen said. "To spite the mother who abandoned you. Don't you think?"

Sawyer refused to engage with her. Maybe there was the tiniest shred of truth in her accusation, but he didn't care. He had enough good reasons to marry Piper. One bad one wouldn't spoil everything. Plus, Gretchen was like a cancer; he didn't want to feed her malignance. With nothing but a goodbye for Harriet, he was out the door.

PIPER STRUGGLED WITH the zipper on the dress she'd found at Hugo's, the only department store in Grass Lake. They'd had one white dress in the maternity section. One. Piper began to question if it was even acceptable for her to wear white. It was obvious she and Sawyer had done things out of order.

"Faith, could I get your help?" she asked through the door.

Faith had reluctantly agreed to take Piper shopping. Not that she'd said she didn't want to go; the look on her face had given her hesitation away.

"Sure," Faith answered. Piper opened the door to let her in the tiny dressing room.

Faith got the stubborn zipper up in one try. The white lace dress was knee-length and had a simple scoop neckline and short cap sleeves. The empire waist was elastic, most likely to accommodate a growing belly. It wasn't Piper's dream wedding dress by any means, but it fit.

"That looks nice," Faith said without much gusto.

"I always pictured myself in something with a long train and detailed beading. I also imagined my dress would accentuate these curves—" she ran her hands down her sides "—not this curve." She pointed at her baby bump.

"I tried on what felt like a hundred dresses before I found the right one," Faith said.

Dean and Faith were getting married this summer. Piper hoped Faith didn't resent the fact that Sawyer was doing it first. "I don't have that kind of time. This one will have to do," she said. "Unzip me?"

Faith obliged. "I feel bad about that. Don't you want to have a wedding the way you always dreamed about? It's not like getting married in a year would really change anything between you and Sawyer if you're both so sure you want to be together forever."

Piper had suspected Faith was not in favor of the timing of things. "That's true, but I also think—why wait? What is really going to be different in a year? I'll be able to fit in a better dress? That's not the point of what we're doing. We're getting married because we want to be committed."

"Commitment is a daily act, it's not something you agree to once and then it's over with," Faith argued.

"I know. The day is simply symbolic. I suppose we'll have to agree to disagree."

Faith was about as confrontational as Piper. She let it go and left the room so Piper could change. Piper tried not to let her thoughts linger on Faith's point, but failed. What she couldn't tell her future sister-in-law was that she feared Sawyer would change his mind if she waited. She believed him when he said he only wanted to get married once. If they did it now, he'd stay committed to her. If they put it off, she might lose her only chance.

None of this was ideal, but it was as good as Piper was going to get. She wanted her son to have two married parents. They bought the dress and headed back to the car.

Downtown Grass Lake consisted of one main road. Piper thought it was adorable. There was a theater with a big marquee announcing the one movie being shown there, a hardware store with a couple of rocking chairs outside where two old men sat and greeted customers as they came and went, and then there was Harriet's Flower Shop, with a window full of roses in every color on display.

"Should we stop in and say hi to Harriet?" Piper asked, pushing the door open before Faith could answer. A bell chimed, and the fragrant smell of hundreds of flowers hit her all at once.

"Maybe we shouldn't," Faith said, chasing after her.

"Oh." Piper hadn't meant to assume Faith had the time to kill. As she turned to leave, her eyes connected with the woman behind the counter. Sawyer's mom.

"Well, it must be family and friends day," Gretchen said. "Don't worry, I promise I don't bite. You okay? You're pale as a ghost."

Piper felt a bit light-headed and her heart pounded. "I—"

"She didn't know you were staying here.

We're going to go," Faith said, gently pulling Piper toward the door.

"Don't leave on my account. Your brother came in and informed us there's a wedding to plan. You must be running around checking things off your list. Buy a dress—check. Order flowers—check. Trap a man into marriage by getting knocked up—check."

"Mom, stop," Faith pleaded.

"He's not ready to get married. You said so yourself, Faith."

Piper wanted to run away, but her legs wouldn't move.

"Sawyer and Piper are adults who get to make their own choices," Faith said. "It's not our place to tell them what to do or to judge them."

"What kind of trouble are you getting yourself into now?" Harriet came out of the back room with a roll of pink tulle. She stopped short when she noticed Piper. "Oh, boy. What are you doing bringing the poor girl here?" she asked Faith.

"I couldn't grab her fast enough."

"You all act like I am going to hurt the girl," Gretchen complained. "I don't want to hurt her, I want her to stop making plans to hurt my son. Is that too much to ask?"

"We're going to go," Faith said, resuming their retreat.

"I'll be by the house later today to make some arrangements for the wedding out of the flowers on the bus," Harriet said. "Everything will be beautiful, I promise, Piper."

"Thank you," Piper managed to mumble. Faith got her out of the store before Gretchen could make her feel any worse.

They walked in silence to the car. Piper's head was spinning with a million questions. She spun her engagement ring around and around. "Do you agree with your mom?" she finally asked.

Faith didn't answer right away, which led Piper to believe she did but didn't want to upset the apple cart. They got to the car and Piper opened the door. "Not completely," she said before getting in.

Piper climbed into the passenger seat. "Not completely, but a little bit. You agree with some of the things she says. Like what? Like I trapped your brother into marrying me?"

"No! Not that. I know you did not plan for this to happen. I know the baby was unexpected."

"You don't think we should get married."

Faith placed both hands on the wheel. "I don't think you should get married in two days. I don't object to you two getting married at some point in time. I think you're a very lovely person and my brother would be lucky to have you as his wife. I just feel like everything is moving at light speed, and that's not the way I want this to be for either one of you. Rushed, impulsive, without the full support of all your loved ones."

Piper pressed her fingers to her eyes to keep herself from crying. Was everyone right? Was this wedding a mistake that would haunt her forever?

"Please don't cry. My brother will never forgive me if he finds out I made you cry."

Piper waved her off. She would do her best to hold it together. Why did two days feel like not nearly enough time to prepare for a wedding but more than enough time for someone to convince them to cancel it?

CHAPTER SIXTEEN

HEATH EMAILED PIPER the prenup the next morning with a warning that he and Piper's mother and brother would be arriving this afternoon. She had waited to open it until she could do so with Sawyer. The whole thing made her feel sick.

"When your brother gets here, I want to ask him if he'll stand up for me. Did you ask Faith if she'd stand up for you? I like the idea of our siblings being our witnesses."

Piper had not asked Faith, because she knew Sawyer's sister did not approve of the marriage in the first place. "How about I ask my brother and you ask your sister? This wedding is already nontraditional, why not mix it up?"

Sawyer seemed puzzled. "You mean Faith would be my best woman and Matty is your man of honor?"

"Why not?" Piper asked.

"No reason. I think it's a great idea. I'll ask Faith the next time I see her."

Piper put her feet up on the chair next to her as they sat at the kitchen table in Faith's kitchen with Scout lounging close by, hoping they'd drop some food. Sawyer scratched the dog's head.

"Do you want to forward this prenup to your lawyer?" she asked.

"Why? I'm going to sign it. I'm sure it says I can't have any of your money or property if we get divorced. I don't need your money or property, so I might as well sign it and get Heath off my back."

"Well, someone needs to read it," Piper insisted. "Your lawyer's job is to make sure you aren't signing something that gives me all your money and property."

"Do you want it? You can have it."

She tilted her head. "I'm serious."

"So am I. We're not even going to need it. We won't be getting a divorce."

His optimism was so refreshing given the negativity everyone else had been spewing. "I couldn't agree more, but you should still have someone read it before you sign."

"Dean and Faith aren't going to have a prenup," he mumbled.

"Dean and Faith also have an engagement that will be more than a year long before they tie the knot. You can't compare us to them. It's like apples to oranges."

Sawyer leaned over and kissed her. "You're right, we're so much better than they are, which is why we're going first."

Piper wanted to believe that was true, but doubt was settling in. Why did he suddenly want to rush to the altar? He'd accused her of doing what her father told her without question, yet wasn't she going along with Sawyer's wishes in the same way? The questions made her stomach hurt.

"What do you say to a horse as the ring bearer and flower girl? I have two horses who would be perfect for the parts."

"I don't have to ride them, do I? I don't think riding horses is on my list of acceptable activities, according to Ruby."

Sawyer's dimples were on display. "Fine, no riding off into the sunset together at the end, I guess. They can definitely just be props."

His phone rang and he hit Decline.

"Who was that?"

"No one important." Aka his mom. Piper wanted Gretchen to stay away from the wedding as much as Sawyer did. She'd actually love it if the woman decided to leave Grass Lake altogether.

"What do you think she wants?" she asked.

"Doesn't matter," he said as his phone signaled he had a voice mail. "Whatever it is, it's irrelevant."

Faith came storming in from the barn. "We have a problem."

Sawyer and Scout both jumped up. The dog barked and Sawyer asked, "What kind of problem?"

She tugged off her work gloves. "Three different people just pulled into our parking lot. They wanted a comment on a wedding that's happening tomorrow."

"What kind of people?" Sawyer asked.

"How in the world would they know there's a wedding happening tomorrow?" Piper asked.

"Well, I'm going to guess paparazzi, given the fact that they thought they could take a few pictures of Piper's bus while they were here."

Sawyer and Piper bolted to the front of the house and pulled the curtains back. Sure enough, Jesse—Helping Hooves' therapist—

was out there directing some guys off the property.

"Great," Sawyer said in an exhale.

"I can't have them taking pictures of my clients, Sawyer. And Dean has some band coming in to record later today. We're both still running businesses in the middle of this." Faith's hands were on her hips. As if she didn't disapprove enough already.

"We'll put up some No Trespassing signs and something that says this lot is only for Helping Hooves clients and guests," Sawyer said, dialing his phone.

"How many more are going to show up in the next twenty-four hours?" Faith asked.

Piper knew from experience that where there was one, there were ten. Paparazzi had a tendency to multiply like rabbits. "We need to get some security down here, as well. I can set that up."

"I can't deal with constant interruptions today, so that would be helpful." Faith went out the front door just as another car drove down the lane.

Someone had to have tipped them off. Or they could have found out about the marriage license. It was public record. That didn't explain how they knew the wedding was tomorrow. The license was good for thirty days—it didn't specify when Piper and Sawyer were getting married.

"Who would have leaked the details of our wedding?" Piper pondered aloud. "The only people who know are the few who are coming. And I can't imagine they would have told the media."

Sawyer hung up his phone. His face was red. "Gretchen."

"How do you know?"

"I just listened to her message. She wanted to warn me that we might have a few 'unexpected guests.'"

The woman was relentless. Piper knew she didn't think Sawyer should get married, but she'd never expected his mother to try to sabotage it by creating yet another thing for them to worry about. They'd have to increase security, and privacy would be more difficult to come by. Seemed each of them had a parent who was determined to delay the ceremony.

"I'm going to run down to the hardware store and get some signs. You stay in the house. With people coming in and out without warning, it's best if you stay out of sight," Sawyer said.

"My face is on the bus out there. It's not like they don't know I'm here."

"We're going to be fine. And if worse comes to worse and this becomes some kind of circus, we'll go down to city hall and get married in front of a judge instead."

That was definitely not the way Piper wanted to get married. It was fine for some people, but she wanted something resembling a normal ceremony.

Sawyer grabbed his keys and took off. Piper peeked through the curtains as he shouted at a new paparazzo to move his car so he could get his truck out.

Everyone working against him seemed to make Sawyer that much more determined to see this wedding through. Piper worried that even his own fears about rushing into this were pushing him to prove them wrong.

SAWYER TOLD JESSE to send one of the volunteers to the end of the drive to keep the trespassers from getting close to the house.

"I'll do it until my next appointment comes in," Jesse said. "But we don't have too many extra hands on deck today until later in the afternoon when the high school gets out."

Sawyer's blood was boiling. He wanted to

stop by Harriet's, but that would only give Gretchen the satisfaction of knowing she had gotten under his skin. He wouldn't say a word to her, because if anyone deserved the silent treatment, it was the woman who had given it to him for the majority of his life.

"Do your best until I can get back with some signs to post," he told Jesse. "I'll stop by the sheriff's office and see if they have a deputy to spare until Piper can arrange for some private security."

He was not going to let Gretchen win. He would handle this minor bump in the road and they would get married as planned.

Earl Bell sat in one of the rocking chairs outside Maddox Hardware. Old man Middleton was noticeably missing. Sawyer tipped his hat. "Morning, Mr. Bell. Where's Hank this morning?"

"Across the street getting us some coffee and sticky buns," Earl replied, gesturing toward the Cup and Spoon Diner. "I hear you're getting married and having a baby. I can still remember when *you* were a baby and your daddy would bring you in here on his hip."

"Time sure flies."

"Faster and faster every year," the older

man agreed. "I also noticed your mother has reappeared. How you holding up, son?"

Small town. No secrets. "I'm fine, Mr. Bell. She might have given birth to me, but she's not really my mother. I haven't been troubling myself with her."

"Well, I don't blame you for feeling like that. Your father had a heck of time when she disappeared the way she did. I'm sure there are some awfully hard feelings. She looks the same as she did before she left, though. It was like seeing a ghost."

Gretchen was definitely haunting Sawyer at the moment. "It was nice talking to you, Mr. Bell, but I have to get some things for the farm," Sawyer said, cutting the conversation short. "I'll see you on my way out."

Maddox Hardware had been around long before Sawyer was born. He, like Mr. Bell, remembered coming in here as a kid with his dad and thinking of it like a toy store. Tools and gadgets galore lined the shelves.

"Sawyer Stratton! Mr. Nashville star. How's it going?" Bud Maddox was the owner and great-grandson of the original Mr. Maddox, who'd opened the store back in the day. "I heard you were in town with your famous friend. Rumor has it there's something big happening tomorrow out on the farm."

Rumors were spreading faster than wildfire. "Oh, yeah? Where did you hear that?"

"Your mom was in here yesterday. Said you were planning a big ol' wedding. Whole town is supposed to be invited."

Gretchen was unbelievable. Not only had she notified the press, but she'd taken it upon herself to get everyone in Grass Lake involved. She must have thought if she created enough hassle, Sawyer and Piper would give up.

"She's seriously lost her mind," Sawyer mumbled in frustration. "Don't believe everything you hear, Bud. Gretchen's been gone a long time. She has no idea what's going on around here."

"Oh, no." Bud frowned. "I didn't mean to—"

"Don't worry about it. I just need to get these signs up before everyone in the entire state tries to get into this wedding."

"Let me ring you up."

"If you hear people talking, feel free to set the record straight. We're keeping it super small. Just family and close friends."

"Will do, Sawyer." If anyone could get the

word out, it was Bud. He would tell every single customer in the store today. By the end of the day, everyone in Grass Lake would get the message that there was no blanket invite. Gretchen would not ruin this wedding.

HEATH AND THE rest of the Starling family showed up while Sawyer was busy hammering the No Trespassing signs into the ground outside the entrance. He knew his future father-in-law was not going to be pleased with the leaks to the press. He liked to control those like he controlled everything else.

The two security guards Piper had hired each had a clipboard and a walkie-talkie. Faith had given them a list of all the people who were expected to show up today so they could let her clients through without much hassle.

"Move aside. I'm Heath Starling. I don't need to show any ID."

Apparently Faith had forgotten to put good ol' Heath on the list.

"They're cleared," Sawyer shouted. "Let him on through."

No thank-you from Heath, but Mrs. Starling waved at him from the passenger seat.

Sawyer waved back, certain all of this was being filmed for posterity's sake.

Some of the photogs' vehicles were parked along the highway in front of the property. They knew better than to try to get too close, but it didn't matter how far Sawyer pushed them back. Their mega-zoom lenses were attached to superpower cameras that must have cost a fortune. Sawyer figured there must be good money in getting ridiculous pictures of celebrities.

The paparazzi weren't about to ruin the wedding day, though. Not if Sawyer had anything to say about it. Let them print pictures of him marrying Piper in every magazine out there. He wanted Gretchen to see his smiling face in all of them.

"I don't want that in there," Piper said as Sawyer walked into the house. She sat at the dining room table with her father, holding a stack of papers. "We strike that and I'll sign it."

"I strongly advise you not to do that," her father said.

"What are we arguing about?" Sawyer asked.

"My father had the attorney put in the prenup that if we were to divorce, you would agree to giving me half a million dollars if you are caught having an affair at any time during our marriage."

Heath was pulling no punches. He'd made it as clear as Gretchen that he didn't want them to go through with this. "Only half a million?" Sawyer asked, trying to let cooler heads prevail.

"The press will have a field day with this and assume I fear him being unfaithful. It paints a terrible picture."

"Anything in there about taking all my kids away?" Sawyer took off his hat and sat next to Piper.

"I learned you can't put anything in a prenup about custody, unfortunately," Heath complained.

"Let's sign it," Sawyer said, grabbing a pen off the table and reaching for the document. "I don't care about a stupid unfaithfulness clause. It's not going to happen anyway."

Piper wouldn't let go of the paperwork. "You need someone to read this for you first. You can't sign it without knowing what it says."

"I trust that your father made sure that in the event of a divorce you will be taken care of and all of your assets will be protected.

That's good enough for me." He held out his hand, waiting for her to relent.

Heath seemed displeased with Sawyer's response. "It won't be enforceable if you sign it without legal counsel. You might also want to think about your family's assets. If you personally can't pay, we could come after your sister."

He had purposely put something in there that needed changing. Heath was anything but stupid. He was a master of manipulation.

Piper flipped through the pages. "You put something about Faith's farm in here? We need to remove that."

"I'll get my attorney to look at it today. It's not a problem," Sawyer said.

Heath grinned. "Well, our attorney won't be able to look at the revisions until next week. Guess we'll have to postpone this wedding to a later date."

"I'll sign it as soon as the revisions are made. We don't need my attorney to look over it again," Piper said in defiance.

"That's not the way this works, sweetheart," Heath said. "The lawyers will work it all out."

"I'm getting married tomorrow whether you like it or not. If you don't want me to sign this prenup, I'm good with not having one at all. If you insist I have one, it's this one with the revisions Sawyer's lawyer makes."

Mrs. Starling came out of the kitchen. "I think your daughter has learned more about negotiating from you than you wanted her to."

Heath rubbed his forehead, struggling to find a way out of this. He needed to accept there was none. Piper had finally found her voice and she was using it.

"How's Matty?" Piper asked.

"He's resting on the couch. He had a seizure on the drive down here," Claudia explained. "This is the first one since the medication change."

"I'm sorry to hear that," Sawyer said. "Did he get accepted into that experimental treatment study?"

"We just got word last week that he has. Thanks to all the work Piper has done to get his name out there."

"And all the money she donated," Heath added.

Until now, he hadn't realized how much this prenup could influence both families. He needed to take it more seriously. "I'll fax this to my attorney," he said, taking the papers from Piper. Time really wasn't on their side. As much as it begrudged him to admit it, maybe they were moving a bit too fast. Sawyer couldn't give up now, though. Not when they were so close.

PIPER COULDN'T BELIEVE the extent to which her father would try to delay the incvitable. Didn't he understand that she was about to get exactly what she had hoped for since she found out she was pregnant? Sawyer was willing to commit to her. He wanted to be a family. Her father could not ruin this for her.

"Did you come here to help me or hurt me?" she asked her dad.

"Helping you is all I ever want to do. But it's hard to sit by and watch you do something that might hurt you in the end."

"With some support from our families, maybe we would have a much better chance of having a successful marriage. A little positivity could go a long way."

Piper's mother put a calming hand on her shoulder. "We're here, aren't we? Your father is overprotective. When that little baby is born, you'll understand how hard it is to bite your tongue when you disagree about something."

"I don't understand why we disagree about this. Getting married is the best outcome we could ask for. It doesn't jeopardize my career. My son will have married parents. What more could you want for me? A prenup that protects money that Sawyer doesn't want anyway?"

Her father didn't answer.

"As long as you love Sawyer and Sawyer loves you, Dad and I will support you two until the end of time," her mom said.

That queasy feeling was back in the pit of Piper's stomach. Anytime someone mentioned the word *love*, the uneasiness struck.

Sawyer flew down the stairs and handed Piper her papers. "I saw from the window that Harriet's here to dismantle the bus flowers so she can repurpose them. Do you want to come out and tell her what you have in mind?"

Piper and her mom followed Sawyer outside. Harriet parked her flower delivery truck next to the bus. It was nice to do something in favor of the wedding rather than against it.

"Good afternoon, my little chickadees. Are we ready to do some magic with our flower friends?" Harriet said, jumping out of the driver's seat. "I brought a few extras in case not everything is usable. We might have to clean up some of the garlands."

Harriet walked to the back off her truck and unlatched the door. She slammed it shut nearly as quickly as she opened it.

"What's wrong?" Sawyer said, coming around back. Harriet had a look of dread on her face.

"Nothing. I brought the wrong flowers. I need to run back to the store." She hurried around to the driver's side door.

"Oh, come on, Harriet," Sawyer said. "I'm sure it's fine. Let's take a look before you go all the way back."

He pulled the handle as Harriet came racing back to stop him. "Don't open that door!"

Sawyer had already wrenched it open. His face dropped and a scowl appeared. Piper came closer to see what the problem was. She couldn't imagine Harriet had packed anything that terrible back there. Piper gasped.

Besides the wedding flowers, there was Gretchen plucking petals from a rose.

"You have a serious problem," Sawyer said.

Gretchen tossed the last petal on the floor. "He loves me not."

CHAPTER SEVENTEEN

"Y'ALL HAVE THIS place locked down like it's Fort Knox. I thought you boarded horses, not gold."

Gretchen was out of control. Sawyer could not handle any more of her nonsense.

"Take her back, Harriet. She's not welcome here," Sawyer growled.

"I didn't know she was in there," Harriet insisted, following a stomping Sawyer to the front porch. "I swear to you I would not have let her come."

He'd never been so angry in his life.

"Just get her out of here, Harriet."

"Gretchen, let's go," Harriet said, but Gretchen had other plans. She was already walking toward the horse stables.

"I need to talk to my daughter!"

"I will call the police and report you for trespassing!" Sawyer shouted from the porch steps.

Heath came outside to see what the commotion was about. "Your mother again?"

Faith was leading one of the horses out of the stable to work in the outdoor arena. Her head fell back in frustration when she caught sight of Gretchen.

Sawyer ran over there. "Can you help me out? She snuck in in the back of Harriet's truck."

"Really, Mother?"

"Hey, ask him what he did before you get mad at me for simply coming here to talk to you. I wanted to see my daughter, and he has guards at the gate. What was I supposed to do?"

"I know what I'm going to do," Sawyer said, pulling out his phone.

"Don't go calling the police with all those paparazzi out there," Faith said. "She can come with me to the arena until Harriet's finished with you."

Sawyer didn't like that plan. Give Gretchen an inch and apparently she would take a mile. "She can't stay here."

"She's not going to stay here. She's going to watch me work while Harriet makes you beautiful wedding flowers for your wedding that's happening tomorrow no matter what *anyone* has to say about it." Faith looked pointedly at Gretchen.

"Sawyer wins. I'm not here to stop him. I'm here to talk to you. I've done all I can to knock some sense into him. I finally understand how my father felt. He's probably having a good ol' laugh up there in heaven. I got exactly what I deserved—a child as hardheaded as I was."

"You and I are nothing alike. Stop saying that!" He hated that she kept comparing him to herself. She was the exact opposite of the kind of person he wanted to be.

"I got this," Faith reiterated. "Go, plan your wedding."

"And don't think you're going to bend Faith's ear and convince her to talk to me on your behalf. She is on my side. She's the one who's always been on my side."

That was all he had to say about it. He was not going to engage with Gretchen again. She could mend fences with Faith and Harriet, but their fences had been obliterated. There was no fixing anything between her and Sawyer.

Piper and her parents were on the bus with Harriet. Sawyer took a deep breath to regain his composure. There was something about that woman that rubbed him all the wrong ways. She was nothing like the mother he remembered. The one who took him hunting for toads down by the lake or told him stories about adventurous space travelers and rambunctious cowboys.

The mother from his memories was someone different. Someone who mattered to him. This Gretchen Stratton had nothing to offer him except her misguided opinions.

"So we can use these around the horses' necks." Harriet had taken down the flower garlands and was carefully placing them in a box.

"Everything coming along?" Sawyer asked.

Piper fixed her gaze on him. She seemed reluctant to speak. He hated that Gretchen intimidated her so much.

"I think we can reuse almost all of this," Harriet said. "Everything okay out there?"

"It's fine."

"How about between you and me?" Harriet asked, obviously afraid he would take Gretchen's surprise visit out on her.

"Did you know she was in the truck?"

"Absolutely not. I told her I was going and she said she would watch the store for me so I didn't have to close early. I forgot your mother is relentless to a fault."

"Then we're fine, as well."

"I'm going to go check on Matthew," Heath said. Flowers and feelings were most likely not on his list of favorite things.

Sawyer made his way over to Piper. He pressed a soft kiss to the side of her head. "Are we okay?" he whispered as Claudia and Harriet discussed the flowers she would pull out for the bridal bouquet.

Piper leaned against him. "I'll be happy when this is all over. Is that bad?"

He smiled and wrapped an arm around her waist. "There'd be no such thing as elopement if everyone loved weddings."

"Tell me everything is going to be fine and I'll believe you," she said.

Her lips were so close and he could feel her breath on his neck. Every time he was around her, he felt the urge to hold her, to kiss her. It was beyond lust or want. It was a connection he couldn't describe with words.

"Everything will be more than fine. I promise."

"You two are so cute. Ah, to be young and in love," Piper's mom said as she and Harriet stopped what they were doing.

"Remember this feeling, sweet peas. Love is what will get you through all the tough times. And trust me, there are tougher times ahead that will make your mother's reappearance seem like nothing."

Sawyer's brow dipped. "That's not very reassuring, Harriet."

"It is if you focus on the part about love getting you through."

LOVE, LOVE, LOVE. Piper felt love for Sawyer that she'd never experienced with anyone else. He was good and kind. He made her laugh and challenged her in ways that made her better. He was the spontaneity she needed in her scheduled existence.

Did he feel it for her? That was the million-dollar question. One she was too afraid to ask straight up. He acted like he was in love. He treated her the way she would expect someone to if they were in love. He didn't say it, though. Wasn't it more important that he showed it? She told herself it was until that annoying doubt crept back in. He was so focused on his mom and proving her wrong. Were they rushing only because Gretchen had reappeared? She hated to think it, but there it was.

"Why don't we show your mom and Harriet where we're going to set everything up for the ceremony?" Sawyer suggested, pulling her out of her dark thoughts.

They all went out back, behind the house and recording studio. The space was surrounded by paddocks and rolling hills that were much greener in the summer. The temperatures were still chillier than Piper would have liked for an outdoor ceremony, but she would have to work with what she'd been given. On Friday it was supposed to be almost seventy degrees. They would survive.

"This is where we'll say our vows. The guests will be over here, and after the ceremony, we'll head inside for dinner," Sawyer said, pointing out the important details.

"It will be lovely," Piper's mom said. "And the paparazzi can't see anything back here, so that's good. You'll have some privacy."

"What in the world are they doing now?" Harriet asked, looking over Piper's shoulder and back toward the barn.

Heath and Gretchen came marching across the property together. Sawyer pulled Piper behind him, placing himself between her and whatever it was those two were about to say.

"We need to talk," Heath said, slightly winded from his walk. "Your mother, although a bit unusual, has a few valid points about this wedding."

"It doesn't matter," Sawyer said. "Nothing she says matters to me. I don't know how many times I can say it."

"Piper, sweetheart, you know you're rushing into something that doesn't need to be rushed," Heath argued.

"Dad, I don't feel rushed. This is what I want." Sawyer had asked her to stand up for herself and this was her chance to prove to him that she could.

"You can't decide to get married one day and have a wedding the next."

"I don't understand this argument," Piper's mother said. "They've been engaged since November and together since August. Marriage was the goal. They aren't taking a lot of time to plan a wedding, but they made the decision to get married months ago."

Piper saw it on her father's face. He was about to say something he couldn't take back.

"Dad, please," she begged.

"It was all pretend. I made them pretend to be engaged to protect Piper's reputation," Heath confessed. "The entire relationship was a fraud up until a little while ago when they decided they should date."

Piper felt like a flower wilting in the sun. She couldn't look at her mother.

"In fact, we discussed telling the media they had set a wedding date when we were in LA, and Sawyer refused because he had no intentions of getting married. He wasn't ready. That was four days ago. Four days ago, he said he wouldn't lie and claim the wedding was this summer because that was too soon."

"Is that true?" Piper's mom turned on Sawyer.

"I don't like it when Heath tells me what to do. It was more about not wanting him orchestrating the whole thing than it was about marrying Piper."

"You were angry with her after she called in to the radio station three days ago and said she wanted a summer wedding. You felt she was pressuring you," her father said, more emboldened by the second. "The only thing that changed was her." He pointed at Gretchen, who actually wasn't gloating. She appeared more saddened by this than anything. "She showed up and all of a sudden he wants to get married."

"That's not true," Sawyer said, sounding less convincing than he had a moment ago.

"Piper Ann, why is your father saying this if it isn't true?" Claudia asked.

"I fell in love with Sawyer at the end of the summer. We made this baby because I was in love with him. I want to marry him because I'm in love with him."

"That's not what I asked."

She knew that wasn't the answer to the question, but she felt it needed to be said. Piper had been in love with Sawyer from the beginning. Yet her heart was breaking because everything her father said was right. She'd tried to ignore it, but the ugly truth couldn't be denied any longer. Sawyer was rushing their wedding to spite his mother.

"What about you, Sawyer? Have you been in love this whole time like Piper?" Gretchen asked. "Or did you decide that you were going to marry her because I showed up saying it was a mistake? If you love her, I'll back off. If you love her, it doesn't matter when you get married."

Piper had a hand on his arm, and his muscles were so tight. He was straining to keep control. "I am not answering you. You aren't my mother. Harriet has been more of a mother to me than you ever were."

"Then answer me," Harriet said. "If I had

asked you a week ago if you wanted to get married, what would you have said?"

Sawyer swallowed hard. "I would have said I wasn't sure. But just because I wasn't sure a week ago doesn't mean I'm not sure now. Maybe Gretchen made me realize that I do want to be married. That making that commitment is important. Not like she would know anything about commitment."

Every answer led back to his mother. Piper wanted to cry.

"What have you two gotten yourselves into?" Piper's mom shook her head and covered her mouth with her hand.

"It was a business deal. Their relationship was supposed to soften the blow that Piper was pregnant. We didn't want to tarnish her brand," her father said.

Claudia would have none of that. "You are the one I'm most upset with right now. Your daughter is a person, not a brand. She has feelings. Obviously she has very strong feelings for this man, and you put her brand ahead of those feelings. She's been forced to pretend to be in a relationship with someone who wasn't sure he felt the same way until three days ago. That's horrible. Have you thought for a second what that was like for her?"

It *was* kind of horrible. But Heath hadn't come up with this plan on his own. "I'm the one who suggested we handle things this way, Mom. I didn't want anything to jeopardize my ability to take care of you and Dad and Matthew."

"It's your father's job to take care of you and your job to take care of yourself and the baby you're carrying. Period," her mom said, pulling her in for a hug. "I am sorry you thought you had to put all of us above yourself."

Faith came sprinting from the arena. "I swear I was watching her. She and Heath were talking and no one was arguing, so I took Freddy to return Winston to the paddock. When I got back, they were both gone." She laced her fingers behind her head and tried to catch her breath. "I'm sorry."

"We were just discussing how your brother and Piper have been lying about everything," Harriet said. "They have been having a fake engagement since the beginning of this mess."

Faith bit down on her bottom lip.

"You knew," Harriet said, reading her like a book.

Faith nodded. "But to be fair, I have expressed my dislike for the fake engagement plan from the very beginning. Heath wanted them to get married right away and I fought to stop that."

"So, on Thanksgiving, you invited everyone here, knowing it was all a ruse? And let us all believe they were a happy couple?" Harriet asked.

Faith threw her hands up. "They weren't an unhappy couple. I do believe that Sawyer cares for Piper. I think he genuinely wants to coparent."

"He cares about her," Piper's mom repeated. "But does he love her?" She swung her attention to Sawyer. "Do you love her? Do you want to spend the rest of your life with her?"

Piper didn't want him to answer that. Not right now. Not in front of all these people. She couldn't take it if he said no.

"Okay, hold on a second. Everyone needs to relax. Whether we decided three months ago, three days ago or three seconds ago, it doesn't change the fact that we decided to get married," Piper said. "Everyone is so worried about what's real and what's not. We decided without Dad's influence to get married, and we picked tomorrow as the day to do it. If y'all don't want to come and celebrate with us, that's your choice. We are done defending ourselves."

Piper took Sawyer's hand and started walking toward the house. "If Dad has been talking to Gretchen this entire time, someone needs to check on Matty."

"Your silence says it all, Sawyer," Heath called after them.

Piper refused to turn around. She kept walking and pulled Sawyer right along with her.

"I'm sorry," he said as they made their way up the porch stairs.

"There's nothing to be sorry for. I should be apologizing for what my father did."

"My sister wasn't wrong." He stopped her from opening the front door and took her into his arms. "I care about you more than I've cared about anyone."

Care but not love. "Do you still want to get married tomorrow?"

"Do you?" he asked.

She wanted to marry him more than anything. "Of course. My mother may be less supportive, but I feel the same way I did when you asked me."

"Then I say we don't change a single thing."

"You want this? You really want this?"

He smiled and placed a hand on her stomach. "We're having a baby. We both want to give him the family he deserves. If I didn't think it could work, I wouldn't be doing it. You asked me to trust you and I'm doing that. I guess now I need to ask you to trust me."

Piper wanted to trust him. She wanted to believe he would never regret what they were about to do.

"Trust me, Piper. I say we get married tomorrow no matter who says they object."

"I trust you. But maybe we should ask the pastor to take that question out of the script," she suggested.

Hopefully they'd all gotten their objections out of the way. They would find out tomorrow, because this wedding was still on.

CHAPTER EIGHTEEN

"Is there a reason that Jason Green told me he's sorry to hear about our mother's Alzheimer's?" Faith asked as she poured herself a cup of coffee the next morning.

"I have no idea," Sawyer replied.

"He said that Bud Maddox told him that you said Mom lost her mind."

Sawyer smacked his forehead. He hadn't realized how what he'd said could have been so misconstrued. Sometimes the town's gossip train went off the rails.

"I did not tell Bud that she had Alzheimer's. She told people the whole town was invited to the wedding and I told Bud to let people know that wasn't true. Maybe when I heard what she did, I offhandedly said something about her being crazy. I didn't mean it literally."

"It's not funny to joke about stuff like that, Sawyer."

"Well, you know what else isn't funny? When your mother walks back into your life after abandoning you twenty years ago and thinks she can mess it up because she knows best."

"She's worried about you repeating mistakes she made. She doesn't know you."

"If the worst mistake I can make is being a father to my son and being present while he's growing up, I think I can live with that."

He was so done explaining why it was important for him to do this. He had overcome his distrust of Piper, and that had been the only thing holding him back. If she could stand by him, he should be able to commit to her.

Faith sat down at the kitchen table with him. "It did hurt my feelings to know that she regretted getting married because they were pregnant with me. She made me feel like I ruined her life or something."

"Don't feel bad. She was quick to take her life back even though she had a great guy who loved her. She also missed out on knowing two pretty interesting people. I mean, I'm always interesting and you're occasionally interesting."

Faith slapped his arm. "How did I not know Mom was pregnant with me before they got married?"

"I guess we never paid attention to when they got married—especially after they were divorced." Sawyer had tried to forget everything about Gretchen once he'd realized she was gone for good.

"Are you really sure about getting married today?" Faith placed a gentle hand on his arm. "I know everyone has been working overtime to get you to reconsider, but I just don't want you to do something because someone told you not to."

"I'm sure."

"You love her?"

"I'm falling in love with her. I know that for sure."

Faith winced. "That's not the same thing. You know that, right?"

"I'm doing the right thing. I'm not like Gretchen. I am not going to desert my family. I'm like Dad. I want to be like Dad. Strong, reliable, loyal."

"You don't have to get married to be like Dad. You can be all those things and date Piper a little longer."

Sawyer shook his head. "She doesn't want to date. She doesn't want to play house. She wants a husband. I'm not going to lose her because I'm afraid to say what I feel might be love. I'm going to give her what she wants and trust that I'll be able to say I'm madly in love with her in the very near future."

"I'm going to pray that's what happens," Faith said, touching his cheek. "I love you."

"I like you most of the time," he said with a straight face.

Faith narrowed her eyes and pinched his leg under the table.

"Ow, ow, ow! Okay, I love you. I love you! You're the best sister ever."

"That's better." She stopped her torture. "I am going to finish my coffee and jump in the shower so I can help Piper get ready for her big day."

At least he'd gotten one person on board with him about this wedding. His sister's opinion mattered more than anyone's. With her support, this day might have a chance.

As Sawyer passed through the front room to head upstairs, he noticed Dean was on the phone, pacing around the front porch. Sawyer went out to see if there was a problem.

"Mom, I'm fairly certain that Gretchen does not have any memory issues."

Sawyer's head dropped. What had he done? This was not going to help keep the wedding day drama-free.

"Did you do this?" Dean mouthed, shaking an angry finger at him.

Sawyer put his hands up. "Not intentionally."

Dean wasn't convinced. "Mom, it's sweet of you, but please do not drop off any pamphlets about living with memory loss at Harriet's. It will not be well received."

If Gretchen found out that Sawyer had started the rumor, intentionally or not, there was no saying what she would do to get back at him. She had already proved her intentions were to disrupt this wedding. "I told you that only family is invited to the wedding. You're lucky you're my family or you and Dad wouldn't have gotten in. Please tell the Woodwards and the Butterfields that it is not true that the whole town is invited."

Great. Not only did people have misinformation about Gretchen, but they still thought they were invited. Sawyer was going to have to turn people away.

"Tell her there's security," Sawyer said.

Dean waved him off. "Mom, there are security guards here who will be making sure only invited guests get in. Piper is a very famous person. We have paparazzi camped outside the farm and media vans showing up two at a time. It's going to be crazy enough without the entire town showing up. I don't know who said that, but they were very wrong."

"Tell her to go into town and spread the word," Sawyer suggested. Maybe someone could set the record straight. Bud had failed him.

Dean gave him a look that clearly meant he should be quiet.

"Okay, I'll see you this afternoon. I'm sure Mrs. Hackney will be very disappointed that she can't get in and you can. Try not to gloat too much." Dean hung up and raised his hands like he was about to strangle Sawyer.

"You are lucky you're the one getting married today, because I would erase you from the invite list for spreading rumors like that."

"I'm sorry. I didn't mean to spread any rumors. I was trying to squash the one about the whole town being invited. Gretchen did that. She was the one attempting to cause mass chaos."

"Well, she might succeed. If everyone in town thinks they're invited and actually shows up, we're going to have our hands full. I might need to get some people to direct traffic farther up the road and help us turn everyone around."

"I can make some calls. Let's not worry about who shows up. Let's be super excited for me. I know you can't wait until your two favorite Grace Note artists tie the knot."

Dean's expression was solemn. "I'm going to speak as your brother-in-law and your friend, not as your record executive. I hope you know what you're doing, because Piper is a really good person and she is in love with you. Don't mess this up."

Sawyer's chest tightened. The weight of Dean's words was not lost on him. "I won't."

"And for goodness' sake, comb your hair."

Sawyer patted down his bed head. "You're just jealous I'm going to be the best-looking guy at my wedding *and* yours."

Dean laughed on his way inside. "Dream on, little brother. Dream on."

PIPER HAD GONE to bed the night before with an uneasy feeling in her gut. It had nothing to do with the baby and everything to do with the baby's daddy.

"Knock, knock," Faith said, coming aboard the bus. "Do you want to use my room to get ready? There's a lot more space in there."

"Thanks. That would be helpful." Piper took her dress off the hook. "Have you seen my parents this morning?"

They'd stayed in the Airstream out back that Dean had bought for Boone to live in last summer. Matthew had stayed on the bus with Piper.

"I stopped by to see if they needed anything, and your mom said they were all good. I made sure they had plenty of coffee and your dad's favorite cereal."

Faith was one of those people who thought of everything. She had a big heart that was programmed to give and give. "You are so kind. Thank you for hosting all of us again."

"You're family now. Or at least you will be in a few hours, right?" Faith gave her a smile and a wink.

Family. Piper was about to be Sawyer's wife. She would be gaining a sister. She didn't know what it was like to have a sister. She assumed it was like having a built-in best friend. She didn't know if Faith would want to be friends, but she hoped she did.

"How's Sawyer?"

"He's good. Ready to get this thing rolling."

"I really do love your brother. I know that not everyone believes me because of the business part of things getting in the way and seeming like the priority, but—"

"Piper," Faith stopped her. "I believe you. You don't have to convince me."

"I don't think he loves me." The words tumbled out of her mouth.

Faith's eyes went wide. "I—"

Piper dropped her head into her hands. "I didn't mean to say that. I'm so embarrassed."

"Don't be embarrassed. It must be weighing heavy on your mind."

Heavy on her heart was more like it.

"I think you were right yesterday when you said he cares about me. I truly believe that. But he's never said he loves me, and whenever someone brings up the word, he gets this look on his face like someone suggested he enlist in the army or something."

"That's a pretty good analogy, actually. Sawyer has had issues with love ever since our mom left. He saw what heartache did to our dad, and he sort of built a wall around his heart so that would never happen to him."

Piper could see that. It was easy to be with

Sawyer on the surface, but the deeper they went, the more guarded he became.

"He's let me in more and more."

"Absolutely," Faith agreed. "But calling his feelings love kind of is like joining the army to him. He could go in and be victorious or he could come home missing a limb, or worse, in a body bag."

"I'm not going to kill him."

Faith chuckled. "I didn't mean that literally. He doesn't want to be hurt."

"I don't want to be hurt, either. I don't want to marry him, then find out a few years from now that he regrets making the commitment. Or hear him say he got caught up in the moment and we should only be friends. I don't know that I could handle hearing he's finally realized he's never going to be in love with me."

Faith frowned. "I wish I knew what to say to make you feel more certain."

"I don't think there's anything you can say," Piper replied. It wasn't Faith who needed to reassure her. There was only one person who could convince her they weren't headed toward heartbreak.

"I do have a little surprise for you that I hope

makes today more like how you imagined," Faith said. "Come in the house with me."

Faith had an enormous bedroom with a four-poster bed and a chaise lounge in the corner. The windows along the back wall of the house looked out at their acres of land. She also had a full-length, freestanding antique mirror.

"I thought about what you said when you were trying on dresses, and you seemed disappointed about not having a dress with a train." Faith disappeared into her walk-in closet. "I know this very sweet lady in town who is probably the most talented seamstress in all of Tennessee. She took two dresses my friend Josie's daughter found on consignment and used parts of both to make a completely new prom dress. It was stunning and one of a kind."

She came out holding a dress bag. "It's tradition to give the bride something old, something new and something blue. I don't know what your mom has planned, but I have the new and old all wrapped up in one."

Faith unzipped the bag and revealed a tulle train complete with beading on the waistband and along the bottom. Piper brought her hand to her mouth. She had no words for this kindness.

"If you don't like the way it looks with the dress, you don't have to wear it. She put it together in a day with tulle she had from something else, and even though she's very good, I would totally understand if you didn't want to wear it."

"It's gorgeous. Of course I want to wear it." The tears in Piper's eyes began to cloud her vision.

This was what it was like to have a sister, to be cared for by a sibling instead of always being the one taking care. Piper swallowed down the giant lump in her throat.

"You two aren't getting started without us, are you?" Piper's mother was at the door with Piper's hair and makeup stylist, Trina.

"We've been waiting for you," Piper said, overcome with emotion.

WITH HAIR AND makeup on point, Piper was feeling a bit more confident about how things might go. Her 1930s Hollywood–inspired finger-wave hairstyle was flawless. She looked like she'd stepped off the pages of *Glamour*. Looking good was an excellent remedy to feeling lousy.

"That train is off the hook," Trina said as Piper posed in front of Faith's mirror.

She almost looked how she'd pictured she would on her wedding day. Minus the bulging belly.

Faith and Trina went to get some snacks for the pregnant bride who needed something to eat every hour, it seemed. Ruby might be worried about her weight gain at the next appointment.

Her mom helped her fluff the train. "We didn't really talk about everything that came up yesterday," Piper said, treading lightly. She knew her mom was disappointed, but her support meant everything. If she had truly lost that, this day wouldn't feel right. "I hope you can forgive me for not being honest about what was happening."

"You lied. Your father lied. Your father told you to lie to me. I'm not happy about it, but I understand he was feeling a bit desperate."

"I wanted to tell you so many times, but I know you have your hands full with Matty, and the last thing you needed was my drama."

Claudia put her hands on her daughter's shoulders. "Piper, sweetheart, I will never be too busy or too overwhelmed to be there for you. You matter to me as much as your brother."

"I know that. I just didn't want to burden you."

She slid her hands down Piper's arms and held both her hands. "You are not a burden. I'm sorry if I ever made you feel that way. Your father has you so focused on your image, he forgets to encourage you to have feelings. You are allowed to be mad, sad, hurt, frustrated, happy, whatever. And it doesn't matter what the press thinks or if the fans will like it or not. You have a right to be human, and that means sometimes you mess up."

Piper was overwhelmed by the comfort her mother's words brought her. For so long, she felt like she had to bury any of the negative emotions she felt. To be given permission to feel was so freeing.

"I don't want to mess up so much that it hurts you. I also didn't want to be a source of embarrassment. I feel like Dad has felt that way this whole time."

"That you're an embarrassment? Oh, Piper. Never in a million years. There is no one in this world that he is more proud of than you."

"I got pregnant before I got married."

"You aren't the first woman to do so and you won't be the last."

"I'm getting married before I'm sure the groom is even in love with me."

Claudia frowned and gave her hands a squeeze. "That has me a bit more concerned. I noticed he wouldn't say the word *love* yesterday."

"Everyone noticed." The lump was back in her throat.

A tear ran down her mom's cheek. "I love you more than you will ever know. It breaks my heart that in this moment before your father walks you down the aisle, you don't know beyond a shadow of a doubt that the man waiting at the other end is going to love you with the kind of fierceness you deserve."

"I think he could."

Claudia caught the tears running down Piper's face. "I think he should."

Faith and Trina returned with two trays of delicious-looking finger foods. Faith had made mini muffins and quiches, and full-sized peanut butter cookies.

"Sawyer told me peanut butter cookies were your favorite," Faith said, offering her one.

"You are so kind." The tears wouldn't stop.

"You can't get her all emotional. It's messing with her makeup," Trina said, setting her tray on the nightstand. "I can fix this."

Piper let Trina clean things up on her face, but she needed to do some cleaning on the inside. "Faith, can you tell Sawyer I need to talk to him before the ceremony?"

"You can't see the groom before the wedding. It's bad luck," Trina said as she reapplied some mascara.

Piper was more worried about the bad luck that would ensue if she didn't talk to him.

"I'll let him know," Faith promised. "We can blindfold him or something if we have to. We'll make it work, Piper. Don't worry."

Don't worry. Easier said than done.

CHAPTER NINETEEN

"TWENTY CARS DEEP. That's how many people are waiting out on Route 12 thinking they are coming to the wedding of the century." Dean had just hung up with Lily, who was helping turn people around before they got to Highway 5.

Gretchen had caused the commotion she had been hoping for. The people who were supposed to be here were stuck in a line of cars filled with people who had mistakenly believed town gossip instead of using their good sense.

"Why would anyone come to a wedding without an invitation? This is unbelievable," Heath said, wiping his brow. It was over seventy degrees in the middle of February. They were probably going to set a record.

"Tell him he can't climb up on the fence!" Dean shouted at the gate guards. One of the paparazzi guys was using the fence to get himself a better vantage point.

Sawyer thought it was ridiculous that they had been taking pictures of him standing in his driveway for the last twenty minutes. Why would anyone want to see him doing absolutely nothing?

He wondered how many of them might be hiding in the trees that surrounded the property. Maybe someone would fly a drone over the house. They hadn't thought about how to stop them from doing that. At this point, Sawyer didn't care who saw him get married. He was ready to let the whole town come on in and witness it. That would sure shut Gretchen up.

"Sawyer, I need you," Faith called from the front porch.

He jogged over to her, hoping there weren't any other fires to put out.

"You look nice," he said to his sister. She had on a pale purple dress and her hair was in a fancy updo.

"Thank you," she said, primping her hair with her hand. "I wish I had a Trina to do my hair every day."

"What's the problem in the house? Because I need to help get our actual guests into the parking lot, but our mother's open invite to the town has made that very difficult."

"Piper wants to talk to you."

That sinking feeling was back. "Right now?"

"As soon as you can."

"Isn't it bad luck for me to see her before the wedding?"

Faith held up one of his old ties with a grin. "I got that covered."

Being blindfolded wasn't Sawyer's favorite thing in the world, but if Piper needed to talk to him, he would have to suffer through it. Faith led him to the room and helped him sit on the bed.

"We'll give you some privacy," Faith said. "Don't you dare take off that blindfold."

Sawyer gave her a salute. "Aye, aye, Captain."

He heard the door close, but Piper didn't make a sound. He wasn't even sure she was in the room. Was it possible his sister was pranking him?

"Piper?"

Something swished to the right of him. He turned his head toward the sound. "I'm here," she said.

He felt her sit next to him and take his hand. It was comforting to feel her, at least. He wondered what her dress looked like and if she wore her hair up or down. Maybe she would let him touch her so he could tell.

"Is everything okay?" he asked, knowing he wouldn't be here right now if it was.

He heard her swallow. "I'm not sure how I'm feeling at the moment. It's sort of a big hurricane of conflicting emotions spinning around my head, you know?"

He nodded, knowing exactly what she meant, because he felt the same way. Anxiety was battling with excitement, while confusion and the guilt he felt over not being able to say "I love you" had their own feud going on.

"I had some really good conversations with your sister and my mom today, and they both made me think about things that I feel like we need to talk about before we go in front of our family and friends and say 'I do.'"

Sawyer gave her hand a reassuring squeeze. "Okay, tell me what you're thinking."

"I need to know what *you're* thinking."

"I'm thinking you smell really good." He leaned in her direction. "Is that your new perfume?"

The sound of her laughter made his heart

happy. She pushed him away. "Stop. This is serious. I know it doesn't feel that way because you have a necktie tied around your face right now, but it is."

"I can be serious," he promised her.

"Yesterday my mom asked you if you were in love with me and I didn't let you answer. But I think I need to know."

Sawyer rolled his head to either side. His shoulders were suddenly so tight. "I am definitely falling in love with you."

Piper was quiet. The silence was killing him. Without being able to see her face, he had no idea what she might be thinking. Had he told her what she wanted to hear? Or had she been hoping for a different answer?

"I love a lot of things about you," he continued. All he could do was be honest with her. "I love your unending positivity. I love how much you care about other people. I love your laugh."

"Stop," she said, pulling her hand away.

He didn't like the way she sounded or the lack of physical contact. Sawyer didn't care about bad luck or what the rules were. He pulled off his blindfold so he could see Piper's face. She took his breath away. She was the single most beautiful woman in the world. He could feel his heart rejoicing at the simple sight of her.

"I do love those things, Piper."

"But you aren't in love with me." There was so much pain in her eyes. "You can't say that you're going to love me every day of forever or that I'm the only person you want to spend the rest of your life with because you can't imagine a world without me in it."

Her voice was definitely shaky. He reached out to her, hoping to hold her, but she stood up and moved away.

"That's a really scary thing to say. I mean, what if you decide one day that you don't love me anymore, while I'm of the mind-set that I can't imagine my life without you? If I think that way, I'll end up like my dad. He had a broken heart, and it killed him way before his time."

"You think your dad's heart attack happened because he suffered heartbreak?"

"Not literally. But he didn't take good care of himself. He ate too much and drank too much because the depression lingered. It was always there, under the surface. I once heard him tell someone that even after almost twenty years of her being gone, he would still take her back if she came home. That's what killed him."

"So we're back to trust. You say you trust me, but you really don't. You have no idea how much I wish there was a way I could prove to you that I won't break your heart. I can tell you I won't. I would even sign a contract promising I won't, but none of that can guarantee anything. You simply have to trust me."

Sawyer felt like a heel for not being able to give her that. "I'm trying here, Piper. And I know you're trying. I have to acknowledge that you've stood your ground even though everyone has tried to make us doubt what we're doing."

The pained expression on Piper's face made him worry something was wrong with the baby.

"Are you okay?" he asked. "Is it the baby?"

Piper sat back down and shook her head. She seemed to be fighting back tears. "Please don't lie to me, Sawyer. Don't lie to yourself. You *want* to trust and love me, but you don't, do you? Not completely."

He longed to be honest, but the truth would certainly hurt her. "I don't want to lie to you. It's been killing me to lie about everything to everyone for so many months now, but I haven't ever lied to you. I don't want to lie to you."

"I don't want you to lie to me, either," she said, pressing her fingers to the corners of her eyes.

He had been so worried about his heart, he hadn't given hers enough consideration. He didn't want to do this, but she was leaving him no choice. "I'm sorry, Piper. Not completely."

PIPER'S HEART WAS breaking in two. All this talk about Sawyer wanting to protect his heart, yet he didn't seem to care about what he was doing to hers.

"So where does that leave us?" he asked.

She felt sick. They had come so far, but were still falling so short. Could they still walk down the aisle? She put her hands on her stomach. All she wanted was to give this baby a happy family.

"That leaves me in love with you and you falling in love with me. And both of us loving this baby."

There were people who settled for much less than that, she told herself. There were those who married for money instead of love.

The ones who married out of fear of being lonely. Piper was fortunate enough to be marrying for love.

She could walk down that aisle today and marry the man she loved. Only she'd be asking him to marry someone he cared about who was carrying a baby that he most definitely loved.

Was that enough?

"And that's all good, right?" He approached her like she was an injured animal that might attack if he moved too quickly. "We don't want to call this wedding off and let Gretchen think she's won."

And there it was. He'd shattered all her hopes in one fatal swoop. "That's your biggest concern right now?" She couldn't stop her voice from rising. "This is all some kind of game you need to win?"

Sawyer's eyes went wide. "No. That's not what I meant. I don't know why I said that."

She stood up, wishing she could throw something at him. "Don't start lying to me now, Sawyer." She paced in front of the bed. "You were completely against the idea of even setting a date for a wedding when we left LA. But your mom showed up telling you not to get married and, boom, here we are today," she said. "Admit you're trying to prove her wrong."

Sawyer heaved a sigh. "How many times do I have to say that I don't care what Gretchen thinks? She has nothing to do with this at all."

"At all?" Piper questioned. "It seems like she has everything to do with everything!" Did he seriously have no idea how much that hurt her? "Do you really think I'm going to buy that? You already admitted that you're afraid to give yourself over to me completely because of what she did to your dad. You built this wall around your heart—those are your sister's words, not mine—because she abandoned you. You asked me to marry you on the day she came waltzing back into your life."

"Because she gave me the push I needed."

Piper wanted to pull her hair out. Why could everyone see this but him? "No, Sawyer. Because you are so afraid that you might be just like her—unable to love someone who loves you."

She could see the sick realization come over him. When he examined his true motivations, he couldn't possibly deny how his immature need to stick it to Gretchen had been pushing him along. "Maybe I've been acting like a child when it comes to my mother. I guess she brings out the worst in me. Maybe my anger has been steering my course more than it should."

Sawyer held his head in his hands. As much as it pained her, there was only one way this day could end.

"I love you," she said. "I think you have an amazing spirit and a huge heart. You live life to its fullest every day, and you make beautiful music while doing it." Piper choked back the tears. "I want to spend the rest of my life with you. But I love you too much to ask you to pledge yourself to me before you're ready to do so. I also can't handle how much it will hurt to be married to someone who doesn't love me back. I deserve better. I can't marry you, Sawyer. I'm sorry."

She backed out of the room as his shoulders shook and the sound of soft sobbing began. Piper held it together until she saw her mom.

"What happened, baby?" Claudia asked as she held her in her arms. Piper couldn't answer—her own weeping made it impossible to speak.

Faith went into the bedroom and shut the

door. At least Sawyer had his sister to help him through this.

"What can I do?" Piper could hear the helplessness in her mom's voice.

She did her best to pull herself together. "I need you to go get Dad and Matthew. I want to go home."

Her mom winced but gave Piper a kiss on the forehead. "I'll go get them. Don't you worry about a thing, okay?"

Piper gathered up her train and headed for the stairs.

"Let me help you," Trina said, picking up some of the tulle.

Piper stared at the beading on the hem of the train as she cradled it in her arms. It had been such a thoughtful gift. She felt guilty that it would go to waste.

Her parents were outside. She watched from the door as her mother told her father what had happened. Not that she knew exactly, but she could guess. Heath didn't look as relieved as she'd thought he would upon hearing the news that she'd called off the wedding.

She watched as her mother went to fetch Matty and her dad made his way up the porch steps. He opened the door and she fell into his arms.

"Let's get you home, sweetheart."

There was a massive traffic jam on the road outside the farm. Piper ducked into the back seat of her father's car, and her mother and brother sat on either side of her to shield her from view. As soon as she had stepped outside, she knew people were taking pictures of her. They'd been waiting for her since yesterday. All of those paparazzi would be champing at the bit to get a shot of her tearstained face as she drove away.

"Keep your head down," her dad said as they made their way to the gates. "Matthew, make yourself as big as you can. Block that side as much as possible."

It was all pointless. Her image didn't matter anymore. What the world thought meant little to her at this point. The one person she wanted to love her couldn't do it. That was all that mattered.

Piper cried into her tulle train all the way home.

CHAPTER TWENTY

"PIPER STARLING, COUNTRY music's new runaway bride, is performing here in Chicago for two sold-out shows starting tonight at the Allstate Arena."

The reporter had on the brightest green tie Sawyer had ever seen. "Her ex-fiancé, Sawyer Stratton, is still scheduled to open up for her. This will be the first time the two of them have been seen publicly since Starling apparently called off their wedding two weeks ago, moments before the couple was set to say 'I do.'" The camera cut to a video of Piper and her family driving away from Helping Hooves. "There has been no formal statement from either side explaining the strange turn of events."

Sawyer turned off the television on the bus. He'd only wanted to see if they were going to cover the story or not, and of course, they didn't disappoint. The news had been having a field day over the quickie wedding that hadn't been quick enough to happen.

"We have to decide if you're going to sing 'You Don't Need Me' so we can finish this set list," Hunter said.

Sawyer had no idea what the plan was. He wasn't in the inner circle anymore, so the information he got from the top was limited. "We'll have to ask Heath. I vote no. But knowing that sadist, he'll probably make us sing it."

That song would be the absolute worst song to sing right now, but singing it meant being onstage with Piper. Getting to see her would be healing and yet torturous at the same time.

Surely Heath wouldn't make Piper sing a breakup song after they'd actually broken up. He wouldn't do that to her.

"Actually, I would leave it off. I doubt they'll send her out for that."

"Do you want me to go to the other side of Bus City to ask, or are you going to text them?" Hunter asked, though he looked a little too comfortable on the couch to be honestly offering to go talk to them for him.

"Fine, I'll text him." He sent Heath the question. After a few minutes with no response, he considered texting Lana. She would at least respond. Before he could, his phone beeped. There was a long text with an attachment.

You will be performing the song tonight. Piper will not. You will use the music video for Piper's part in the duet. Attached are the specifics for setting that up. Also, meet and greets will be with Piper only from now on. Your presence is no longer required. Please do not try to engage with Piper once we are all in the building. Do not stand outside her dressing room or bother her staff to pass messages. Thank you for your cooperation.

That was probably the first time Heath had thanked Sawyer for anything. And he'd done it before Sawyer actually did what was asked.

"Looks like we need to put it on the set list. I will be performing it with recorded Piper."

"Ouch," Hunter said. "Sorry, man. I know you wanted to see her."

He did and he didn't. He wanted to see her to make sure she was all right. He didn't want to see her because he was not.

It was very weird to go from seeing a person every day to not seeing or speaking to them at all. She couldn't avoid him forever, though. They were still having this baby together. They were still going to share custody and coparent.

His heart ached at the thought of raising their son without Piper by his side. He'd had that vision of them living together as one big happy family, and now that wasn't a possibility. Sawyer would get his time and Piper would have hers. He hated the idea of it and feared their son would, as well.

"I say on our next long tour break, we head to Vegas and live large for a couple days. Go to some clubs, hit some casinos. What do you think?" Hunter was ready for Sawyer to fall right back into his old patterns. They were young and wild and free. No strings, no fiancées (fake or otherwise), no wives.

That last one stung the most.

"I don't know. I can't think about vacation when I'm staring down a month of shows." Truthfully, he couldn't think about anything other than Piper and the baby.

"Well, you think about it. I will go wherever you want to go if it will help you get your mind off things."

Things such as what in the world was wrong with him? He'd had the perfect girl and all he had to say was *I love you* and not be such an immature jerk. Sawyer still couldn't wrap his head around his own idiocy. He had put Piper in the path of pain to fulfill his selfish need to get back at his mom. He was no better than Gretchen and had only himself to blame.

"I'm going to take a walk around the arena. I can't sit here anymore," Sawyer said, standing up and giving his legs a stretch.

"Want me to come with you?" Hunter asked. "If you need me, I'm there."

"Thanks for the offer, man. But I think I need a little time by myself."

"I'm just a text away," Hunter reminded him.

Sawyer appreciated his friend's concern, but he needed to be alone with his thoughts. He had no idea where Piper was. He couldn't be accused of trying to engage with her if he happened to stumble upon her. He went inside the Allstate and decided to find his dressing room. There were three doors in a row. The right one had Piper's name on the door and the left one had Sawyer's. There was no one in the middle. He couldn't help but wonder if Heath had asked them to do that. God forbid she and Sawyer share a wall.

The door to Piper's dressing room opened, and Lana stepped out. She startled and held a hand against her chest. "Didn't you get Heath's text?"

"Yeah, I got it."

"No loitering outside her dressing room."

Sawyer rolled his eyes. "I'm loitering outside my dressing room, not hers." He pointed to the door with his name on it.

"She's coming out soon to do sound check. Don't be out here when she does. This is hard enough for her already, okay?"

He felt horrible for being the cause of her pain. He had promised Ruby to help reduce Piper's stress, but all he had done was raise it to what were probably unhealthy levels.

He decided he'd go hide in the upper level and watch sound check. They couldn't say he was trying to engage her in conversation from the nosebleed section.

The arena was so still when there was no one in it. Sawyer closed his eyes and took a second to enjoy the peace and quiet. His eyes opened the moment she stepped out onstage, his body had sensed her presence before his brain registered it.

He was up so high it was hard to see anything. She adjusted her earpiece and the background track began to play. Her voice came through loud and clear as she sang a couple bars of a song.

This was the feeling he had been avoiding since he had woken up that one morning in September with her lying next to him. There she was on the stage. So close yet so far. He could see her, but he couldn't talk to her. He couldn't hold her or kiss her. It was the worst kind of torture.

Still, he didn't regret letting things go as far as they had. As much as this hurt, he couldn't wait to meet that baby growing inside her.

It *was* painful, though, and suddenly he couldn't sit there and watch her from afar a second longer. He headed back downstairs and backstage to his dressing room. When he opened his door, he noticed an envelope at his feet. He picked it up, figuring it was something from the arena staff until he saw the handwriting on the front.

It was from Piper.

He ripped it open. Inside were several sheets of notebook paper. The first one was a note, the rest song lyrics.

Sawyer,
I need your help with this. I want it to be
good, and you're the only one who can
make it that way. Any feedback would
be appreciated.
Piper

No *Love, Piper* or *xoxo, Piper*. Just plain
ol' *Piper*. He glanced over the song she had
written. It took him a minute, but he realized
it was the one he had seen her working on
that day they'd fought about setting a wedding date. This was the song for their baby
boy. A love song and a lullaby all in one.

Sawyer wouldn't let her down. Their son
should know how much both of his parents
loved him no matter how they felt about each
other. Sawyer's love for his son was something he had never been confused about. In
fact, it was the one thing he had been sure
about from the beginning.

He'd make this song the greatest one ever
written.

PIPER WAS TRYING to get in the right mind-set
for this show, but it was harder than she'd
feared it would be. Every time she moved
from one place to another in the arena, she

worried she would bump into Sawyer. It was only a matter of time. They would eventually have to see each other. She just didn't want it to be a surprise.

"Let's get your hair and makeup done for the meet and greet. After that, we need to make sure you eat something. You've got a healthy boy in there who needs his mom to help him get bigger," her dad said as they made their way back to the dressing room.

"Sawyer's not coming to the meet and greet, correct?" she asked for clarification.

"Correct."

"Because he didn't want to come or because you told him not to come?"

"Because I told him not to. No reason to make you and the fans uncomfortable. There's nothing more awkward than standing there with two people who recently broke up."

"But did we sell the experience to people with the promise of meeting both of us?"

"Yes, but—"

"But nothing. If everyone in the room thinks they are going to meet both of us and they only get to meet me, they will leave blaming me for not getting the full experience. Down, down, down. That's what will happen to my reputation." She had her hand do a nosedive for a visual. "You won't want that, Dad. I know you."

"Believe it or not, I do not care about your reputation as much as I care about your feelings. Your mother would be so proud if she could hear me right now."

Piper smiled. He had come out of this experience a different person, as well. "I appreciate that, Dad. But he and I have to be in the same room at some point. Might as well get it over with. Rip the Band-Aid off."

"I'll let him know," Heath said. "If you're sure. We could always set him up in a separate room. You're the star and he's the opening act." Well, it hadn't changed him completely.

"It's fine." The baby kicked, almost like he knew he was going to be near his daddy again.

THE MEET-AND-GREET ROOM in the Allstate was much larger than some of the other ones they'd been to. There was plenty of space for them to spread out.

Piper found herself bracing every time the door opened, thinking it was going to be Sawyer. She went to spin her engagement ring around her finger, but it wasn't there. She fiddled with her bracelets instead, trying not to let her emotions get the best of her.

"Can I get you anything before this starts?" Lana asked. "Water? Snack?"

"Did Dad tell Sawyer he should be here?"

"He said he did," Lana answered half-heartedly. Sometimes what Heath said wasn't exactly what he did.

"Did Sawyer reply and say he would be here?"

"I don't know, Piper. I can go check and see if he's in his dressing room. You want me to do that?"

Before she could answer, Sawyer came through the door, tucking his shirt in. He looked like he'd only just gotten the message and had raced to get there. Piper's heart skipped a beat as their eyes met. Her heart had definitely not gotten the memo that it was over between them.

"Sorry, I was busy writing a song and lost track of time," he said. His eyes never left hers.

He was working on her song. The thought made her smile. At least there was one thing she could count on—he would love their son. But that smile didn't last long. Just seeing him hurt in a way that almost took her breath away. How would they handle raising their little boy if this pain didn't ease?

"What's the plan if someone asks us what happened?" Sawyer asked, giving his hair a tousle.

"No comment," Heath said. "We will not be commenting on personal matters. That will already be communicated to everyone who will be allowed in here. If someone decides to ignore my rules, they will be escorted out by Mitch."

Sawyer's eyes got as big as saucers. "Boy, he is not messing around."

Again, he made her smile. "No, he is not."

Since the Nashville debacle, Heath no longer let all the fans come into the room at the same time. Each group would come in one at a time and leave before the next set was allowed in. It was like he was afraid Sawyer had a few more long-lost relatives who might crash the party.

The first pair of fans came in—a mother and her teenage daughter. They looked so much alike.

"Hi there," Piper said, giving the young girl a hug first. Immediately, the teen began to cry.

"I can't believe I'm meeting you. I love you so much."

Those famous three words. They were like daggers into her broken heart. As much as Piper loved to hear them, there was only one person she wanted to hear them from.

SAWYER NOTICED THE slight change in Piper's expression when the fan told her she loved her.

"Well, I love you right back," Piper said, regaining control. "And I am so glad you came out to see the show tonight."

Sawyer shook hands with the mother and posed for the pictures with the three ladies. Piper put the fans in between them.

Being this close and still not being able to touch her was excruciating. It was like all his feelings for her had quadrupled since she'd walked out on him. He couldn't explain it, and he certainly didn't know what to do about it.

Everyone seemed to be following the rules Heath had laid out. No one asked any questions about the wedding, although they got a few curious glances and Sawyer noticed there was a lot more whispering when people went to the candy bar to get their treats.

Two young guys about Sawyer's age were up last. They had big grins on their faces when they saw Piper. One wore a button-down shirt and khakis, while the other was sporting a Chicago Blackhawks sweatshirt and jeans.

"You are more beautiful in person than I imagined. Wow, look at you," Khaki Pants said, taking Piper by the hand and making her spin around so he could get a good look at her.

Sawyer didn't like it one bit.

"Can I get a hug?" the Blackhawks fan asked. "I have been dreaming about being this close to you for years."

Piper went in for a quick hug, but the guy didn't let go. "Oh man, you smell good."

"She does, doesn't she?" his buddy said. "Let me get a hug."

Sawyer cleared his throat. "Hey, that's enough, guys." He couldn't stand to watch them treat her like a piece of meat.

"What's the matter? Is the ex a little jealous?" Mr. Khaki Pants asked, throwing his arm around Piper. "When you're ready to be with a real man who will treat you like the princess you are, I want you to come find me. I've been told I'm one heck of a kisser. Maybe you want to find out if that's true…"

Every muscle in Sawyer's body was tense. He was about two seconds from punching them both in the face. He grabbed the guy's arm and not so carefully removed it from Piper's shoulders.

"You're done," Sawyer said, getting in his face.

"I'm done?" Khaki Pants questioned, giving Sawyer a push. "The way I hear it, you're done. She left you and this is the way you treat her fans?"

Sawyer shoved him back, and then the guy's friend joined in the tussle. Security stepped in and escorted both fans out. Sawyer was breathing heavily. The worst part was that the guy was right. He was done. Piper had let him go.

"I appreciate that you were trying to help, but next time let the security guys take care of jerks like that," Heath said.

Sawyer glanced back over his shoulder to where Piper and Lana were huddled together.

"Are you okay?" he asked her.

She nodded and came closer. "Don't do that, okay? There are going to be people looking to get a rise out of you. I don't want you to mess with your fun-loving, easygoing image. You're everybody's buddy."

Of course she was more concerned about his image than her well-being. "Well, I don't want two punks to think they can manhandle you because you're a beautiful woman without a fiancé. If you don't want me to step in, make sure your security gets in the mix a lot sooner."

"I will make sure that happens."

"Guys like that need a lesson in respect. Celebrity or not, no one should touch you without your permission."

"I got it."

Sawyer still felt a bit fired up. "I'm going to make sure our son knows how to treat a lady with respect. You can count on that."

Piper put a hand on his chest. "Relax."

He would have been able to if she weren't touching him. His heart raced under her hand. His skin burned. He wanted to hold Piper against him so he could feel warm all over. Considering the lecture he had just given her, though, he thought better of it.

"I still care. A lot."

"I see that." She dropped her hand. "We both have to figure out how to navigate these new waters."

He'd definitely felt lost at sea the last couple weeks. He was desperate to navigate the storm that was raging inside him. How was he supposed to find his way home when it was becoming clear that she was always going to be his true north?

CHAPTER TWENTY-ONE

"Deep dish or thin crust?" Lana asked.

"It's our second day in Chicago, we have to get deep dish," Piper said, rubbing her belly. The baby would thank her later.

"Do you want me to cancel the interviews we have set up in Minneapolis or should we send a list of acceptable questions and hope they play nice?" her dad asked from the other side of the bus.

"I think I'm going to have to face the music. If I keep avoiding it, the hungrier they're going to get for something salacious."

"Honestly, I can't believe how hard the media is being on you," Heath said. "This is why I wanted him to be the one to call it off when I had control over this nightmare. Apparently you're the runaway bride, and I read somewhere today that you called it off because of your diva-like tendencies. You thought getting married on a farm was beneath you. I'm ready to start suing for slander."

"Your album is still selling on pace to break records," Lana chimed in. "The shows are all sold-out through the end of the first leg. When the baby comes this summer, everyone's attention will be on him. I don't think we need to worry too much. This could be nothing but a little bump in the road."

As much as Piper appreciated the optimism, she wasn't sure how to feel about Lana referring to her greatest heartbreak as a small bump in the road. She was still in love with Sawyer. He was still on tour with her. He was still the father of her baby. She would be feeling this hurt day in and day out for a long time to come.

It didn't surprise her that the album was selling at a record pace. It had Sawyer's fingerprints all over it. He had brought something out in her she hadn't known existed. Everything they had done to protect and build her brand had backfired, but the music still shone. In the end, she'd lost the one thing she hadn't realized she wanted more than her career.

"They said they can deliver enough pizzas for the whole crew by noon today, but they want to know if you'll sign a menu for them to auction off at their next fund-raiser event?"

"Done," Piper said. An autograph was by far the easiest request to honor.

"How are you feeling about the show tonight?" her dad asked.

"Fine." It had been a bit strange not to sing with Sawyer. She wasn't sure the song went over very well without her there in person.

"What about the meet and greet? Maybe having Sawyer in the room was a bad idea."

"It's going to take some time to figure out our new boundaries."

"I know yesterday must have been tough for him, but he can't go around assaulting fans. He needs to leave that to the guys we pay to do that."

"He doesn't take kindly to men who disrespect women."

"Or one woman in particular, at least," Lana said.

Piper was tired of people acting like there was hope. "I think you missed the part of our wedding day where he basically told me he's not that into me."

"I think you don't notice the way he watches you when you do those meet and

greets," Lana said. "He's completely enamored. And yesterday he looked like it pained
him to be so infatuated."

She didn't want anyone to use those words
to describe how Sawyer felt about her. She
couldn't think about him being enamored
or infatuated. She wanted him to be in love
with her, but he wasn't.

"Sawyer made his choice, and we both
have to live with it."

"Well, I never did think he was very smart.
This proves it," Heath said, getting up from
his seat. "Anyone who doesn't fall head over
heels for you is an idiot." His gave her a kiss
on the top of the head.

"I'm not trying to give you false hope,"
Lana said when Heath stepped off the bus
to take a phone call.

"Then don't tell me about the way he looks
at me. He can look at me any way he wants,
but he told me clearly that he is not in love
with me. That's the only part that matters
to me."

"I know what he said. I just don't believe
him."

"Well, my heart doesn't have the luxury
of pretending to know better than he does,"
Piper said.

"You need to talk to the crew at lunch today." Her dad climbed back on the bus. "You've got several people out there messing around on the golf carts. They nearly ran me over."

Piper took a look out the window. "They're trying to have some fun. The boredom is the worst."

"Someone is going to get hurt."

"I'll have a golf-cart safety lesson at lunch, okay?"

Heath huffed. "I'm dealing with a bunch of children."

Piper's phone chimed with a text.

Been thinking about your song all night. Collaborate?

She had made her peace offering by giving Sawyer the song lyrics she'd written. A song was what had brought them together in the first place—maybe a new one would heal the wounds of this breakup and help them find a new normal. Piper needed to find it fast if she was going to make it through this tour without dying of heartbreak. There was also that minor issue of raising a child together.

Which would go a lot smoother if they could stand to be in the same room together.

Sawyer's opinion on the song meant a lot. He hadn't said if he liked it or not. She sent back a quick reply.

My bus or yours?

"CAN YOU PICK up after yourself just a little bit? Is this what it would have been like if we had lived together in college?"

Hunter was a complete slob, and it wasn't like Sawyer had high standards, either.

"What is the big deal?" Hunter didn't bother to move while Sawyer focused on putting all the garbage in a bag.

"Piper's coming over to work on a song."

"Is that a good idea? Shouldn't you two give each other some space?"

"I want her to come over."

"You want to torture yourself," Hunter accused.

Maybe that was true. Sawyer deserved it. He had forced her to call off the wedding because of his behavior and lack of consideration for her feelings.

"We're working on a song for the baby. I need to do this."

Hunter didn't argue. When it came to the baby, he knew to keep his mouth shut. Sawyer's son was his number one priority from here on out.

There was a knock at the door, and Sawyer ran up front to push it open.

"Come aboard," he said. "Now remember, this bus isn't as tricked out as yours." He snatched a dirty sock off the top of the microwave. "And my roommates are not as clean as Lana."

"No one is as clean as Lana."

Hunter sat upright. "I heard rumors that we're getting lunch today. Any chance I can get the scoop on what we're eating so I can impress a certain wardrobe director with my inside knowledge?"

"I don't know, what do I get in return for this favor?"

"Anything you want."

Piper didn't even need to think about it. "I want you to teach me how to do an epic drum solo so I can challenge anyone and win."

Hunter seemed impressed by this request. "You got it. I didn't realize you were that cool."

Sawyer threw the dirty sock at him for

his backhanded compliment. "Maybe you shouldn't tell him anything."

"Come on. I knew she was cool, just not *that* cool," Hunter said.

"It's fine. I am that cool," Piper said with a wink. "You can tell Darla that I ordered you guys about fifty deep-dish pizzas from Lou's."

"Thank you very much!" Hunter said, slipping on his shoes. "Excuse me while I get in good with the woman who mends my pants."

Piper had her hair up in a messy bun and a worn-out Boone Williams T-shirt on under her unzipped pink sweatshirt. He loved that whether she was glam or grunge, the style seemed to suit her.

"You wanted to show me what you added to the song?" she asked, snapping him out of his stupor.

His faced warmed with embarrassment. How long had he been standing there staring at her? "Yeah, let's go back here."

He hated that things had to be so awkward between them. One of Piper's best qualities was her way of making everyone feel comfortable. What he wouldn't give to go back in time a few days. Before he messed everything up by trying to rush to the altar.

They passed the empty bunks on their way to the back. Sawyer set his guitar on the floor and pushed the video game controllers aside so Piper had somewhere to sit.

"I'll admit I was surprised you wanted me to look at this."

"Why? I wrote it for our son."

"It's just so soon after…" The fact that she'd even be standing in the same room with him seemed like a big deal given what had happened.

"After we broke up?" she asked.

He was shocked at how detached she sounded. Not that he expected her to get all emotional being around him, but he did imagine she'd feel something. "Well, yeah."

"We're having a baby. Whether we're together or not, I want to be able to talk to you about him."

Sawyer tried backpedaling. "I'm glad. I just thought you'd need some time."

She cocked her head to the side. "More time than you?"

Apparently not.

"No. I wasn't saying that." He wasn't gaining any ground with her this way.

"Maybe it's too early for both of us to talk

about the breakup," Piper suggested. "Let's focus on the song. What did you think?"

Much safer territory. "I think you were really paying attention when we talked about selling the song's message in the verses and using the chorus to add that unforgettable punch."

She smiled down at her lap. Piper had every right to be proud of how far her songwriting had come.

"I didn't think you needed to change anything. I thought maybe I could add a bridge before going into the final verse."

He picked up his guitar and started strumming. "Did you have a melody in mind?"

Piper sang the first verse, giving him chills. He had her sing it again, and this time he tried to play along based on what he had heard. They spent the next hour going back and forth and jotting down the notes that worked best.

Piper had written a beautiful song about fear and hope, about how much she needed their son to know that unexpected didn't mean unwanted. It was a special song for a special baby.

Piper's phone rang. The pizza was here. "I have to go. I need to give a little speech thanking everyone for their hard work." She stood up and tucked a loose piece of hair behind her ear. "Thank you for helping me put this together. I love the way it sounds with the guitar, and I think the bridge is perfect."

"I love it, too."

Her teeth clamped down on her bottom lip. "I'm glad you love it," she said.

That word was clearly a trigger he hadn't meant to pull. He should probably get used to sticking his foot in his mouth around her.

She left. Sawyer stayed behind, picking up his guitar and working on the song a bit longer. Piper would be a wonderful mother. He had no worries about that.

It was crazy that he had been so afraid she would be like Gretchen. Neither one of them was like his mother. They both wanted to put the baby first. They both wanted to love without fear. Only Piper had been braver than he had. She'd been willing to take the risk, to trust, to believe that what she felt for him and their unborn baby was love.

Sawyer added one more verse to the song. This one, if Piper kept it, would have to be sung by him. When he finished, he went outside to see if there was any pizza left.

He started walking toward the group of

pop-up tents on the other side of Bus City. It wasn't unusual for band and crew members to gather outside. Sometimes people skateboarded or played some hacky sack. Occasionally, the dancers created dance circles. It wasn't out of the ordinary for people to be whooping it up.

However, as Sawyer got closer to the tents, he heard someone yell something about getting help. One of Piper's backup singers was crying as she ran past him. His anxiety kicked into overdrive as the sound of shouting was replaced by sirens. An ambulance drove by, headed in the same direction as Sawyer. The hair on the back of his neck stood on end as another ambulance pulled up.

He imagined every scenario that could have led to not one but two ambulances being called. Every time he thought of something, it was Piper he pictured going into the back of one of them. Full of panic, he took off running.

"What happened? Is Piper okay?" he asked the first group of people he came across.

"Golf cart accident," one of the stagehands said. "Some people were messing around and one of them tipped."

"Piper?"

The guy shrugged. "I don't know who it was, but she was over there."

Sawyer took off again, pushing his way through the people standing around gaping at what had happened.

"Have you seen Piper?" he asked one of the women wiping tears from her face.

"She just got in that ambulance," she said, pointing at the first one.

Just before Sawyer got to it, the emergency vehicle took off with its sirens blaring. He tried to get it to stop but failed. Out of breath, he bent over with his hands on his knees. The other ambulance was still there, helping some of those with minor injuries.

"Are you going to the same hospital as that ambulance?" he asked one of the paramedics.

"Sure are."

"My pregnant fiancée was in that one. Can I ride with you?"

Thankfully, they agreed to let him tag along. Sawyer climbed in the back with one of Piper's background singers. The poor guy definitely had a broken leg. He was wailing from the pain as the EMT gave him a shot of what Sawyer hoped was some seriously strong pain medication.

When they got to the hospital, Sawyer hopped out and ran into the ER. It was packed with people waiting to be seen. He searched for someone who could tell him where Piper was and if she was okay.

He found the registration desk and cut to the front of the line. "Excuse me, I need to find the woman who just came in on the last ambulance. She's pregnant. Blonde, about five and a half feet tall."

"Sir, you're going to have to wait in line," the nurse said.

Sawyer's heart was racing, and his hands shook. "You don't understand. She's pregnant. Her name is Piper Starling, she's a country singer. Her ambulance must have gotten here minutes ago. I just came in on the other one that was sent to the same scene."

"Sir, I understand you're feeling panicked. Please get in line, and when we get your information, we can see if your loved one is here."

His *loved* one. It was clear as day. That was what she was. If anything happened to Piper, he'd never forgive himself for being so blind to his feelings for her. Everyone had said he would simply know when he was in love. They'd said it wasn't something they could describe, that he would just know because he wouldn't be able to imagine his life without that person.

That person was definitely Piper.

He couldn't wait in a line that was five people deep. He needed to find her and tell her he was in love with her. A nurse hit a button on the wall and opened the doors to the exam rooms. Sawyer waited until they were almost closed and slipped through.

"Sir, you can't—"

"Piper?" he called out, poking his head in every room. He needed to find the operating rooms. She must have been seriously injured. He stopped at the nurses' station. "Can you help me find my fiancée? She was in an accident at the Allstate Arena. She was just brought in."

"He's not allowed back here," someone yelled from down the hall.

"Please. She's pregnant. I need to find her."

No one would listen as security descended and pulled his arms behind his back. Sawyer kept yelling Piper's name in hopes she could hear him. If nothing else, at least she would know he had been here looking for her.

"Piper!"

"Sawyer?" A perfectly intact Piper stepped out of the crowded waiting room back where he'd first come in. "What are you doing here?"

"Is this who you're looking for?" the uniformed security guard asked.

Sawyer's face nearly split in two from grinning so big. "That's her."

The guard let him go, and he ran to her.

"What are you doing here?" she asked.

He didn't bother with those minor details. He grabbed her face and kissed her long and hard. He kissed her in a way that would make it clear why he was there. He had come to tell her he was in love with her.

CHAPTER TWENTY-TWO

PIPER NEEDED TO come up for air, but the way Sawyer kissed her in the middle of that loud, crowded hospital waiting room must have given her superpowers.

As the kisses got slower, Piper let herself get lost in the feeling of his strong hands holding her face firmly in place, contrasted with the soft and gentle way his lips moved against hers. When he ended the kiss, he kept his face close. His nose brushed hers.

"You're safe," he said as if he had doubted it the moment before.

"Of course I am." She didn't care that she wasn't supposed to be this close to him anymore. She kissed him again, her fingers tracing the hard line of his jaw. She loved his jawline.

He pulled back. "I was so scared. The thought of anything bad happening to you or the baby made me lose my mind."

The love haze she was under began to lift.

The reason for her being there came back to the front of her mind. "I'm fine. It was Hunter. He's been hurt…bad."

Sawyer released her and his face fell. "Hunter?"

Piper grabbed the clipboard of forms she had been filling out before a ranting and raving Sawyer was dragged out by security.

"I don't know any of his information. I've been trying to call you, but it kept going to voice mail."

Sawyer took the clipboard from her and scanned the first sheet. "I can fill most of this out. What happened?"

"He was fooling around on the golf cart with Milo and they flipped it. I think Milo might have broken his leg, and Hunter hit his head. He was unconscious when the ambulance first got there. I didn't want him to come here alone."

Sawyer kissed her again. "Thank you for being so sweet."

Between the two of them, they were able to fill out Hunter's registration forms and get ahold of his family. Sawyer was frustrated with his careless friend. At the beginning of the tour, he and Hunter had been out of sync, but since the wedding had been called off,

Hunter had proved to be the friend Sawyer knew he was. Hopefully his injuries weren't as serious as they seemed.

After Hunter had a CT scan, Piper and Sawyer were allowed to go back and sit with him. The doctor quickly assuaged Sawyer's fears.

"Six stitches, a broken arm and a mild concussion. He should be able to head out as soon as we get that arm in a cast."

"My life is over," Hunter complained.

"I think you're lucky it wasn't worse," Sawyer said.

"Lucky? How am I going to play the drums with only one arm?"

"Wasn't there a one-armed drummer in some '90s rock band?" Piper asked.

"He had a special drum kit. Looks like I'm off the tour," Hunter lamented. "Just when I was this close to getting a date with Darla."

"Too bad Piper didn't ask for those drum lessons earlier. She could've been in my band." Sawyer put his hand on her knee.

"Thanks for staying with me, Piper. You are way cooler than I gave you credit for. I've never met a famous person who's so down-to-earth. I mean, I'm nobody, and you're Piper Starling."

"You're not nobody. You're a member of Sawyer's band and his best friend."

"I haven't been very fair to you. I've spent this whole tour trying to convince this guy he's better off without you. I was jealous and I'm sorry. I think karma paid me back."

Piper seemed to appreciate his apology. Sawyer did, as well.

"I'm glad you realize how amazing she is. One, because she deserves it, and two, because I'm in love with her and you're going to have to be the best man at the next wedding we have."

Hunter began to laugh and pointed at Piper. "I'm not surprised, but it sure looks like someone else is."

Sawyer crouched in front of her. He took her hand. "I've been a fool. I told myself that all these things I felt weren't love—until I thought something had happened to you. That's when I realized there was nothing else it could be. All my stupid defenses fell away and this feeling burst out."

"Love?"

"Without a doubt love."

PIPER DIDN'T SEE an ounce of uncertainty in Sawyer's eyes. They were the clearest they'd ever been. There was no confusion, no fear. And she was looking.

"I also have to apologize to you for putting my anger ahead of your feelings," he said. "I promise you that I am going to make things right between me and my mom. I know now that I have to work these feelings out if I want to move forward with you."

She put her hands on his cheeks and bent down to kiss those lips one more time. His honesty made her heart feel like it was about to bust at the seams. "I forgive you."

"I love you, Piper. I want to be a family. Will you be part of my family?"

"I still love you, but I'm not marrying you unless I have enough time to plan my dream wedding." This time, nothing would be rushed. Both of them would savor every moment.

One side of Sawyer's mouth curled up. "You can have as much time as you need," he said. "When we get married, I want everything about it to be right."

MAKING THINGS RIGHT for Piper meant making things right back in Grass Lake. Sawyer needed to resolve his issues with Gretchen before he brought Piper into the mix.

He accompanied Hunter home in between the shows in Minneapolis and Detroit. Faith was riding Sassy in the front paddock. She waved at her brother as he parked the car.

"How's Hunter doing? Did he survive the flight okay?"

"He's fine, but he was hogging the armrest the whole way home with his cast."

"Your sympathy for his pain is admirable," Faith said with a laugh. "I might have baked some of your favorite cookies, so you'd be in a better mood when Mom comes over."

Cookies would help his growling belly. It was unlikely they would help him feel less anxious about talking to Gretchen. If he was going to be completely free of fear and distrust, he had to confront the woman who had put those two things in his heart.

"I'm going to take Sassy to the tack room and clean her up. I'll meet you inside in a few?" Faith asked as she dismounted.

"How about I take Sassy? Maybe doing a little manual labor will help me clear my head."

Sawyer loosened the girth strap and took the lead rope from his sister. "Come on, girl. You remember me?" Sassy nudged him with her nose. "Of course you do."

He removed the saddle and pad and gave Sassy a good brushing. After checking her hooves, he led her back out to the pasture to graze.

Harriet's car was parked up by the house. Sawyer's heart rate was already elevated from grooming the horse. Confronting Gretchen increased it a few more beats per minute.

If he was going to be the best husband and father he could be to Piper and the baby, he needed to put his anger with his mother to rest once and for all.

The three women sat at the kitchen table with a plate of cookies in front of them. No one was eating, however. He knew those cookies weren't capable of ridding anyone of this kind of anxiety.

"Hey, sugarplum," Harriet said. "How was your flight?"

He went to the sink to wash his hands. He could feel Gretchen's eyes on him. "It was fine."

"How is the tour going after everything? Is the press being kind?" Harriet was the only one of them brave enough to make conversation.

"The media loves to twist everything, but

we're good. We're great, actually. I think calling off the wedding was exactly what we needed to get on the right path. Piper and I are actually happier now than we've ever been."

"I knew you'd be happier when you were free," Gretchen said.

"Piper and I are happy *together*. She loves me and I love her. Someday, we'll get married and our son will have a bunch of brothers and sisters."

"Oh, sweet pea!" Harriet said. "I don't know how you got here, but I am glad you're happy. If you're happy, I'm happy."

"You're still going to marry her." Gretchen shook her head.

Sawyer took a deep breath and reminded himself why he was here. He couldn't give in to the anger she seemed determined to drag out of him.

"When I was little, I used to think that if I ever found you, I would ask you why you left and demand an answer." He sat down across from her at the table. "I realize now that the reason doesn't really matter. You left, and no explanation can change the way that shaped who I am today. What I really want to know is why you came back. Because that will help me decide if I'll let you influence my life moving forward."

Gretchen averted her eyes and shifted in her seat. She folded and unfolded her hands. "I told you, I came back to stop you from making the same mistakes I made. It would have been a mistake to marry someone you didn't love because she was pregnant."

"And for all intents and purposes, you accomplished that goal when Piper called off the wedding, but you're still here."

She took a cookie off the plate and broke it into smaller pieces. "Well, I've been catching up with Harriet and spending time with Faith."

"So, another reason you came back was to reconnect with Harriet and Faith. Anything else?"

"It's not like you want anything to do with me, but I might have come back to get to know you a bit, too."

"Getting to know me is another reason. Is that correct?"

She nodded.

"Anything else? Do you need money? Are you dying?"

Gretchen's brow furrowed. "Lord, no. I

don't need your money, and I am healthy as a horse."

"Is there a reason reconnecting became important to you all of a sudden? Twenty-one years is a long time. You can't blame me for being suspicious after so much time has passed."

"I don't have a good answer. I wanted to talk to you all for years, but I guess hearing you on the radio and reading about you in the news gave me the push I needed to actually do it instead of thinking about it."

Sawyer was surprised to hear her say she'd wanted to reconnect for so long. He had assumed Gretchen's reappearance had something to do with his fame, but knowing she had wanted to reconnect him before that was a relief.

"Why not sooner?" Faith asked.

"Your father was a great dad. He knew what to do no matter what you two threw at us. It was like he was born to be a dad."

Sawyer could only hope to be half as good at parenting as his dad was, but he wasn't sure what this had to do with his mom staying away.

"We were very lucky to have him," Faith said.

"Me, on the other hand, I was a terrible

mother," Gretchen continued. "I'm not nurturing. I don't know what to do when kids cry. I hate bodily fluids. I didn't want to be a parent, but I loved your dad and he wanted a family. I gave him what he wanted even though I knew I couldn't rise to the challenge."

"I don't remember you being a bad mom," Faith said. "I remember chasing fireflies and sleep-outs in the summer. I remember how you'd take us to the lake and teach us about nature."

Gretchen actually smiled. "I'm glad those are the things you remember about me, because I remember locking myself in my room while you were crying until your father came inside. I remember yelling at you both to stop touching me. I remember telling you to make your own dinner when you were like six years old."

Faith and Sawyer exchanged glances. Sawyer had been way too young to remember that stuff, but Faith had been ten when Gretchen left. She had to recall their mom being so distant.

"I don't remember any of that," Faith said. "When Dad and I talked about you, we only talked about the good things. He would tell me stories when I was missing you."

Gretchen pinched the bridge of her nose and shut her eyes. "That man." She got up and grabbed the box of tissues on the counter. "That man was a freaking saint."

Sawyer leaned back in his chair. His dad, a man who had had every reason to bad-mouth Gretchen and paint her as the villain, never had. In fact, he'd done the exact opposite. He'd made sure that the only memories that stuck were the ones that made Sawyer and Faith feel loved.

"I wish I would have figured out how to be present in your lives more. At the time, I thought it was an all or nothing decision. But that was unfair to you two and to your father," Gretchen said, dabbing her eyes. "I'm sorry I didn't come home for his funeral. I should have come and paid my respects, but I didn't want to cause you two any more grief than you were already dealing with. But your dad was the best man I have ever known. Better than I deserved."

Sawyer was torn. He had been angry about her not coming, but she was right that her presence would have taken away from their grieving process. Sawyer would miss his fa-

ther every day for the rest of his life, but he
had successfully moved into the acceptance
phase. Big John lived on through Sawyer and
Faith. Now, it was time for Sawyer to heal
the part of his heart that had broken when
Gretchen left. The only way to do that was
to give her a chance to start over.

Maybe she would let them down, maybe
she wouldn't. Sawyer had to trust that he'd
survive either way.

"I have some good news for you," he said,
turning around to face her. "Faith and I don't
need to be parented anymore. We cook our
own dinner. Well, Faith is very good at cooking dinner, and I can boil water, which is use-
ful at times."

"We no longer have issues with crying for
no reason or wanting to touch people who
don't want to be touched," Faith added.

"We're just really cool people," Sawyer
said. "People you might want to get to know
and hang out with sometimes."

"I'd like that," Gretchen said as the tears
fell a little faster.

"Now, don't make me go lock myself in
my room until you stop crying," he teased.

Gretchen burst out laughing. "You are an
impressive young man."

"Thank you. I had the best role model in the world."

"Yes, you did. And he would be very proud of the man you are."

After everything Sawyer had been through in the last couple months, he felt pretty confident that his dad would have been happy with how he'd chosen to handle everything in the end. He'd made some mistakes, but he had set out to right the wrongs and mend the fences he had mistakenly thought had been destroyed beyond repair.

Nothing was ever lost forever.

CHAPTER TWENTY-THREE

THE FOURTH OF July parade in Grass Lake was one of Sawyer's favorite events in his hometown. This year he was blessed to be riding alongside his gorgeous fiancée.

"Are you sure you packed enough water bottles?" Piper asked as she moved slowly around the kitchen. At nine months pregnant, she was due to give birth at any moment. In fact, Sawyer was a bit concerned that their little guy was going to make an appearance before they got to be grand marshals of this year's parade.

"If you drink too much water, you're going to have to wear a diaper, because they will not stop the parade so you can go to the bathroom."

Piper scowled at him.

"Be nice to her. She is a woman on the edge," Faith warned him.

"If she was on the edge of anything, she'd fall in. It's amazing she can stand upright."

"Please swat him in the back of the head, Gretchen. I can't move fast enough to catch him," Piper said.

Sawyer's mom rolled up the newspaper she was reading and chased him around the island. "Be nice to her. You have no idea how miserable this part of pregnancy is."

Sawyer came up behind Piper and wrapped his arms around her and that big belly. "I love you. I tease because I love."

"Try loving me more and teasing me less. I seriously feel like if you poked me with a pin this thing would pop."

"It won't be long now." He kissed her neck. "Let's just hope it's long enough to get us through the parade."

"Let's go, family. The Grass Lake Fourth of July parade coordinators wait for no one. Not even the grand marshals," Dean said.

"You're telling me Marilee Presley would start the parade without me?" Sawyer asked, grabbing the cooler he'd packed with plenty of water for Piper.

"My mother would start the parade without me, and she loves me."

"Your mother would start the parade without me, and she loves me even more than she loves you," Faith teased.

"Of course she loves you the most. You're the most lovable." Dean lifted her off the ground and spun her around until she giggled.

Dean and Faith had been married for about a month. They'd held their wedding in Grass Lake Community Church surrounded by not only family and friends but practically the entire town.

Piper had taken extensive notes on how to do a wedding right. She and Sawyer were planning to get married in the fall right before they headed back out on the second leg of their tour. Heath already had Piper's tour bus babyproofed.

Main Street was in its full red, white and blue glory. Flags were flying and people lined the streets.

"How you feeling, Mama?" Sawyer asked as they got out of Dean's car. "You gonna make it?"

"I can't let you be grand marshal by yourself. We're in this together, right?"

There was no one he wanted to be in it with other than her. "Then let's get this parade started."

Marilee was running around checking off everyone in line. She squealed when she saw them approach. "You made it! I was worried that maybe that little fella disrupted your plans."

"Not yet," Sawyer said. "We're ready to go."

She led them to the head car, a bright red Mustang convertible that would be driven by Mr. Presley. On the sides of the car were signs with Piper's name in giant letters and Sawyer's in tiny print underneath.

"What in the world? How come my name is so small?"

Marilee cringed. "Sorry, the girls who painted them misjudged how much room they would need to fit both names."

"It makes sense, if you think about it. I am literally ten times bigger than you right now," Piper said.

He kissed her forehead and helped her into the back seat of the car. They sat on the back and waited for their cue to go.

At twelve on the dot, Marilee started the parade. Piper and Sawyer waved to the crowd. Everyone cheered and snapped pictures of them. Sawyer had ridden in the parade last year by himself. How things had changed in such a short time. Not only did he have a hit album, he was marrying one of the greatest country singers in the world. His mother was part of his life and Dean was officially his brother-in-law.

There wasn't much more he could ask for.

Piper gripped his arm, digging her nails into his skin. "What's wrong?"

"Oh man, I think that was a contraction," she said once it passed.

"One contraction doesn't mean anything. Just breathe through it." Ruby had sent her home twice after having contractions for hours.

About two minutes later, Piper had another one. And two minutes after that, another. Piper, still the consummate professional, did her best to mask her discomfort. Sawyer kept smiling and waving. There was nothing else he could do.

"Ahhh!" Piper moaned as yet another contraction hit. That was four contractions in a row that were about two minutes apart. Redfaced, she could no longer hide her pain. "Oh my gosh, Sawyer."

"What?"

She turned to face him. "My water just broke."

This was not a drill. He didn't want to freak out while on display for the entire town of Grass Lake, but Sawyer needed to get Piper to Ruby immediately. He tapped Mr. Presley on the shoulder and told him the problem.

Ted Presley was known for having a bit of a lead foot. That was about to come in very handy. Sawyer helped lower Piper down into the back seat and buckled her in before Ted took off like it was a NASCAR race. Safety first. The Grass Lake residents probably had no idea what was happening as the car sped down the street. Astonished faces quickly became nothing but a blur.

He texted Ruby to meet them at the hospital ASAP. He texted Faith and Heath. He texted Hunter and Lana. In between texts, he encouraged Piper to breathe through the pain.

"Would you tell someone who was shot to breathe through the pain?" she screamed. "Breathing. Doesn't. Help!"

Ted got them to the ER in a matter of minutes. Sawyer jumped out of the car and ran around to open Piper's door and help her out. They went inside to check in.

Two hours after they arrived, John Heath Stratton came into the world. He weighed a whopping eight pounds, three ounces, and was twenty-one inches long. Ruby said Piper was a champ and Sawyer could not disagree.

As he held his son in his arms, he was reminded of yet another huge blessing that had been bestowed upon him this year.

"You look good holding that baby," Piper said from her hospital bed.

"You look good, period." He leaned over to kiss her.

"We did it," she said. "We made a baby and he's kinda perfect."

"My dad would have been out in the waiting room doing backflips over this little guy."

Big John would never get to hold little John in his arms, but Sawyer's son would know everything there was to tell about his namesake.

"Thank you," he said to Piper. "Thank you for not giving up on me even when I gave you so many reasons to."

"Thank you for loving me."

That was nothing. Once he got the hang of it, it was the easiest thing he'd ever done.

THREE MONTHS AFTER John was born, Piper and Sawyer were back on tour. Their wedding had been a lavish affair. There was a horse-drawn carriage and dove release. Fireworks at the end of the night and a dress with a ten-foot train that had been custom-made by Piper's favorite designer. And if the wedding itself hadn't been miracle enough, little Liam from North Carolina had been able to attend as the ring bearer. He beamed with pride as his father wheeled him down the aisle. Cancer would win eventually, but not until a few more of Liam's dreams came true. It had been a day she would never forget.

"You want Mama? Is that what you want?" Sawyer held John over his head and had him giggling up a storm. "Well, let's get her."

Holding him like an airplane, Sawyer flew John right into Piper's arms.

"Did you like that?" she asked him. "Daddy plays all the fun games, doesn't he?"

"Are you ready for tonight? I think the sleep deprivation could be a problem," Sawyer said through a yawn. "I can't remember any of the words in the second verse of 'Out All Night.'"

Piper could top that. "At rehearsals, I sang the chorus of 'Walk On' even though they told me to sing a snippet of 'Better Days.'"

"We're both losing it," Sawyer said with a laugh.

"Maybe it's part of our new brand. The

tired-and-incoherent-new-parents brand. Maybe we can pick up a diaper company as a sponsor."

"I can see it now," Sawyer said. "Piper Starling and Sawyer Stratton, brought to you by baby wipes."

At least they could laugh about it. They had each other, and that was all Piper needed to get through.

"You two ready for the meet and greet?" Heath said, coming aboard. "Hello, my favorite little baby in the whole world." Grandpa took his grandson away from Piper. "You are getting so big. Yes, you are."

John thought Heath was even more hilarious than his own father, which really rubbed Sawyer the wrong way.

"How do you get him to laugh like that? He only does that for you. I don't get it."

"Babies love me," Heath gloated. "I've got him. You two need to go to the meet and greet. Right after Piper changes her shirt, because you have spit-up on your right shoulder."

Piper glanced down and, sure enough, she had been hit. "You little stinker," she said, giving John's nose a poke.

After a quick outfit change, security led

them down to the meet-and-greet room, where Gretchen waited with the fans. Being a traveler at heart, she hadn't been able to resist the temptation to join them on their cross-country trek. She refused to babysit anything other than the candy bar, but Sawyer had caught her making silly faces at John to get a laugh more than once.

As for mother and son, things were actually going better than expected. Sawyer didn't always like to admit it, but he and Gretchen had quite a bit in common. They had similar taste in music and a love for zombie television shows. They both had contagious laughs and knew how to put together some pretty impressive pranks while on tour together.

Meet and greets were less stressful these days. People were always friendly. Piper and Sawyer didn't have to hide anything or lie about their feelings. It was all sunshine and rainbows.

During Sawyer's set, Piper made an appearance to sing "You Don't Need Me" with him. She sang it like she meant it but was much happier knowing that song didn't represent who they were to each other anymore. It would be something they'd always have to sing since it was their first hit and it was what had brought them together—and it was part of the reason little John was hanging out backstage with his granddaddy.

The song that Piper would happily sing every show for the rest of her life was the one she and Sawyer had written for John, for each other. That song was how they closed each show. Just her and Sawyer onstage with a slideshow of pictures running behind them on the big screens.

"How y'all doing tonight?" Piper asked the crowd in Dallas, Texas, for the last time that evening. "Did you have a good time?"

The lights shone on the crowd, who responded with their loudest screams.

"Well, we've got one more song for you tonight. This song is near and dear to my heart, so I have to bring a little piece of my heart out onstage with me. Can y'all welcome back my handsome husband, Sawyer Stratton?"

The crowd erupted once again. Sawyer walked out with his guitar strapped to his back and his white cowboy hat on his head. There was nothing sexier than that boy and his hat and guitar.

"So, everybody knows this man is the love of my life, but there's another little man who's the other half of my heart." On the screen behind her, they put up a picture of John smiling from ear to ear.

Again, the crowd went wild. Piper could guarantee that if someone needed a stadium of mostly women and young girls to lose their minds, all they had to do was show them cute boys in cowboy hats and babies with dimples. It was a proved fact in Piper's world.

"I am the luckiest lady in the whole wide world. I have the love of a good man, a sweet baby who calls me Mama, and I have all of you. Thank you for spending the evening with me. Let's do it again real soon. This song is called 'For the Love of a Boy.'"

* * * * *

Get 2 Free Books,
Plus 2 Free Gifts—
just for trying the Reader Service!

Love Inspired®

LI17R3

Get 2 Free Books,
Plus 2 Free Gifts—
just for trying the Reader Service!

YES! Please send me the **Home on the Ranch Collection** in Larger Print. This collection begins with 3 FREE books and 2 FREE gifts in the first shipment. Along with my 3 free books, I'll also get the next 4 books from the Home on the Ranch Collection, in LARGER PRINT, which I may either return and owe nothing, or keep for the low price of $5.24 U.S./ $5.89 CDN each plus $2.99 for shipping and handling per shipment*. If I decide to continue, about once a month for 8 months I will get 6 or 7 more books, but will only need to pay for 4. That means 2 or 3 books in every shipment will be FREE! If I decide to keep the entire collection, I'll have paid for only 32 books because 19 books are FREE! I understand that accepting the 3 free books and gifts places me under no obligation to buy anything. I can always return a shipment and cancel at any time. My free books and gifts are mine to keep no matter what I decide.

268 HCN 3760 468 HCN 3760

Name	(PLEASE PRINT)	
Address		Apt. #
City	State/Prov.	Zip/Postal Code

Signature (if under 18, a parent or guardian must sign)

Mail to the **Reader Service:**
IN U.S.A.: P.O. Box 1867, Buffalo, NY. 14240-1867
IN CANADA: P.O. Box 609, Fort Erie, Ontario L2A 5X3

* Terms and prices subject to change without notice. Prices do not include applicable taxes. Sales tax applicable in NY. Canadian residents will be charged applicable taxes. This offer is limited to one order per household. All orders subject to approval. Credit or debit balances in a customer's account(s) may be offset by any other outstanding balance owed by or to the customer. Please allow 3 to 4 weeks for delivery. Offer available while quantities last. Offer not available to Quebec residents.

Your Privacy—The Reader Service is committed to protecting your privacy. Our Privacy Policy is available online at www.ReaderService.com or upon request from the Reader Service.

We make a portion of our mailing list available to reputable third parties that offer products we believe may interest you. If you prefer that we not exchange your name with third parties, or if you wish to clarify or modify your communication preferences, please visit us at www.ReaderService.com/consumerschoice or write to us at Reader Service Preference Service, P.O. Box 9062, Buffalo, NY. 14240-9062. Include your complete name and address.

Get 2 Free Books,
Plus 2 Free Gifts -
just for trying the Reader Service!

Get 2 Free Books,

Plus 2 Free Gifts—

just for trying the Reader Service!

YES! Please send me 2 FREE Harlequin® Desire novels and my 2 FREE gifts (gifts are worth about $10 retail). After receiving them, if I don't wish to receive any more books, I can return the shipping statement marked "cancel." If I don't cancel, I will receive 6 brand-new novels every month and be billed just $4.55 per book in the U.S. or $5.24 per book in Canada. That's a savings of at least 13% off the cover price! It's quite a bargain! Shipping and handling is just 50¢ per book in the U.S. and 75¢ per book in Canada*. I understand that accepting the 2 free books and gifts places me under no obligation to buy anything. I can always return a shipment and cancel at any time. The free books and gifts are mine to keep no matter what I decide.

225/326 HDN GMWG

Name _____ (PLEASE PRINT)

Address _____ Apt. #

City _____ State/Prov. _____ Zip/Postal Code

Signature (if under 18, a parent or guardian must sign)

Mail to the **Reader Service:**
IN U.S.A.: P.O. Box 1341, Buffalo, NY 14240-8531
IN CANADA: P.O. Box 603, Fort Erie, Ontario L2A 5X3

Want to try two free books from another line?
Call 1-800-873-8635 or visit www.ReaderService.com.

HDI7R3